Let Me Be the One

LILY FOSTER

This is a work of fiction. Names, characters, places and incidents are either the product of the author's imagination or used fictitiously. Any resemblance to actual persons, living or dead, events, or locales is entirely coincidental.

Let Me Be the One
Copyright © 2014 by Lily Foster

Cover by Cover Me Darling

First paperback edition September 2014
IBSN 9780990594109 (paperback)

Shorefront Books

This new edition of my debut novel, *Let Me Be the One*, includes a series prequel. Up until now, this short story has been available for newsletter subscribers only.

Settle in for Nick Brunner's story. Angry young man, heir to a surf apparel fortune, forgotten son. He sets a chain of events into motion that will change the lives of so many...

Where It All Began

NICK'S STORY

I had my first drink when I was eleven.

Most people will tell you they hated that first sip—the sour tang of flat beer, the burning sensation that makes your eyes water when you throw back a shot of hard liquor—but I'm not most people. I just remember feeling warm. I remember the bourbon snaking its way through me, easing something coiled up tight inside my skin.

It felt like a hug.

By the time I was fourteen, sneaking sips from my mother's stash wasn't cutting it anymore. And I'd already been caught trying to swipe an entire bottle of expensive tequila from my dad's place the year before, so he was keeping a closer eye on his inventory.

Side note: My father didn't act surprised, lecture me on the dangers of drinking, or threaten me with punishment. Not his style. He cracked the seal on the bottle and slowly set about cutting a lime into wedges. Pausing between shots, he gave me a once over and then said something like: *Thieves are lower than scum,* very Clint Eastwood-esque in his delivery.

I was nothing if not resourceful, so that summer between eighth grade and high school I started paying some creepy middle-aged guy who lived in my neighborhood ten bucks every time he made a beer or liquor run for me.

No one noticed.

I drank at night mostly. I'd do a shot or two as I played video games before bed, or I'd drink a few beers, feeling very grown-up when my mother left me home alone eating takeout for dinner.

The divorce still wasn't final at that point.

He moved out when I was in third grade and the never-ending custody battle started soon after.

Should make me feel special, right? Both parents, so desperate to have their precious little boy to themselves that they'd spare no effort or expense to claim him. They'd spend hundreds of thousands of dollars between the two of them before it was all said and done. Lawyers, private detectives, the court-appointed psychologists—all because they wanted me.

But they didn't.

They hated each other. And I'm not talking about your garden-variety animosity, like when a spouse cheats or money's tight. My parents truly abhorred one another. If I'd been a toddler just learning the language, I probably would have thought my father's name was Fucking Idiot, as my mother rarely referred to him as anything else. And let's just say I knew what the C-word meant early on in life. It's the term of endearment Nick senior favored when talking about his wife.

At one time they were business partners, and if you listen to him tell it, she had no hand in Trim Gear's success. He was the surf rat, and it was his idea to manufacture a line of board shorts made from a superior, more flexible quick-dry material. Hell, the company's name (surf lingo for shifting your position on the board for maximum velocity), that was his idea too.

I was in fourth grade before I learned the more widely accepted definition of trim.

My mother will tell you that the ridiculously sexist, albeit clever and catchy name is the only thing my father contributed to the growth of the brand. She was the brains behind the operation. She negotiated with the factories overseas, developed the marketing strategy, established their online presence and got them prominent exposure in the upscale retail outlets.

Legend says that when they started the company they were living out of a beat-up minivan on the outskirts of Santa Barbara proper. They showered at friends' houses and lived off the generosity of others. It's hard to imagine.

I've only known a life of luxury, calling that bleak box-like structure overlooking the Pacific Ocean home from the time I was a born. We had a private chef to whip up dinner every night, a husband and wife team who came in to clean two or three times a week, and I had a babysitter.

What I wanted was a brother or a sister, but I wasn't getting one of those.

I do have some good memories from that time. I remember the parties my parents threw in that house when everything was new: the success, the wealth. Looking back, those parties were more like drug-infused, sun-drenched orgies, but I recall feeling supremely happy as I was passed among friends and strangers alike. Those adults asked me questions, tussled my hair, sang to me, made me feel...wanted.

If I really focus, I can get back to that place. I can hear Soundgarden or Oasis playing in the background mixed in with the sounds of laughter. I can inhale the coconut goodness of the women and the sweet aroma of herb wafting through every room. I can see the topless, long-haired beauties in the pool perched atop their boyfriends' shoulders, and I can make out the shadows of bodies moving against one another as the sun dips lower and darkness takes over.

During those parties my parents were different. They were happy, or they acted happy—I'm not sure which.

It's when everyone went home, when you woke up the next day

to dirty glasses covering the countertops, to the discarded bongs and the remnants of peoples' clothing on the pool deck—that's when it got bad. That's when there was no breakfast if the babysitter wasn't scheduled to work, that's when no one rolled out of bed until the sun was high up in the sky, and that's when they went back to default mode: pissed off and dissatisfied.

It was a relief when my father finally packed his shit and left. Silence was preferable to the screaming matches, and those months leading up to the official separation were the worst.

The stomachache would start up on the bus ride home. I'd take my time climbing the stairs to our front door, listening intently as each step brought me closer, a nine-year-old doing his best to determine whether or not the coast was clear. There were entire days I'd stay holed up in my room. I could turn the volume up on my television, make it loud enough to drown out the happy loving couple.

A few months after they split, my mother decided she wanted to move back up north to be closer to her family. Dad reclaimed the beach house right after she pulled me out of school mid-year and settled us into a big house in Monterey.

I'd never met my grandparents, so I was excited about that, but the excitement wore off after a few months passed and we never had so much as one visit from them. I was to learn later on that my mother was estranged from her parents and her sister, who did live in northern California, but in a far less affluent, rural area. Turns out she hadn't spoken to them in over a decade, and contrary to what she'd told my father, Mom had no plans for a reconciliation.

The best thing about leaving my childhood home and my father? No more pressure to surf. I just wasn't good at it. He could say it was no big deal until he was blue in the face, but his disappointment sat heavy on my shoulders.

Narcissistic prick made no effort whatsoever to teach me. Nope, grace and athleticism on the waves came natural to him, so it should have been second nature to me too. He'd just stand on the shore, arms crossed, shaking his head every time a perfectly good set passed me by. The future face of Trim Gear couldn't paddle fast enough to catch a wave, let alone execute a flawless pop-up or ride the barrel.

The day I stopped pretending was the day I caught him mouthing the word *weak* as he watched me from the shoreline. Sitting on my board, bobbing out there in the ocean alone, the words burned hot in my throat: *Fuck you, Dad.* But I was a coward, so I waited until he left before paddling in and dragging my board across the rocks and wet sand on my way back home. My lame little rebellion because, *You carry that board like it's a goddamn Stradivarius, son.* If memory serves me right, I returned up north to Mom's the next morning, and that was the day I had my first blessed taste of Maker's Mark.

It was like a ping pong game, with me being the ball from the time I was nine years old until I was around sixteen. I moved back and forth between them, changing schools three different times in those six years. The summer before seventh grade, my father had a private investigator dig up evidence that Mom was dating a drug dealer and hauled me back to SoCal. Being that some of his closest friends dabbled in the trade, I was confused as to what the big deal was. A few months later Mom "won" me back, and I still feel shitty about the part I played in that.

They had an epic blowout when he dropped me off for Christmas break, my mom getting in his face and cursing him out so badly that he had no choice but to shake her and push her back. She had to mask her satisfied grin later on that night when I snapped those photos, the make-up enhanced bruises proof that my father was an abusive monster. I kind of agreed with my dad, that she incited the whole ugly incident, but whatever, the judge went for it and I liked being up north better, so it was a win all around.

Hold up, another side note: Laying hands a woman is wrong. I know that. Even if my mother did manipulate him, even if she was looking for a confrontation that would all but guarantee she'd regain custody (as well as the hefty child support payments my father would now be on the hook for), even if she stirred the pot, he was wrong to react with physical violence. There's never a valid excuse.

I'm proud to say that I've never hit a woman. At times I've been so angry at the women in my life that I've put holes in drywall and taken a bat to a certain one's car, but I've never physically harmed anyone. Sometimes you love a girl with everything you have, though, love her so hard it makes you crazy. But no, I won't stoop that low. I'm not like him.

I'm getting off topic again.

Long story short, I went back and forth, the two of them divvying up school vacation days like they were negotiating the terms of a Middle East peace treaty, minus the peace.

Funny thing was, they never spent much time with me once they had me in custody (the prison reference is intentional). I was left on my own a lot, a scrawny kid who found it hard to talk to people. Maybe if I hadn't been bounced back and forth so often I would have been able to make friends. Or whatever, maybe I was just born this way.

When I was sixteen my father got remarried to a Hawaiian girl nearly twenty years his junior—baby on the way—and my mother was fully immersed in her newest venture, an organic line of haircare products. Trim was sold, netting them both a modest fortune, so they had no need to be in contact with one another. And just like that, it was over. They were done fighting, and done fighting over me.

The therapists I've had in the years since have told me that my drinking was a cry for help. I don't dispute that, even though I would have laughed in anyone's face had they suggested that theory back in the day.

I was caught with a flask in my locker freshman year of high school, wrecked my mother's car in our driveway when I was a sophomore (it's a pretty long driveway), got my stomach pumped after a particularly bad night (junior prom—my date was a fellow alcoholic in training), and was given a citation for drunk and disorderly when I got into a bar fight with one of my cousins on the night of my aunt's funeral. Each and every fuck-up along the way was covered by a donation to the swanky private school I was attending at the time or to a local police charity. The lawyers handled everything. So if it was, as my therapists assert, my parents' attention I was seeking, then I'd failed miserably.

Quick note on that funeral: I still have no idea why my mother dragged me to the ceremony. I mean, I'd never met the woman (never met her son before either, the one I head-butted in the bar). I did get to meet my grandparents that day, but there was no dewy-eyed reunion, no affectionate bear hug for the grandson they'd never laid eyes on. Definitely wasn't the Norman Rockwell painting come to life that I'd once dreamed of. Nope. Those two fuckers, with their cheap clothes and bad teeth, they were as cold as ice. Kind of felt bad for Mom that day.

Luckily, my gene pool did provide me with a leg up, intellectually speaking. School came easy to me, and all those hours spent alone trolling the internet led to some measure of skill with computers. By the time I was seventeen I'd developed some basic hacking skills, enough to gain access to my parents' accounts and personal records.

A light bulb went off when I stumbled upon that one encrypted file. Trust funds in my name. One from each parent. Irrevocable.

Bingo.

At the age of twenty-three I would be coming into roughly twenty-million dollars.

I didn't stop drinking, but this information did give me some incentive to avoid wrapping my car around a tree, or accidentally driving off the PCH in a drunken stupor. I began to envision a different version of myself: a successful, popular, winning version. And what better way to reinvent oneself than to move clear across the country and start over?

I probably could have made it into an ivy based on my college entrance exam scores, but those schools also want to go over your high school transcript with a fine-toothed comb. They're not into kids who vacillate between top honors one semester and skirting the line of failure the next. They also want to scrutinize your extracurricular resume to make sure you regularly feed the hungry, train emotional support dogs for combat veterans, and/or develop a cure for cancer in your spare time.

Ridiculous.

A second-tier, albeit very competitive school in Boston accepted me with open arms. My parents were proud of me, I guess. I did overhear my father tell Miguel, his financial advisor-slash-friend, that I was a "smart kid" that summer before I left, but he threw the compliment out absently. I was standing there on the shoreline with the two of them, but Dad was clearly more interested in watching Miguel's son as he took nice long rides on the barrel every damn time he chose to drop in on a wave.

My dad clapped the kid on his back when he came out of the water, the two of them speaking their own language, that surfer lingo I was fluent in but despised. He was around my age, maybe a year or two younger, with sun bleached hair that hung half-way down his back and an expertly crafted tattoo of a wave on his bicep. Smiling to myself, I noticed it bore a striking resemblance to a well-known surfboard manufacturer's corporate logo.

Posers, each and every one of them.

They all act as if they'd be happy living in a tent on the beach, subsisting on coconuts and fish tacos—*As long as the waves are rad, bruh*—when in reality, they're jonesing for that fat endorsement deal. They all want to live in a house like my father's, they all want to score some young honey from the Big Island, they all want a standing reservation at George's in La Jolla. They all want the life.

The smile on my father's face was so pure when he spoke to that kid. Until that day, I didn't really understand what people meant when they described a smile as reaching the eyes. My father's eyes were smiling when he spoke to that boy. They were twinkling, for God's sake. And when the kid spoke, calling my dad Dude (original) and peppering his sentences with words like shacked, soup and keg, I imagine my father was thinking to himself: *This one, why couldn't he be my son?*

I was eager to board that plane already, but not even halfway through my farewell weekend trip with Dad and Tiffany, I was itching to bolt.

Tiffany, yes, you read that right. Were you expecting some tropical, goddess-inspired name? I know I was. I remember sharing a good belly laugh with Mom when we found out that my future stepmonster was named after the lead actress on *Saved by the Bell*. But never fear, those two phonies were about to rectify the situation. After losing the last one to a miscarriage (my father actually cried when he broke the news to me over the phone—boo fucking hoo), Tiff was now fat as a walrus with twins on the way. They weren't going to find out the sex, Tiff shared as the three of us sat on the deck that night, but they were hoping for "two little brothers" for me.

"We even have names picked out," she said, reaching over to squeeze my knee. And I hate to admit it, but even with the round belly and those tits, marred by stretch marks and swollen to the size of melons, she still looked hot. I had to ask Tiffany to repeat herself, so lost in my recurring fantasy of nailing her that I missed the big reveal. "Kainoa and Kamalei."

I typed each one into my phone. Kainoa translates to namesake... nice. Kamalei means adored son...even better.

"Do you like them?"

Wide-eyed and smiling, she reached over to take my hand. Always the naïve and hopeful half-wit, so eager for my approval. My father, meanwhile, with his gross insensitivity knowing no bounds, looked on at his child bride, smitten.

Irrevocable. Right then and there it became my favorite word.

Powerful, non-negotiable, venomous—an iron-clad guarantee that those two little fetuses could never get their grubby little paws on my money.

I managed to make it through the rest of the evening, even smiled and congratulated the happy couple.

The flute of champagne I downed the next morning after claiming my seat in first class tasted like freedom. And for a while, it all went according to plan.

I arrived at school with a new sense of purpose, pumped up with confidence. I'd look in the mirror and see a good-looking guy staring back at me. A rich, good-looking guy, I'd remind myself. Yep, no matter what, there was twenty million waiting for me at the end of the rainbow.

In Boston I could be the face of Trim Gear. I could exude Cali cool, could assume the identity of someone I was not.

I made friends in this new place, became part of a tribe that hung out, lived and partied together. A mix of athletes, clowns and musicians, they all had one thing in common: they kept their heads on straight. They managed to party like animals on the weekends, yet maintain decent grades. They lived lives of balance.

I learned a lot from them, tried to be like them. I wanted what they had. Take my roommate Vic, for example. Played varsity lacrosse, managed good grades even as a double major, and he had a girlfriend. Yeah, I had a thing for Suzanne. She was as nice as she was pretty. I'd listen in when the two of them were hanging out in our suite's common room, fascinated by their easy back and forth, with the natural way they had of being affectionate with one another. If I couldn't have her, I wanted someone just like her.

Then there was my good friend Chris, a Boston native. He lived in the dorms with us but would head to Brookline for a home-cooked meal at least twice a month. When I finally got the chance to tag along over Thanksgiving break, I never wanted to leave. His parents fussed over him. I'd never witnessed anything like it. His father looked on at him with pride, treated him with respect. And his mother hugged him more times in that one weekend than I'd been hugged by my mother over the course of my entire life.

Observing my new friends left me feeling empty sometimes, but I'd tell myself I could make myself over, have that life someday.

I didn't label myself as an alcoholic back then, and for a while there, I did have my shit under control. I drank more than my friends —overdid it at parties now and then, maybe snuck a few shots midweek when I was studying alone in my room—but I wasn't a disaster like I had been back in high school. I went to my classes consistently freshman year, handed in assignments on time and earned decent grades without much effort.

It wasn't the academics that took effort, it was all the other stuff. The socializing, the *it's all good* act, the mask of relaxed content that I wore. I was exhausted from it.

Sophomore year I met the love of my life, and that's when the train went off the rails.

It's the opposite for other people, isn't it? You meet *the one*—the one who lights you up, makes you smile for no reason, makes you want to be a better person—and it's supposed to be good. It's supposed to last. But Darcy Donovan didn't last, and while we were together, the bitch definitely did not encourage me to be what those self-help books refer to as my best self. No, that bitch reduced me to ashes.

Here we go again.

Side note: I retract those last statements. It's wrong to refer to women using that word (even if the shoe fits), and I know my negativity is borne out of a lingering sense of resentment towards my mother (another nugget courtesy of my years in therapy).

I made some mistakes, I fully acknowledge that, but I never really stood a chance. It was like the deck was stacked against me from day one. Even in the beginning, when I made Darcy happy and she looked at me like I was her person, I just knew she wouldn't hang in there and go the distance with me. At the end of the day she turned out to be no different from the others. She turned her back on me.

Nevertheless, I tried to change for her. Even now, knowing I've lost her, I'm still trying, still fighting to be someone worthy.

It's been nearly two years since I've seen her in person, a year since I've hacked into her emails, and roughly six months since I've stalked them on our graduating class's alumni page. And, uh, yeah, I've managed to go cold-turkey for an entire week now—eight days to be exact. Haven't once scanned through the pics she's always posting in Insta, even though I'm itching to click on her profile.

Wasn't going to include that last item, but why start lying to you now?

Sitting in the basement of Saint Augustine's parish hall earlier tonight, a place I visit every Monday and Thursday without fail, I earned my bronze chip. One year of sobriety, that's what it signifies. It felt like a victory until I realized I've had more success quitting drinking than I've had trying to quit her.

My name is Nick Brunner. I am a son, a brother, and yes, I am an alcoholic. I am a work in progress.

But this isn't my story, it's Darcy's. To her, I know I'm no more than a distant memory, a bad waking dream, a blip on the radar from her past.

She looks happy, and I want that. I want her to be happy.

I just wish she could have been happy with me.

*　*　*

Let Me Be the One

Chapter One

TOM

I want her.

It's not easy to reconcile, not easy to see myself as a fundamentally good person while coveting what my friend has, this perfect woman he does not deserve.

Screw principles, screw ethics, screw that bro code bullshit. An hour in her presence would lead the best of men to veer off the high road. And the rules don't apply when your friend is a jealous, manipulative liar who also happens to be an alcoholic in the making.

Nick Brunner doesn't deserve her.

Sitting here across from the two of them, I find myself wondering how I came to be friends with Nick in the first place. I don't like him. I don't like the way he slicks back his shoulder-length hair, as if he can't decide who he's channeling today: surfer dude Nick or business mogul Nick. Don't like the way he peppers his speech with words like gnarly and stoked. He may have grown up in southern California, may be the heir to a surf apparel fortune, but he's a poser. His carefully curated look, his speech, his mannerisms? It's all an act.

I especially don't appreciate the way he watches my girl—damn, I mean his girl. He's eyeing Darcy like he's the wolf and she's Little Red. He wants to eat her, consume her, wants her all to himself.

He planted his hand on her thigh the moment she sat down. Wants her to think he's being covert about the whole thing, that it's a private affair, but I know Nick. I know that he wants my full attention when his hand, concealed by the table, begins to inch up, slow and steady on its way to the promised land. He wants me to know he possesses her, wants me to see her squirm. I see her cheeks flush when he reaches his destination, watch in despair as her chest rises and falls. Darcy looks to him, one eyebrow arched, annoyed more than she's turned on. Good. I'm as close as I'll get to being satisfied when I see his hand begin its retreat back down to her knee.

Baby. He calls her that a lot. Normally I'm not opposed, but I see she doesn't like it, so I'm mad at Nick on her behalf. This whole time we've been sitting here—and I'll admit I've been in the girl's presence for less than an hour—she seems like she's not entirely happy. She's restless.

"Why would you say that?" Now she's flat-out pissed. "That word is sexist, it's demeaning, and it's just wrong. If I broke up with someone to start dating you, would that make me a bitch?"

What did I miss?

Nick's trying to look cool and unaffected, but he doesn't like being challenged. "It's simple. Morgan strung him along and then fucked him over. In my book that makes her a bitch. Sorry if I offended you, baby. C'mon, you're nothing like her."

She's not appeased. Her expression changes when she turns to me and reaches her hand across the table to rest it on top of mine. I respond like an abandoned puppy receiving affection for the first time in its life. I'm so lost in how good her skin feels touching mine that my ex's name barely registers. I tune in half-way through, catch only half of what Darcy says next.

"—not entirely awful. It looks like she was someone special to you, so she must have *some* redeeming qualities."

I'm able to piece together that Darcy and Nick have attributed my spaced-out state to seeing my ex walk by. Like the mere sight of her would crush me or something. Uh, no. I was thinking about Darcy, envisioning the two of us tangled up in the sheets, waking up with my arms wrapped snug around her body. Morgan wasn't even on my radar.

"Don't go feeling bad for Tom, he hasn't been lonely. Two tables over to the right is Holly." He shoots Darcy a greasy smile, and goes on talking about me as if I'm not here, not sitting two fucking feet across from them. "She was Saturday night. Holly's friend Dawn, sitting right next to her?" He gives a knowing nod. "St. Patrick's Day."

"Not true," I protest as I look over and try to pin down the time-line he's stating as fact.

Holly is a yes.

My mind goes back to last Sunday morning, to that moment when I shifted my body the way I always do when I want to leave someone's bed unnoticed. I breathe a quick sigh of relief when she doesn't stir, then locate my clothes and dress without making a sound. I want out, want to escape without having to say goodbye or thank you. Yes, one time I actually said thank you—awkward as fuck. One quick look in the mirror tells me it was one of those nights. My eyes are red-rimmed and there's dried blood at the base of my nose. I give myself the day-after pep talk that's becoming routine: *Way to go, asshole.* Reaching for my phone on the nightstand, I catch her reflection in the window. She's awake, and from the look on her face I can tell she's mired in regret, same as me. I turn away, pretend I don't notice.

I don't want to look at the other girl right now, her roommate.

Pretty certain I'll recall saying something lame like *Kiss me, I'm Irish*, although knowing me, my pick-up line was a tad more raunchy.

When Nick adds, "I'm surprised he remembers Morgan's name after the year he's had," I want to lunge across the table and choke him out.

I'm like the clueless public defender you see on those cop shows, trying to mount a defense but coming up empty. I look to Darcy, open my mouth to speak but say nothing. She's looking down at the table. Our easy back and forth is over, it's awkward now. She mutters something about getting to class and leaves.

"What the fuck was that about?"

Nick is all wide-eyed innocence. "What do you mean?"

"You do that a lot...Make jokes about how many girls I've been with. You make it sound like I'm with someone new every night."

"Hate to break it to you, guy, but you're known as the biggest man-whore in the school's history."

Is he expecting to get a laugh out of me with that dig? When I don't respond, he shakes his head and raises both palms to placate me. "Didn't mean anything by it." Popping another fry into his mouth, he adds, "I'm actually kind of jealous. I'm stuck with the same girl in my bed night after night, while you get to sample all the fine tail on this campus."

Lie. Another one to add to the pile. I was coming to see that Nick stretched the truth, exaggerated, and flat out lied on a regular basis. The other day he told me he had "several" venture capitalists interested in the new e-commerce start-up he was developing. I was impressed for about thirty seconds until he was unable to answer the most basic questions related to his non-existent business plan. And he loved bragging about how he was "raking in the Benjamins" with online poker. Odd that he couldn't manage to win so much as one hand when playing among friends.

Nick was also in the habit of angling to make himself look good at someone else's expense. He took the moral high ground in public, commenting on other's faults to boost his own profile, when in reality he's one of the biggest degenerates I know.

And now I've become his fall guy. I'm the guy Nick keeps close. Those jabs disguised as compliments are meant to make me look bad standing next to him. That I'm in the same league as him nowadays —what does that say about me?

The year he's had. It's only been six months since Morgan dumped me. Six months since I walked up to the guy who was helping her move her stuff into the dorm and introduced myself. For real, I assumed he was her cousin or something. The light bulb didn't go off until I saw Morgan freeze in place, panic-stricken when she came back outside to find the two of us unloading her car together.

She went home after freshman year, after spending pretty much every waking moment outside of class with me, and got back together with her high school boyfriend. She'd been pulling away from me all summer, but I didn't see it at the time, hindsight being twenty-twenty and all that. The phone calls she cut short, the invitations to visit that she skirted, the short goodnight texts she wrote signing off with *Love ya,* when I'd gone full-on *Miss you, Love you, Can't wait to see you.* A complete and total dumbass, that's what I was. And following that oh so awkward moment in the parking lot, I went on the bender to end all benders.

Nick would lead you to believe my life has been like a bad country song ever since—whiskey, women and whining—as if I spent every day pining away like a loser for someone who obviously doesn't give a crap about me. And maybe it's partly true. There's been too much drinking, too little studying, too many meaningless hook-ups. At first, screwing around did the trick—took my mind off my misery—but feeling good in the moment doesn't make the morning after any better. Like I said, Nick tends to exaggerate, but waking up in a strange bed more than a couple of times is a couple of times too many.

Nick sees a guy from one of his classes and bolts after him, probably looking to scam notes or a test outline out of him. He's got his schmooze face on, clapping the guy on his back like they're long lost pals. He makes me sick. I look away, inadvertently locking eyes with Holly. I give her a half smile and a wave, a lame substitute for the apology she deserves. Her eyes are sad when she smiles back. I imagine mine are too. The nagging sense of self-loathing that's taken root and begun to grow inside of me intensifies.

I am not proud.

This isn't me.

I give myself the time it takes to walk from the cafeteria to the dorms to wallow in self-pity. I've been dealt some shit cards in this life, but I always push through. Morgan's betrayal hurt, but my reaction has been borderline pathetic. I've been through much worse. And besides, I'm over it, haven't thought about her in weeks. Didn't even notice when she walked by me today. Couldn't take my eyes off Darcy to spare Morgan even a passing glance.

Darcy.

It's more than desire, more than just wanting what I don't have.

I need the happiness, the sweet glow of kindness—I need whatever it is that she's giving off.

I need *her*.

All the stupid shit I've been doing? It ends today. I'll change for her, do everything in my power to show her I'm the better man, that I deserve to be the one.

Chapter Two

DARCY

"Is that you, Donovan?"

He's smiling from ear to ear and I find myself doing the same. I scramble to grab the one shopping bag that dropped when we collided, but he reaches down and picks it up before I can.

He looks dazed and dreamy, stunned in a good way when he says, "I can't believe it's you."

Tom Farrell also looks hot, let's not leave that part out. Still too amazed by this happy coincidence to speak, I take him in from head to toe. The tailored suit, the crisp white dress shirt opened at the neck, the stubble just now making an appearance on his strong jaw after a hard day's work—my mind drifts to kissing along that chiseled jaw of his.

"Who's this?" the older gentleman standing next to him asks. One look at his face and I know this must be Tom's father. He's good looking, with playful eyes and a kind smile.

"I'm Darcy." I say it at the same time Tom says, "Dad, Uncle Rob, meet Darcy Donovan. We go to school together." Turning back to me, he shakes his head and smiles. "It's crazy running into you like this."

"Totally crazy. I'm just staying in the city for a few days to get some shopping done. I leave next week."

"You live nearby?"

Hands full, I gesture uptown with my chin. "Not far."

"Can you join us for dinner, Darcy?" his father asks.

I look down at my outfit: flip flops, yoga pants and a tank top, and then look to the attendant standing guard outside the restaurant. A laugh escapes before I say, "I don't think this would fly at Jean Georges."

Tom looks me up and down. I can feel my skin heat, can feel the flush that spreads across my cheeks. He turns to his father, shoots him a look that's pleading, like he wants his dad to come up with some sort of solution. It's kind of adorable.

"Your parents aren't in town?" When I shake my head, his father smiles as if he's won. "Well, if you're in the big city alone, as a fellow parent I have to insist we look after you and take you to dinner."

If he only knew that I'm more than happy to play along. "I guess I can suffer through a Michelin star-rated meal. Be back in a few minutes, I live just a couple of blocks away."

Mr. Farrell wears a satisfied grin. "Escort her, Thomas. We'll hold dinner for you."

Ohmygod, ohmygod, ohmygod. My heart is beating a mile a minute. He's taken my bags, so I'm left empty-handed, feeling awkward as I walk alongside him. But it's not like me to feel unsettled like this. *Snap out of it, Donovan. He's just a boy.*

"Is this your brownstone?" he asks when I come to a stop.

"Yeah, this is home." I fumble with my keys and shake my head. "Sorry, I don't know what's the matter with me. Maybe I do need to eat."

Inspecting the many bags now in his possession, he says, "It looks like you took that saying *Shop 'til you drop* to heart."

Tom follows after me into the entryway. His shoes click loudly on the tile and the sound echoes. It's unusual for this house to feel so empty. I'm suddenly grateful that I won't be sitting here eating takeout dumplings by myself tonight.

"Want me to carry these upstairs?"

"Don't bother. I'll just take this one." I take the Trina Turk bag. I want to wear a new dress tonight, for him. It's an off-white linen, so it shows off my tan, and it fits me like a glove. Now I'm glad I let the salesperson talk me into the gold strappy sandals, knowing they'll look perfect together. Taking the stairs two at a time, I look back down at him and tease, "You can pass the time looking at my baby pictures."

And I think he does just that as I give myself the quickest washcloth wipe down in history, throw my hair up into a pretty stylish looking topknot, swipe on some lip gloss and then dress. *Not bad*, I tell myself as I look in the mirror. *I wish I had more time to get ready, but not bad.*

He's standing in front of a portrait as I make my way downstairs, then moves onto another, studying it. When I can make out the picture, I cringe because it's a winner.

"I'm still amazed my father let me dye my hair lavender."

"Huh?"

I gesture to the picture he's standing in front of. "Looks especially hot with the mouth full of braces, right?"

He doesn't answer, says nothing as he takes me in. I shift on my feet, unsure of what to do or say.

"You look great." He smiles. "I mean, really, really great."

Oh-kay. "Thank you."

And when he offers me his arm like a formal gentleman on the walk back to the restaurant, I think I might be in danger of swooning—like eighteenth century, in need of smelling salts swooning.

"Your home is beautiful." Before I can thank him, he adds, "It looks formal and stately on the outside, so I was expecting, I don't know, all marble and chandeliers on the inside, but—"

"But it's not."

"It's homey and lived in. It's nice."

"Yeah, most of my friends' houses are of the marble staircase, chandelier, expensive artwork variety. Growing up in Manhattan is—"

"Different."

I nod. "I love it here, don't get me wrong, but spending the summer at the beach is a nice break."

"So that's where everyone is?" He bumps my hip gently and teases, "Let me guess, you're an East Hampton girl."

I shoot him a side-eye. "Never. My Dad hates the scene out there, and the traffic would basically eat up his entire weekend. There are plenty of beach towns in the five boroughs. Not too many people know about them, which makes them perfect. And yeah, my parents are at the beach now. My father always takes a few weeks in August."

"A life of leisure." He fingers the lapel on his suit jacket. "Some of us have to slave the summer away in the city."

I hip check him right back. "I worked five days a week this summer, with the lives and safety of thousands of beachgoers on my shoulders. Don't go hating on me just because I happen to get a killer tan while I work."

"A lifeguard?" When I nod, he laughs. "I love it."

He opens the door for me before the attendant can do it, then guides me to his family's table with one hand on my lower back. The contact makes me lightheaded.

Later on that night I'll wonder if I made a decent impression on his family, or if I came off as flighty. Tom makes it hard to focus. When he looks at you, he looks at you with intensity, and when you speak, he hangs on every word. Every smile, every innocent touch is disarming. When he reaches over and uses his napkin to wipe some wayward sauce from my cheek, I slip my hands beneath the tablecloth to check my pulse. The pre-med student in me is ready to diagnose tachycardia, even though I know it's Tom setting my heart racing.

His uncle pours us a glass of wine to have with dinner, and after the adults leave us to go have desert in the lounge, the wine feels like it's having a truth serum-like effect on me.

I barely know you, but I can't stop thinking about you.

When your name comes up in conversation, I lap up every bit of information I can about you.

Is it true what they say about you?

I have a crush on Thomas Farrell.

Thank the Lord I don't say any of that out loud.

I didn't, did I? He looks uncomfortable. It takes me a second to tune back in, and then I'm the one who's uncomfortable.

"I don't know everything, Darcy, but I heard enough. I wasn't prying or anything, it's just that I'm good friends with Dan and Jenna's your roommate, so I heard things." When I don't offer anything, he asks, "Is this because of Nick? Are you really leaving because of him?"

I shake my head, even though the answer to his question is an emphatic yes.

Yes, I'm scared of him.

Yes, he's ruining my life.

Yes, I'm running away.

But I don't say any of it because I'm trying to take on a different persona. No, I'm trying to be more like the girl I once was. I used to be fearless, confident and outspoken. It took just a few months with Nick Brunner to strip it all away.

"It has nothing to do with him. I mean, I'm so excited for Spain." I smile through my practiced speech, but it feels forced. The crease in his brow tells me he's not buying it, so I pour it on. "And I'll be hitting just about every major city in Europe while I'm there...Paris,

Amsterdam, Florence, Prague, Lisbon. I already have a million side trips planned."

He closes his eyes for a moment and then takes another sip of his drink. I get the distinct impression he knows more than what he's letting on. No doubt he's heard what Nick's been saying about me. Probably believes there's at least some measure of truth to all the filthy lies he's been spreading. Does he know I was too scared to leave my dorm room towards the end of last semester, that I was a blubbering mess, crying nonstop and always looking over my shoulder?

I close my eyes too, but from shame.

He reaches over and squeezes my hand, and when I look to him, I see nothing but understanding and kindness in his expression. "I wish I signed up for study abroad. I'm totally jealous of you."

I take a deep breath and nod. "It's going to be great."

I find myself speaking in affirmations a lot lately: *I'm so excited, It's going to be great, Can't wait.* I'm trying to convince myself, when in truth, living in a foreign country and traveling with a group of strangers was never on my bucket list.

"It will be." He studies his glass, moves it in a way so that the ice cubes circle and make a clinking sound now that it's empty. He's stalling, so I assume he's not ready to let this go. He cocks his head to the side when he looks back up at me. "I'm glad you're going. It is going to be a great experience. But I just want you to know that I kind of hate him for it, and I'm not the only one."

I do my best to make light of it. "Guess you've been talking to Jenna?"

"She's obviously beside herself." He smiles. "She feels like she's losing her twin sister." Tom's father catches his eye and looks down at his watch. "Let me tell them I'll get the next train."

I check the time on my phone. "Is there a later one?"

He sighs. "Probably not. I still have time to walk you back if we leave now, though. I'll meet them at Grand Central."

"I'll be fine. It's just a few blocks."

He stands and then takes my hand to help me out of the booth. "I'm walking you home."

People from New York will tell you there's a mass exodus from the city between Memorial Day and Labor Day. The locals head for their summer homes while Manhattan is inundated with tourists crowding the sidewalks. Between the heat, humidity and the crowds, the city is unbearable.

They have a point, I guess, and I definitely prefer sandy shores to hot asphalt, but I love this city in every season. Take tonight. There's a cool breeze signaling the end of summer, planters and window boxes are overflowing with multicolored blooms, and I've got a gorgeous man walking alongside me, his arm linked with mine. It's not intimate the way holding hands would be, but there's something so warm and familiar about the way he leads me. It's protective, and I decide that I like it. After what I've been through, I'll take protective over possessive any day of the week.

Tom looks down at his phone and frowns.

"You have to hurry, don't you?"

He shakes his head. "I'll grab a cab on the corner, I'll be fine. I just don't—"

"Want the night to end?" He nods as if I've read his mind, but I'm only saying what I'm feeling. "I know, I wish we had a few more hours. I'd like to take you on a walking tour of my little corner of the city."

"Where would you take me?"

"Hmm...Maybe I'd take you by my high school, show you where I ruled the lacrosse field."

"Lacrosse? I pictured you as a tennis player."

"Competition was fierce at my school. I'm decent, but I wasn't close to being good enough to make that squad. And full disclosure, our lacrosse team rounded out the bottom of our private school league every year. I didn't ride the pine or anything, but I'm not what you'd call a gifted athlete."

"I think you're just being modest...Bet you're a baller."

I burst out laughing. "Not even close."

He nudges my elbow. "Where else would you take me?"

"Around the corner from my high school there's a bar we used to sneak into when we were seniors."

He's wide-eyed. "Underage drinking? I'm appalled."

"Yep, I'm a law breaker. My father loves the burgers there, so I go there with my family at least twice a month when I'm home. If we're there late enough on a Friday night, I get to see the new crop of high school seniors flashing their fake IDs."

I should prompt him to go. I know he's cutting it close, but he's looking at me like he wants more, and I want that too. But already feeling lonely for this boy I barely know is probably not a good thing. I've been a mixed-up mess these past few months, and getting hung up on a fantasy is not the first stop on the road back to stability. It's time for goodnight.

"Last but not least, I'd take you to the best late-night dumpling spot in the city. I was actually planning to order takeout from there tonight before I ran into you."

"I hope you're not disappointed."

"Are you kidding? That was one of the best meals I've ever had. And that's saying a lot because I'm like a crack addict when it comes to my pork and chive dumplings." I raise my hand to hail the cab driving down my street. "The company was really great too."

Tom leans in and gives me a hug. I have to stop myself from snuggling in closer to breathe him in. He holds me for an extra beat before breaking away. "I'm so glad I ran into you tonight."

"Me too."

He lowers the window as soon as he gets into the taxi. "See you in January, Darcy."

Chapter Three

One year later...

TOM

What the hell?

I'm fixated, studying this beautiful girl as she makes her way across the far end of the field. I need to verify that she is, in fact, my Darcy, and not just some apparition, every fantasy I've had over the past year screwing with my sanity. When I see Jenna and the rest of the girls rush over and grab her into a group hug, it's all the proof I need. I'm smiling, think I even hear myself laugh out loud, so overcome with happiness and relief and the promise of something good to come. That's when I get hit square in the gut with a soccer ball.

Doubled over, I can hear myself choking out that nasty combination of stomach lurching, wheezing and coughing that you make when you get the wind knocked out of you.

"Sorry." Dan laughs as he jogs towards me. "I didn't mean to nail you so hard."

"What was that for?" My voice doesn't sound like my own.

Dan offers a hand to help me up. "I needed to knock that dazed look off your face." He gestures towards the group of girls gathered on the edge of the field. "You're drooling, Tom."

One year. That's how long she's been gone, how long it's been since she ran off.

"What is she doing here?"

"She came back."

"You said—"

"Last I heard, she was transferring."

Dan shrugs like the difference between her coming back here for senior year or finishing school someplace else is no biggie, and I want to slap the shit out of him for acting so indifferent.

I look over to Nick. His eyes are on me, studying me before he shakes his head and gestures in her direction. "Look who's back." His face is a mixture of aggravation and pain. "My life would be a lot easier if the bitch just stayed away."

"Don't even start, Brunner. I'm only going to warn you once."

"I'm over it, Dan, so you can relax."

Nick rolls his eyes once Dan's back is turned, and then looks to me, shaking his head as he lets out a tired breath. Is he assuming I'm on his side? That we're brothers in arms or some shit?

If you asked anyone last year, they'd have told you Nick Brunner and I were friends, good friends even. And there was a time when I did gravitate towards Nick and people like him, a time when my own life was in the gutter and I was making bad decisions—birds of a feather and all that. But I'm not that guy anymore.

Friends. Pretty sure no one would describe us using that term now, except maybe Nick.

The guy is delusional. I think he actually believes we share some kind of bond. Darcy dumped him, Morgan dumped me, so we both know the pain of being discarded, both had to suck it up and watch as someone we loved moved on. When he's drunk—so basically I'm talking every time we run into one another—he wants to commiserate, but I'm not having it. He's still angry and spiteful where Darcy is concerned, whereas I never once felt the desire to get back at Morgan, to hurt her.

I'm not anything like you, Nick. I never was. I've said those exact words to him.

And since Dan and the others have filled me in on more of what he put Darcy through, I can barely stand the sight of him.

"You all right?" Dan asks after Nick walks off.

"Why didn't you tell me?"

"I honestly wasn't sure she was coming back. After Darcy bailed on last semester, I didn't talk about it much...Didn't want Jenna getting her hopes up."

Just like I'd gotten my hopes up.

I worked out like a madman, swore off booze, and was as celibate as a monk for the first half of junior year. My preparation for the return of Darcy Donovan earned me my highest GPA ever and a set of six-pack abs to boot—I should thank her for that. But when I came back to school after Christmas break only to hear she'd decided to stay abroad for the entire year, I'll admit to feeling crushed. I literally felt worse than I did that day in the parking lot when I helped Morgan and her boyfriend move in, and that's saying something.

And while I didn't backslide completely, I did say *screw it* on occasion. Old habits die hard.

I watch her walking towards the rest of the group now, trying to sort out what it all means. Does she remember that night last August? Was I the only one who felt it? When I said I'd see her in January, she answered back, "See you next semester, Tom." It sounded like a promise. Almost as if we were concocting a plan without either one of us having to say the words out loud.

Her laugh carries across the space that separates us, wakes me up and draws me in. My desire for Darcy hasn't abated. Time and distance have done nothing to lessen the pull I feel towards her.

Dan grabs our t-shirts off the ground and tosses mine to me. "Beer?"

"I'm down."

He's smiling and shaking his head. "I'll bet you are, especially since a certain someone is standing right next to the keg."

"Guilty as charged."

I hang back a few feet when Dan moves in on Jenna, kissing her cheek. "Hey, babe." He moves on to Darcy then, lifting her up off her feet and taking her into a bear hug. "You're a sight for sore eyes."

She pokes his chest. "Have you been taking good care of my girl?"

"Absolutely."

When Darcy looks over his shoulder, her eyes land on me and she smiles. "Tom."

She's got me, a guy who's normally borderline cocky, standing here shuffling my feet with my hands stuffed in my pockets. I shake off the nerves. "Glad to see you've finally come back."

"I'm really happy to be back."

"I want to hear all about your trip," I take one step closer and lower my voice, "when I take you out on our second date."

Darcy smells like musk, like vanilla, like a bonfire—like the best sex I've ever had. I held back last summer. Standing less than a foot away from her, drawing every moment out just to put off saying goodbye, I wanted to kiss her more than I wanted my next breath, but I held back.

No more of that.

Now I move in close, breathe her in. I'm so close I can feel her shallow breaths, can see the flush creeping across her skin. She's affected by me and I love it.

Darcy takes a step back then, manages a casual laugh. "Our second date? You mean when your parents took me out, that was our first date?"

I touch her shoulder because I can't keep my hands to myself when she's this close. "I guess that's debatable, but I'm going to go with a yes."

Jenna and Beth pick this moment to crash our little party of two. As they drag her off, I can hear Beth asking, "What was that?" referring to me, and Jenna telling her some nonsense about being careful, something about setting Nick off.

Screw Nick. Any good will I had towards him has evaporated.

I'm not going to stand down. I'm not going to hold back to spare his feelings. I'm not letting anything get between me and what I want.

And I want her.

* * *

"I'm not telling you what to do, brother, but you were pretty obvious about it right out of the gate. You know this is gonna get ugly."

Chris is our team captain and one of Nick's roommates, although I don't get the impression there's a close bond there anymore. Chris is a big guy and doesn't fuck around, but he's thoughtful and even-tempered. When he has something to say, people tend to listen.

I know he's right, it's definitely going to get ugly, but I don't care.

"Remind me again why we're even having this conversation? Nick has a girlfriend, does he not?"

Chris tosses me the ball, harder than he did a moment ago. "If you're referring to that sophomore, yes, he has a girlfriend, but you and I both know where his head's at now that Darcy's back."

"It looked to me like he had his tongue jammed down that poor girl's throat yesterday. Didn't look like he was hung up on Darce at all."

Chris laughs in my face. "Darce? You've got a pet name for her already?" When I shrug, he sobers. "You know he thinks of you as one of his closest friends, right?"

"He was never my friend," I toss the ball back just as hard, "and you know that. Why are you defending him right now, anyway? You know what he did to her."

"I'm not defending him." He sits down on the grass, reaches for his water bottle. "I don't know, it's complicated. I've always felt bad for the guy."

"I'm kind of over feeling bad for him."

"Right in the middle of that shitstorm sophomore year, when I was dragging his drunk ass home every night, his father paid him a visit. Took us all out to that really expensive sushi place on Comm Ave. Totally over the top, way too much sake, and it got awkward. Within ten minutes of sitting down at the table, you got the impression that he just wasn't all that interested in Nick. I know it sounds weird, but I'd even go as far as to say he doesn't like Nick. Every time Nick went to start a conversation, his father cut him off, spoke right over him. He paid more attention to me, Denny and Vic. His dad was engaged and interested in whatever mundane crap any one of us had to say, except if Nick was talking."

"That sucks."

"It was embarrassing."

"Still doesn't give him a free pass for what he did."

"No, it doesn't." Chris looks to me, shaking his head. "When we got back that night, you know what Nick said to me?"

"Not a clue."

"He's making himself a sandwich, and I ask him how he can eat after that feast. He says, 'I hate sushi.' I ask him why we went for Japanese then. Nick says, 'He picked the restaurant, and before you ask, the answer is yes, he knows I don't eat sushi.' Isn't that crazy?"

"It's shitty."

"So that's why I haven't cut him loose. Even though I hate what he did to Darcy, even though I wanted her brother to beat Nick's ass when he came to campus looking for him last year, even though he doesn't deserve anyone's sympathy."

I look to him and nod. "I get it, but don't ask me to back away just to spare his feelings. I'm already in too deep where she's concerned, so I'll handle the fallout."

In too deep. That I was.

I fell fast and hard for Morgan, and what I felt for her pales in comparison to this. I think about Darcy all the time. And it isn't just that I'm daydreaming about what it would be like to be buried inside of her, although I'm doing that on a very regular basis. It's more. I want to take her places, hold her, talk to her, just be with her.

I spotted her on her way to class this morning. Still with that end of summer tan, long waves hanging halfway down her back, and a body that would render any man stupid. I was fixed in place, staring at her. When she dropped whatever she was holding, I had to fight the urge to sprint across the quad to grab it off the ground for her. And when she laughed at something her friend Caitlin said to her, I smiled, happy that she was happy. In that moment I knew I was falling for her.

Too much, too soon.

Maybe Chris has a point. Maybe I do need to slow down.

Chapter Four

DARCY

I'm probably the only person on campus relieved the weekend is coming to an end.

It's quiet as I take a few minutes to stretch, this Sunday morning no different from any other. Most of my friends crawled back home just a few hours ago, and they'll be asleep until the first Sunday football games get underway this afternoon.

Running along the river, I replay the events of yesterday, try to make sense of what happened.

I wish I'd never gone to watch his game. Definitely wish I would have skipped the after-party at the rugby house. One minute he's looking at me from across the room, smiling at me like we share a secret or some inside joke, and the next minute he's got another girl sitting in his lap, laughing as she whispers in his ear.

At least I didn't stick around to let him make a complete fool out of me.

Not that the alternative was any better. I should have listened to my inner voice, the one telling me to go home and eat some cookie dough, but instead I listened to my roommates, who proceeded to drag me to a party where I was welcomed by Nick and his new babe. He downed his beer when he caught sight of me, and his girl shot daggers my way, as if it was my fault he was drinking his weight in beer. *He's been doing that long before you arrived on the scene, honey.* Ten minutes later and some over-served fool was insinuating I had a stick up my ass because I wouldn't dance with him. The guy could barely stand upright. That moment was the cherry on my craptastic sundae.

The worst part? I was nice to the guy. When he wouldn't take no for an answer, when he accused me of being stuck-up, even when he pulled me close and tried to make me dance with him against my will, I didn't stand up for myself. No, Beth did that. Beth got in his face and told him to back off. Beth—all one hundred and ten pounds of her—stomped on his foot when he kept it up. Beth hugged me afterwards and assured me the guy was a jerk.

I'm still that girl? Weak, afraid, unable to stand up for herself?

I tell myself that I'm not.

I feel strong when I run. The rhythm of my breathing soothes me and the repetitive tap of my sneakers on pavement helps to center my thoughts. I can work through any dilemma when I run.

Today I keep going past my normal turn-around, push myself, feel like I could run a marathon. By the time I circle back to campus, I'm humming along to Pink's *U+Ur Hand* while mulling over the merits of taking a self-defense class, and I've come to the conclusion that guys in general just aren't worth it.

I gave Tom too much credit. He's clearly earned his reputation. Whatever. I'm here to get through senior year and prepare to head off to medical school. I'm not wasting my time drooling over someone like Tom Farrell.

Jenna doesn't bring him up and I refuse to fish for information when we walk into town. More important things on my mind today, such as lasagna. I'm actually a pretty excellent cook, if I do say so myself. Plus, cooking always gives me a peaceful, contented feeling. How can all not be right in the world when your house is filled with the scent of cake baking or chicken roasting?

After laying into me for leaving without telling her and Dan where I was going last night, she tells me about her run-in with Tom. According to her, he looked devastated when she told him I'd left with some other guy. I burst out laughing and hug my best girl. Jenna always has my back. I doubt he was truly heartbroken, though. Tom Farrell, from what I've gathered, is supremely confident around women and has plenty of willing ones to choose from.

That's what's really bothering me. When we were together in the city last summer, Tom seemed so genuine. He was kind, funny, down to earth—someone I could see myself with. But now I'm getting mixed messages. Tom seemed to get off on all that female attention yesterday, while he all but ignored me. And that first day back at the field? Those flirty, breathy things he whispered in my ear that made me ache? Is the real Tom Farrell nothing more than a phony Casanova who just wants to score? I won't be that girl for him. Not happening.

We spend the better part of the afternoon sautéing onions and garlic, making a homemade Bolognese sauce, and layering two large trays of lasagna. It smells awesome in our place, and Jenna, my sous chef, is enjoying some Chianti with me. This is exactly what I needed.

As we're taking the garlic bread out of the oven and the rest of the girls are coming to the table to feast, the front door opens. Dan, Ben and Tom walk in.

"Damn, it smells like heaven in here. I'm not above begging for a home-cooked meal." Ben looks to me and Jenna, hands in prayer. "Please tell me you can feed me."

Dan shrugs. "I'm eating. You're all cutting out the carbs, right ladies?"

"Cutting out carbs, my ass," Caitlin snaps.

Dan talks right over her. "I'm just looking out for you by taking some of this off your hands."

I can feel Tom's eyes on me, but I'm not about to turn around and look at him. I can't. I'm mad at him for blowing me off, but I'm more angry with myself. Why do I feel so hurt? There's nothing between us. Not a kiss, not a past, nothing. I feel ridiculous.

Everyone at the table falls into easy conversation while Jenna and I fetch odds and ends from the kitchen. I notice Tom hasn't taken a seat.

"What are you waiting for, Farrell? Dig in," Ben sputters between bites.

I can't resist, can't keep my mouth shut. My common sense flies out the window as anger bubbles up inside of me. Does he think I'm a fool? You're going to lead me on with some whispering in my ear nonsense one day, then have me stand by and witness some random girl wiggling into your lap the next? No, he can kiss off.

"I'm sure Tom's got places to go, people to see. He probably has one of his many babes cooking for him as we speak."

The chit-chat stops, the room falls silent, and the awkward vibe hangs in the air. From the corner of my eye I can see him lower his head, turn around and leave.

Now I feel like a witch.

And I can't stomach one bite of that damn lasagna.

* * *

TOM

Hands in my pockets, I raise my face to the sky, let the driving rain pelt me hard. I walk past my place with no destination in mind.

The look she just shot me? I think if I *had* gone ahead and made myself a plate, Darcy might have stabbed me with that knife she was wielding. It smelled like garlicky, cheesy goodness in there, and damn, now I'm starving.

I went there to check in on her, to make sure she was all right. When I ran into Beth at that after-hours party and she told me some jerk was hitting on Darcy and getting aggressive about it, I nearly lost it. I got no answer when I knocked on their door last night, so I was hoping I'd have an opportunity to talk to her now. Guess when it comes to me, Darcy and her bestie for life are like-minded. After screwing with my head, telling me Darcy left our party with another guy, Jenna basically called me pathetic.

One of his many babes. Did it look like I was into those girls yesterday? I didn't think so. I didn't put a hand on anyone, didn't flirt. I wanted to go straight to her, but I stuck with my plan to take my time with Darcy, to go slow.

Maybe she isn't interested in me.

Nah, I don't believe that for a second. I felt her body react when I touched her, and it was the same for me. The pull was real.

Obviously, my plan is backfiring. I just have to lay it out there. No risk, no return.

* * *

Easier said than done, because she goes full-on ghost mode for the duration of the week. She's not at lunch with her girls. I have Dan scoping for me, so I know she's not at home after dinner. I troll the library with no luck. Desperate, I hunt Jenna down Thursday night and go for a casual tone when I ask what "all of you girls" have been up to this week. Jenna knows me well and can therefore see right through my bullshit. She shoots back, "When you say, 'all of you girls' I'm assuming you mean, what's Darcy been up to this week?"

"You gonna make me beg?"

"No. I just don't want you jerking her around if you aren't serious. She had a terrible year, and I know she's still skittish about being back here. You know I love you, Tom, but you don't have the best track record."

"Wow."

"Wait, I'm not trying to be mean or to put you down. It's just that I've known you since freshman year and you've changed. The guy you morphed into after you and Morgan split up isn't someone I'd want my sister hooking up with, and Darcy is my sister. I can see that you're into her, but what does that mean? You looked like you were back to your lame lady killer ways on Saturday."

The mention of Morgan dumping me has me rubbing some phantom ache in my chest. It's been so long since the memory of that day in the parking lot filled me with hurt and with shame. Jenna goes to rest a hand on my shoulder, but I'm not having it. I don't want her comfort. I shrug her off and walk in the opposite direction.

I hide out in the library for a while, stewing, not wanting to face anyone. I'm the first to admit that I acted like a complete jackass for a while there, but have I really earned that poor of a reputation? Sophomore year was one thing, but junior year—save for a few trips down memory lane—I was a damn choir boy. Jenna makes it sound like I'm some clown who isn't capable of being in a real relationship.

I have no intention of jerking Darcy around, and I'm going to prove it.

Chapter Five

TOM

Saturday night, and the party is at our place. I've been watching the door all night. I watch as Jenna, Beth, Caitlin and Rene come in sometime around eleven. She's not with them, but I'm patient. When my phone reads twelve-thirty, though, I get a sinking feeling. She's not coming, and it's because of me.

Go big or go home.

I tug a sweatshirt over my head and make my way towards the door, determined to go to her and lay it all out there. Two steps from the side door and ready to make my exit is when I spot her, tucked into a corner at the base of the stairs talking to my friend Mac. I also see Nick out of the corner of my eye. He's standing off to the side staring at the two of them. He downs his full beer and then takes the spare he poured himself from the table behind him—always double fisted.

In Mac's defense, it's loud in here, but does he really need to move in so close every time he says something to her? I mean, he's practically tongue-fucking her ear. It's bringing out that evil, eerie look in Nick's eyes and it's getting on my nerves too. I see Darcy take a slight step back when Mac inches forward. Her body language tells me she's not into him, thank the Lord.

Darcy walks towards the bathroom when Mac gestures that he's getting them a refill. He has two full cups in his hands when Nick pounces. Everyone within ten feet of them is doused in beer, girls are screaming and fists are flying. Mac lands a few good ones to Nick's face and then pushes him down to the ground with ease.

"You're such a loser. You think *your* girl likes it when you fight over Darcy? Get a fucking grip."

Everyone turns to Nick's waif of a girlfriend. She looks mortified, but like a mouse, allows Nick to grab her wrist and haul her out of the party. I see Chris follow them out, so I know she'll be safe, but the way Nick handles her makes me seethe. Darcy told me last summer that he'd never laid a hand on her, but what does that mean? Was Nick rough with her the way he is with this new girl?

The music starts pumping throughout the room again, and conversations start back up with people yelling over the music. I see Mac looking around for Darcy but I know from past experience that she's probably already bailed. I catch up to her just as she's fumbling with her key.

"Are you okay?"

Her back is to me, but it's obvious she's crying from the way her slumped shoulders rise and fall.

"Tom, just go."

"No." I'm careful in the way I approach and put my hands on her waist. "Please, just look at me."

She turns slowly, her eyes wet with tears. "I shouldn't have come back. I can't take another year of this."

I want to scoop her up, pull her close and hold her. I lower my face so that we're eye to eye and cup her cheeks in my hands. "No, Darcy."

Those are the only words I manage to get out before Mac comes running up behind us out of breath. She backs away from me.

"Hey, there you are. He's a douchebag, don't let him ruin the night. Come on, let's go hit another party."

She flashes him a weak smile. "Thanks, but I'm heading to bed. That was enough drama for one night. G'night, guys."

When she closes the door, Mac zones in on me. "What was going on there?"

"Stay away from her, Mac."

He puts his hands up, palms facing me. "Relax. Are you with her? If you are, I'll back off, but if you're not..." When I give him nothing, he asks again, "Are you with her?"

The truthful answer is one I don't want to admit, so I just shove my hands in my pockets, turn and walk away.

* * *

DARCY

Another Sunday, another long run to process the mess from the night before, and another day cooking my problems away.

I can't stomach much of the cafeteria food, for the most part it's greasy and gross, but the real reason I spend my Sundays cooking is that it reminds me of being in the kitchen at home with my mom. I'm always happy there.

Today Beth is my kitchen sidekick and roast chicken is on the menu. She's the worst cook in the house, but she can't do too much damage chopping up celery and onions for the stuffing.

"So," Beth starts in cautiously, "are we going to talk about that massive brawl over you last night? What I wouldn't give to have Mac and Nick slugging it out over me. That was hot."

"That was so *not* hot."

"Mac looked like he was ready to kill for you, and he is seriously beautiful. If I wasn't with Marcus, the things I would do to that boy."

"Please, you and Marcus make me gag you're so in love. But last night was just…" I shake my head, turn away from her, take one of those deep cleansing breaths I learned in yoga class. "I just want to fly under the radar. Nick, all that drama…I just can't do it."

"I hear you," she says, wrapping me in a hug.

And then speak of the devil himself, Nick knocks once before walking right in like he owns the place. He barely makes eye contact before looking back to the floor. He's nervous.

"Can I talk to you for a minute? I just want to apologize."

Wide-eyed, Beth looks over to check with me. When I nod, she shoots Nick a death glare before heading upstairs.

Nick paces, raking his hands through his hair. "I *am* sorry, Darcy." He pauses, looks to me like he's pleading for understanding. "I don't know why I did that last night. I want you to feel comfortable around me, to be happy." His head drops when he adds, "You know I still love you. I just, I mean…Why can't you be happy *and* be with me?"

I take a seat across from where he's standing, shell-shocked and alarmed. He wants to be with me, for us to be a couple again? Is he insane?

Nick studies me, gauging my reaction. He shakes his head, one fist now tapping against his thigh. "I can see that's not what you want."

Weary, angry and…scared. I'm still scared of him, and the realization sickens me. *Stand up to him*, my inner voice cries. No more being gentle to spare his feelings. He's only ever read my kindness as submission.

"I won't do this anymore. I feel bad that you're hurting, and you know I'll always care about you, but we're over." I remind myself to be crystal clear. "We're not getting back together."

"Seeing Mac all over you last night? I wanted to tear his fucking head off. I'm trying here, Darcy, but you're not making it any easier. Hooking up with my friends? What, are you looking to get back at me or something?"

"We're done here." I stand and move towards the door. "You're not telling me who I can and can't be with. It's been over a year since we broke up. We go to the same school and we share the same friends, so I'm not promising you anything. I'm done tip-toeing around for you."

"I'll ask you again…Are you, or are you not with Mac?"

Just like old times, I feel like I'm on the stand being cross-examined. He's challenging me, menacing me. Same old Nick—gentle and pleading one minute, angry and intimidating the next.

Hands clasped behind my back so he can't see them shaking, I stand my ground. "It's not Mac, but there is someone and you know him. I'm not with him, but I have feelings for him."

He smirks and shakes his head. After a long, tense moment he takes one step closer. "If it's not Mac then it's Tom. I see how he looks at you." He raises his voice when I remain silent. "Seriously, one of my best friends?" He paces the floor again, walking away from me and then coming back to face off. "Gonna spread your legs for him? That's how it's gonna be?"

He's so close I can feel his breath, and for a moment I think he might be angry enough to lash out. When he reaches for my arm, I must flinch, because his eyes widen and he steps back, puts his palms up to reassure me. Shaking his head, he says, "Tom's a master bullshit artist. He'll get what he wants and then you'll be nothing to him." He lowers his voice, deflated. "I would never do that to you. I'd never treat you like that."

I see Beth starting to make her way back downstairs, but I motion for her to stop. I don't want a rescue from her or from anyone else.

"I want you to leave, Nick."

After a few strained moments of silence, Nick turns and practically takes the door off the hinges on his way out.

Five minutes with Nick and my stomach is in knots. That familiar nervous energy is coursing through my veins and my hands are shaking. I have to warn Tom, let him know about the storm heading his way.

Dan picks up on the first ring. "Can you give me Tom's number?"

He pauses before answering, "Sure, Darcy. Are you okay?"

"I'm fine, I just need to tell him something, kind of right away."

I nearly drop my phone when he answers.

"Hey Tom, it's Darcy."

"Well, to what do I owe this pleasure?" Lord, just the sound of his voice. "Are you calling to apologize?"

"Huh?"

"You know, for denying food to a starving boy last week. I'm still fantasizing about how good that lasagna smelled."

"Um, no, you have yet to earn my lasagna." My nervous laugh gives way to panic. "Seriously, I'm calling to tell you that Nick is probably heading your way and he's really angry. I'm sorry, I just wanted to give you a heads up."

He sighs, sounding irritated but not the least bit concerned. "I can handle him. Exactly why is he acting psychotic today?" He adds, "Not that he ever needs a good reason."

"He came over to my place, we talked, it didn't go very well, and he kind of got the impression that I might be into you."

"You *might* be into me? Hey now, that's definitely worth taking a punch for."

I cringe. "I'm about to die of shame and embarrassment right now."

He laughs. "Well, thanks for the warning 'cause here he comes. Wait...Darcy?"

"What?"

"You've made my day."

Maybe I'm setting myself up for heartbreak, but I can't stop myself from wanting him. I pray Tom is a changed man because I'm officially a lost cause. Just hearing his voice and hearing him say my name messes with my head.

Since that night we spent together talking over dinner last year, I would often find my memories morphing into daydreams about Tom. And no, those dreams didn't revolve solely around us doing the deed. I also envisioned just being with him, being someone special to him. But staring out the window today, absentmindedly stirring the gravy, I am definitely thinking about him kissing me, touching me, taking me.

By typical standards, I'd be considered inexperienced for a college senior. Since my high school boyfriend, there's been a long dry spell in that department. After graduation, Matt and I stayed together through most of freshman year, even though he was in Chicago and I was here. Then Nick and I imploded long before I was ready to take that step with him. So no, I've never had the earth-shattering, body-rocking experience I've dreamt of, or read about in romance novels.

In my dreams, Tom always tells me he loves me before he touches me. Guess I'm a hopeless romantic. "You know I love you, right?" He whispers this in my ear as he presses into me, his front against my back. I nod my head, too breathless to speak. He drops kisses along the column of my neck as one hand makes a path up beneath my shirt and the other hand undoes the button and slides beneath the waistband of my jeans. His touch is better than anything I've ever experienced. I reach behind me to fumble with the button on his jeans and—crash back down to Earth when I hear Beth stomping down the stairs. Cheeks flushed and breathing heavy, I have to lean against the counter for a minute until I can stand on my own again.

There's no relief. I want him. Not just in that way, though. I want all of him. I want him to fall for me.

* * *

TOM

Look at this dumbass, standing less than a foot away from me with his hands fisted, practically foaming at the mouth.

"What's up, Nick?"

"I'm telling you to stay away from her."

"Can't."

His jaw stiffens. "Did you fuck her?"

"Man, shut up. She's not like that to me."

He laughs like a crazed hyena. "She's not like that to you? How is she, Tom?"

"I really like her." I shrug, pop the top off the beer I'm about to enjoy, and turn my attention back to the television. After what he put her through, I don't believe he's owed more of an explanation. "I'm sorry, but don't count on me backing off."

Nick looks like he's weighing his options as he stands in my living room surrounded by my friends. He makes a wise decision not to go at me, knowing I could destroy him without breaking a sweat. He decides to glare at me instead, as if that's a threat, and then turns and leaves, slamming the door on his way out like a twelve-year-old. Jackass might be backing down now, but I know he's not letting this drop.

I do feel bad about Nick, but at the same time I'm walking on air. Hearing her sweet voice on the phone, knowing she was looking out for me, knowing she—how did she put it—might be into me? I get up, pour my full beer into the sink, smiling as I watch the contents go down the drain because I'm crazy happy.

Approaching her place, the smell of whatever she's cooking wafts out through the open kitchen window and overwhelms me. It smells like home, warm and safe. This time, I *will* be staying for dinner.

I walk in the door to the sight of Darcy lifting a huge bird out of the oven. Even that's sexy when she does it. She sets the pan on the counter and then reaches up with the back of her hand to move a loose strand of hair from her face. I am full-on mesmerized. She has her back to me, standing barefoot in some workout pants and a form-fitting tee. Every curve is on full display.

"Hey, Darcy." She turns at the sound of my voice. When she goes to speak, I put one hand up to stop her. "Don't say anything. Just let me get this out." Deep breath. "I've spent the last year thinking about no one but you. I'm trying to figure out how to show you that I'm different, that I've changed, but I'm failing. I just want a chance with you."

She lets out a tired breath. "How long have you been standing there?"

"I like watching you."

Her eyes are hard, scrutinizing me. I want to go to her, get closer, but the look on her face keeps me in my place.

"Have you changed, Tom? When I saw all those girls around you last weekend..." She trails off, shaking her head. "I won't do that. If it's me, then it's only me."

"It's only you."

"I want to believe that."

I move in and lean down to press my forehead to hers. "I promise, it's only you."

DARCY

He makes me feel beautiful.

I'm dressed in sweats, a t-shirt stained with gravy, and my hair is in a ponytail. But when he looks at me, I see happiness in his eyes, kindness and desire.

He lets out a burp that practically shakes the ground and goes on for a full five seconds. This knocks me out of my lust-induced fog.

"That was gross."

"It's my compliment to the chef. That's the best meal I've had in a long while."

"In that case, thank you."

"You're a good cook."

"Thanks, I enjoy it."

"I want lasagna."

"Come again?"

"I want lasagna the next time you cook for me. I felt cheated last week. I even went and got takeout from that Italian place on Beverly Road."

"Ouch, even their pizza is terrible."

"Yeah, I got baked ziti and it was pretty bad. So, when you deem me worthy—"

"When you've earned it, I'll cook it."

I get a pinch on the hip for that.

We've been out here for nearly an hour. Instead of eating with the girls, I made us plates and we ate on the deck chairs littering the "yard" we share with four other senior houses. I wanted to be alone with him, wanted to get back to the way it was between us that night last summer.

And it's good. It feels real when it's just the two of us. He's stripped down, honest and open. He asks me questions, makes me laugh, lets me in. He tells me about his parents, his three brothers, about his dream of eventually joining his father's firm and making a name for himself in finance.

When we talk about my family, he comments on the picture of me as a baby sitting in my mother's lap.

"I can't believe you remember that."

He shrugs. "I remember everything about that night. And I don't mean for this to sound creepy, but I remember thinking how beautiful your mom is, and how you look exactly like her now."

I try to keep my emotions in check, but for some reason it's not so easy to do tonight. "Thanks. I actually love it when people tell me that I look like her."

"I'm sorry, did I say something wrong?"

"No, I love that picture too. It's just…It's one of the last pictures of the two of us together before my mother died."

He rakes his hands through his hair and whispers, "Shit, I didn't know. I'm so sorry."

"Not too many people know. If it comes up, people usually act weird about it and then don't know what to say to me. And really, I'm fine. I think the hard part for me is that she died when I was so young. I'd just turned two, so I don't really remember her at all. The *not* knowing her is what hurts, you know? Missing someone you really never had the chance to know."

He looks off into the distance, collecting himself, quiet for a moment. "I always say that I have three brothers. I mean I do, but Charlie, the one who was closest in age to me, died when he was eleven and I was thirteen. I don't bother telling most people either because I...Sometimes I just don't want to tell the story."

I take his hand, lean over and kiss his cheek. It feels like such a weak gesture, when what I really want to do is wrap him up in my arms and blanket him with kisses.

Minutes pass before he breaks the silence. "Charlie died of leukemia. Do you mind me asking how your mom died?"

"She died in a car accident."

He lowers his head, which is usually my cue to stop, but for some reason I press on, wanting him to know the details, to know *my* story. "My parents loved to ski. My dad worked long hours at the hospital back then, but whenever they could get away for a few days we went up to a little ski house they rented in upstate New York. My mother was just taking a quick trip to the store to get something she needed for dinner our first night there, and..." I trail off shaking my head. "There was some ice on the road. A driver in the opposite lane lost control and hit her head-on. My dad said she died instantly."

He looks broken taking this all in. "Like I said, I don't remember any of it. I do get sad thinking how it must have been for Caleb and Luke. Sometimes I'll see a family with boys who look to be about the same age they would have been at the time of the accident, just seven and nine. They must have been so scared that night."

"Shit. I can't imagine your dad trying to cope with losing her while raising three little kids."

"Yeah, I know. I mean, we definitely went through some tough times. My brother Caleb especially, he struggled for years. But I don't remember home as a somber place growing up. My house was always filled with music, laughter, and there were always a lot of people around. At first my grandparents stayed with us in shifts to help my father out, and then Dad married Sarah. I call her Mom too."

Realization dawns on his face. "Oh yeah, I saw another woman in the family pictures. Dark hair, really pretty, but didn't look like you."

Thinking of her makes me smile. "Yeah, Sarah's great. I absolutely adore her. I always think she was an angel my mom sent to our family."

I don't stop to think it through before blurting out, "Hey, next month my father has a conference in Boston. They're coming in a day early to take me out. Come with me and you can meet them." As soon as I say the words, I want to suck them right back in. I cover my face, laughing but kind of mortified. "Sorry, that was totally weird. I just asked you to meet my parents and we're not even dating. Please forget I just did that!"

He laughs and grabs my hands. "No way! Now I'm definitely coming. You can't take that back. And you already met my parents, so now we'll be even."

* * *

It's got to be two or three o'clock before I finally drift off to sleep. I cannot stop thinking about him. I feel his loss, mourn for the boy he was losing a brother like that. And I feel special, honored that he'd share something private and so painful with me. It makes me feel close to him.

Other people don't understand why I'm reluctant to bring up my own sad past, but Tom does. It just defines you to other people and I resent that. When I was younger, I was "that poor girl who lost her mother." I'd hear teachers talking about me that way, other kids' moms—it brought the sadness on all over again. Now that info is strictly on a need-to-know basis. If you're not close to me, you don't need to know. But Tom? I want him to know everything.

* * *

TOM

I can't sleep.

I want her here, right next to me.

My heart sank when she told me about her mother. From the very first day I met Darcy, for reasons I can't explain, I felt protective towards her. And now that I know the kind of pain she's endured, I want to do everything in my power to keep her from hurting, to keep her safe from harm.

My thoughts drift back to Charlie. I can still remember the smell of the hospital, the stale air. The sick kids and their sad parents—they're everywhere. And no amount of balloons, posters of kids with smiling faces, or *get well soon* cards can make this place feel festive. Not anymore. Not now, when Charlie's skin looks grey, when he's too weak to get up by himself to take a piss, or when it looks like it's taking everything he has in him just to draw breath.

Sometimes I can't walk into the room. I won't cry in front of him, and seeing him in my mother's arms like she's cradling a baby makes me so fucking sad that I can't see through my tears. I take a walk, buy him a comic book while I buy myself some time.

We all know what's coming. Just Brendan and Terrence, they have no clue. They ask me at least ten times a day if the doctors and nurses "fixed" Charlie yet. Jesus, how do you explain to a five-year-old and a three-year-old that their brother is never coming out of that awful place, that he's never coming home again?

All of my prayers went unanswered that year. My brother didn't get better. He didn't live.

Darcy understands that kind of loss, and it makes me feel closer to her. Makes me believe I can let her in.

U all right?

She's typing her reply right away. Guess she can't sleep either.

A little down before, but I'm really happy too. Think I'm a weirdo?

Lol. Same here. Just as weird as u r.

I see the screen bubble come to life and then disappear.

Can I see u tomorrow?

A nanosecond passes before she answers yes.

Promise I'm not a stalker, but I know u have class in Warby Hall at 11. Meet me after?

LMAO. Meet u in the quad.

Score.

Sweet dreams, D. See u tomorrow.

She has no idea. I *need* to see you tomorrow, need you right now. Want you in my life, want you in my bed. She'd run full speed in the opposite direction if she could read the crazy thoughts racing through my mind.

Chapter 7

DARCY

Turns out, Tom *is* a stalker.

He runs into me, accidentally on purpose, almost every day. He might be in the quad when I come out of class, he shows up for morning yoga on Tuesdays now, and he stumbles upon me in the library like he's surprised to see me. As the days turn into weeks, spending time with Tom becomes a part of my routine.

I like this new routine.

"What, Donovan? Did I just hear you correctly? You can't drive?"

Tom is telling me about the repairs he had to make on his truck when I casually mention that I have a permit but still don't have my driver's license. For some reason, this cracks him up.

"So? I live in Manhattan. I have no need to drive."

"No, no, no...You definitely need to be able to drive, sugar."

Okay, the sugar thing? It simultaneously makes me lightheaded and makes me want to rip his clothes off.

He stops cold, turns me to face him and takes me by the shoulders. "I have to rectify this situation."

"Really now?"

"Yep, I'm going to teach you."

"Are you sure you trust me with your precious truck?"

"Absolutely. Anyway, this gives me an excuse to have you all to myself."

He smiles and then reaches down to take my hand. A warm sensation snakes its way throughout my entire being. I'm not sure how I manage to keep putting one foot in front of the other. There is something so intimate about holding hands, and it's a public declaration. He's putting "us" out there for the world to see.

Before Tom breaks off to go to class, he gives my hand a gentle squeeze. "First lesson is tomorrow afternoon."

I'm fighting an almost dizzy feeling, but somehow manage to tease, "You're pretty bossy. I hope you're a nice teacher."

"No, I'm tough. You better bring your A-game."

"Hmm, what are you going to do to me if I don't follow your instructions?"

He leans in, taps me on the nose and whispers, "Take you over my knee for a spanking." He cocks one eyebrow and smiles knowingly. "I think you'd like that."

He pulls moves like that a lot. He's a flirt and a tease. Every touch is like foreplay, and lately I'm wound as tight as a top.

That first weekend he came by before us girls were heading out and tagged along. The second week he came by early on Friday and asked me to grab dinner with him before we hit parties. By week three we were arriving everywhere together.

He always escorts me home and lays the hottest kisses on me before saying goodnight. He gives me nothing but kisses. The way he kisses leads me to believe he possesses some serious skills in related departments, but Tom doesn't push to go further. His show of respect is appreciated, but I want him, badly. I'm basically a pool of liquid when he so much as looks my way.

* * *

TOM

Darcy is easy to talk to, and she doesn't make her parents out to be uptight or old-fashioned, but I'm anxious nonetheless. Could it be that I, Thomas Farrell, am concerned about making a good impression? I let out a breath and smile, knowing that's exactly why I'm on edge. I do want her parents to like me, which tells me something I already know: Darcy is important to me.

I get to her place early, hoping to hang out for a few minutes before her parents come to pick us up. It's quiet downstairs, seems like the place is empty, but I can hear music coming from upstairs. "Darcy?" I'm careful to make my presence known so that none of the other girls come out of the bathroom in a towel or something and look to slap my face for invading their privacy, but I get no response. No response when I knock on her bedroom door either, but that's where the music is coming from. Step in and call her name...nada. But as I'm turning to go, I hear hangers drop to the floor. Except for some black lace underwear, Darcy is as naked as the day the Lord made her, and she is, hands down, the most beautiful creature I've ever laid eyes on. I'm standing there like a halfwit, staring at her with my mouth hanging open for the better half of a minute before I come to my senses.

"Shit, I'm sorry, I swear, for real, I knocked!"

I'm a babbling imbecile, rendered dumbstruck.

My back is to her when she says, "Turn around." When I don't move, she says, "Tom, I *want* you to look at me."

I can feel the air shift, know she's moving closer.

What's it been, five weeks? Five weeks of getting to know her, of holding back, not so much as even trying to get past first base? And it's not like I've been suffering through it. It's more like I'm my old self again, enjoying the slow build-up, being ok with the pace of things, wanting to make sure she's ready. God knows I'm ready.

When I turn, mere inches separate us. She takes one of my hands and moves it to cup her breast. She's doing her best to look confident, but her eyes tell me she's nervous when she says, "I want to feel your hands on me."

I'm like a fifteen-year-old watching porn for the first time, unsure of what to do, so overwhelmed that I want to plead for mercy. But I close my eyes then, enjoy the feel of her soft skin, fill both hands with the heavy swell of her. "Damn, you're so beautiful." I breathe the words into her skin as I move down to taste her, lick and nip at her breasts as I hold her ass in my hands, pulling her in closer to me. She's letting out these little moans, and I'm so hot for her that I'm about to come. *If she'd just grip me right here for a second*. I'm thinking this as I take her right hand and lead it down south.

I don't hear the knocking at first, but Darcy hops back, her eyes wide as she stifles a laugh with her hands.

"Huh?" That's the only word I can manage in my current state. But then the knocking gets louder and realization sets in. "Oh, shit."

"Just go down there and let them in. Pretend you were waiting on the couch."

I point down to my crotch, shaking my head. "No fucking way!" She's laughing hysterically now, while I'm descending into panic mode. "I can't meet them like this!"

She catches her breath, but then starts laughing harder. When the knocking starts up again, she comes to her senses. "All right. Go downstairs and let yourself out the back door. Wait a few minutes and then come around and knock on the front door. I'll be quick."

She looks back down at my raging boner and starts laughing again before throwing on a robe. I hear her calling down to her parents from her bedroom window, telling them she'll be there in a second. Meanwhile, I tiptoe down the stairs and slide the back door open like a military operative on a covert mission, quiet and careful.

Fear has taken care of my hard-on, so I take the next few minutes to just breathe deep and calm myself before knocking on the door and greeting her parents like I wasn't just upstairs molesting their daughter a few minutes earlier.

And they do turn out to be totally cool, so I'm able to revert back to my normal, relaxed, charming self during dinner—at least I hope I'm giving off that vibe.

Darcy, though, has her Irish up. Sarah and I are looking back and forth between her and Mr. Donovan like we're spectators at a tennis match. They're not really going at it, but their energy is intense. Sarah, sitting across from me, catches my eye at one point and gives me a look that's meant to reassure me, to say: Don't worry, they do this all the time. But this is compelling stuff, so I'm taking in every word. Darcy is on the road to becoming a doctor—I knew that. But what I didn't know, until now, is that her father, a doctor himself, isn't too enthusiastic about her plans for the future.

Mr. Donovan puts his hands up in surrender. "I know you can do anything you set your mind to, it's just that the field is so different now. There's so much you have to give up. Years you can't get back. I hear these mid-thirty-somethings questioning their decision all the time. And I know you think I'm saying this because you're a woman, but I said the same thing to Caleb and Luke."

She rolls her eyes and laughs. "Enough! Can we please change the subject?"

Sarah chimes in, "I almost forgot! Luke and Kate are coming over after we get home Sunday. They said they have important news."

Darcy's eyes go wide. "Do you think?" Then she winces. "I pray that it's good news. If Kate has another miscarriage, it's going to devastate her."

Sarah takes Darcy's hand. "Maybe I shouldn't have said anything, but from the tone of Luke's voice I didn't get the impression that it was bad news. I'm very hopeful, sweetie."

"Please, either way, I want a call as soon as you hear anything."

* * *

Darcy and I walk the half-mile home instead of taking a ride.

"Thanks for asking me to come to dinner. Your parents are really nice."

She squeezes my hand, looks up at me and smiles. "I'm glad you came."

"So, what was that between you and your dad?"

Darcy seems confused momentarily, but then shakes her head and says, "Oh, you mean about medical school?" When I nod, she says, "I think he's afraid I'm going to work myself to the bone and study non-stop, only to wake up at age thirty-five, exhausted, husbandless and childless."

"Did either of your brothers choose medicine?"

"No. Luke was heading in that direction, but when he was in high school he was involved with a Jesuit volunteer organization that put him to work on home building projects in impoverished areas. He's very outdoorsy and really got into carpentry and building. He worked for a contractor throughout college and then went out on his own a couple of years ago. He met Kate when she was interning, assisting the architect on one of his projects." I can only see her profile, but notice she's teary-eyed. "I just...I love her." Letting out a breath, she adds, "So they're married now and they have a business together."

"An architect and a general contractor?"

She looks to me and smiles. "A perfect match, right?"

"What about Caleb?"

"He never had any interest in being a doctor. Caleb is in your future line of work, sort of. He's a commodities broker."

We walk then, silent, lost in our own thoughts. I'm thinking about the thirty-five and exhausted comment, not really liking the sound of it, and obviously she is too when she breaks the silence.

"Don't get me wrong, maybe I won't admit it to my father, but I do think about what he says. His interns and residents are always at our house. Sarah takes the ones who are new to the city in like stray kittens, makes sure they have somewhere to eat a home-cooked meal. I hear what they say. I do think about it."

"I think if it's what you really want to do, you can make it work. Can you get through the program at your own pace so you can have a life while you work towards it?"

"It's competitive. You've got to be willing to put the long hours in." She waves the thought away. "Whatever, it's a long way off."

As soon as we get back to her place and determine it's deserted, she fists the fabric of my shirt and pulls me close. "I know you have an early game tomorrow, but will you come upstairs for just a little while, puh-lease?"

I think this girl is trying to kill me.

* * *

DARCY

Tom holds my hand under the table during most of dinner. Is it for reassurance? I mean, he doesn't come off as nervous about meeting my parents. If anything, it's the opposite. Tom sitting here at the table with my family feels totally natural.

Tom is answering my father's questions about his summer internship, and then the conversation moves onto lighter topics like surfing and rugby. My father is like the unofficial, reluctant orthopedist for my brothers' club team, so he knows a lot about the sport.

While they're deep in it, Mom leans in close. "He's wonderful, Darcy. Seems like it's serious."

"No...I mean, I just started seeing him, but I do really like him."

"Well the feeling seems to be mutual, and you look very happy. Any run-ins with 'he whose name I won't say'?"

"Um, nothing too bad, but Nick and Tom used to be friends, so that's a little weird."

I nod in reply when she says, "Just please promise me you'll reach out if you need us this time."

I love seeing my parents, but I'm itching to get back to my room to pick up where we left off before. I know the girls are all out and my place will be empty, so I barely stop when we get inside the door. I lead him upstairs and he follows. Tom is smiling like he knows exactly what's on my mind, and once we're in my room, he advances on me until the backs of my legs hit the mattress and I'm falling back, laughing as he lays his body over mine. He rests his weight on his forearms, teasing me so that we're not making contact where he knows I want it.

"I like your parents," he whispers.

I part my legs slightly, encourage him to rest his lower body against mine. I run my hands down the length of his back, over the fabric of his shirt. "I can't think about them right now."

When he gives in, I can feel him, so hard against me. His mouth turns up at the corners when he sees how lost I am. "I wish you could see how beautiful you look when you're needy like this." He breathes the words into my neck as he rolls his hips into mine. "Can you feel what you do to me?"

I'm breathing some heady, drug-laced oxygen. Can't do anything but nod, breathless. I put my hands on his hips and draw him closer.

"Fuck," he whispers as he grinds his hips and then put his mouth on mine. I love the way he kisses me, like he's simultaneously worshipping me and consuming me. I get lost in it. But just when it's getting good, he shifts so that his hips aren't pressing into mine. He whispers in between soft kisses, "Darcy, I meant what I said before. You're special to me. I think you know that. So we don't have to rush this. I can't believe I'm saying this, but I don't *want* to rush this."

When he moves, he leaves me cold and wanting. "I'm ready. I trust you."

He lifts himself up and sits next to me on the bed. I move to cover my face, totally embarrassed, but he takes both of my hands in his so that I have no choice but to look at him. "Hey, believe me, it will be good and I can't wait for that day. I just want it to be different with you." He breathes in deep. "I need it to be different with you."

I'm still a little embarrassed by the fact that I've thrown myself at him, *twice* in one night, but his words mean something. His words and his actions contradict everything Nick's been saying about Tom. This is special. I feel it and so does he.

"Come here," he says, pulling me onto his lap. "Can I ask you something?"

It feels so good sitting here with his arms wrapped around me. No, it's way better than good. He tips my chin up, prods me out of the dazed state I'm in.

"Hmm?"

"Please don't answer if you don't feel comfortable. It's just something that's been nagging at me."

"Go on, ask me."

"Uh...did you and Nick ever—" He shakes his head. "You know what? Please forget I said anything. I shouldn't ask you that."

He looks surprised when I laugh. "The answer is no, but I am aware he told just about everyone that I was quite the sex fiend. I'm pretty kinky from what I hear." Tom stares at me wide-eyed. "Jenna filled me in. Dan wanted me to call him out on it, but I won't."

"Just so you know, everyone thought he was talking shit anyway."

"Then why did you ask?"

He shrugs, shakes his head and gives me a half-smile. "Simple curiosity? Jealousy? Morbid obsession with you? I don't know." His expression changes, hardens. "But the thought of Nick lying about you, saying you did things with him, it makes me want to beat the shit out of him even more than I did before."

"I don't feel anger. It's more like I'm ashamed of having been with him in the first place, and maybe a little ashamed of myself for being such a poor judge of character, you know?"

"You couldn't have seen all that coming."

"That's what I tell myself. And what he did was pathetic, but I guess he's not the only guy who's ever lied about sex. Anyway, I'm over it."

"You're a lot more forgiving than I am, Darcy."

"What else do you want to know about me?"

His smile is wide, apologetic. "Everything."

"Well, I'm not a virgin. I didn't mean to give you that impression."

"That's not important. And you don't have to explain anything to me."

"I'm not explaining myself. I just want you to know me. My only experience was with my first boyfriend, Matt. We were seventeen that first time and he begged me." I can't help but giggle. "Like he was going to *die* if we didn't have sex. I wasn't ready, but felt kind of obligated to him because we'd been together for so long. It wasn't great. I did it because he needed it, not because I wanted to. The only relationship I've had since Matt was with Nick, and even though he makes it seem like we were together forever, it was only four months. After just two months I was having serious doubts about us, so no, we didn't."

"I'm sorry I even brought it up." He looks at me with the most open and loving expression. "I want to be the one for you. I don't want to scare you off, but I...I have strong feelings when it comes to you. And I want you to know me too, but," he laughs half-heartedly, "I think if we talk about my past, you'll run for the hills."

"You're not going to scare me off, but I really don't need to know."

He pulls me in close and just holds me before we say goodnight.

When he leaves, my twin bed feels too big without him.

* * *

TOM

She's been in my dreams all night long, and she's on my mind first thing this morning.

Today we're playing an away game in New Hampshire, so we're heading out early. Chris is driving a small bus filled with a mixture of the very hung over, the somewhat hung over, and me—the one not hung over guy. I sit up front bullshitting with Chris for the entire ride, as everyone else is either asleep or still somewhat drunk and talking nonsense. Chris is in charge of the line-up, so we spend most of the drive talking about how we match up against the opposing team.

I've been fighting the urge to ask about Nick, but eventually I cave. "How's our boy Nick been doing?"

"Eerily quiet about the whole you-and-Darcy thing. I'd keep a shiv under my mattress for when he comes at you. No doubt it's gonna happen."

"I know. I feel like he's lurking, biding his time. He's going to pull a Kato-on-Clouseau ambush one day soon."

Chris laughs. "Yeah, I can picture that." He goes on, "You're better for her. I mean, I've known her since freshman year, but I got to know her a lot better when they were together. Truly a nice person, a very cool girl."

"Yeah, I'm totally into her."

He nods. "That's fairly obvious." He looks lost in thought for a moment before saying, "Nick just messed that up so badly. He's one of those people who should be forced to watch a video of their own drunk-ass nonsense. I don't think he knows what an absolute dick he can be." He looks to me as if he's just had a revelation. "Why didn't I ever think of taping him one of those nights when I had to drag him away from her place?"

"Um, I'm guessing because you were preoccupied? How bad was it?"

"Ugly. He was a disaster, screaming and slurring. Then when me, Dan or Denny would get there, he'd start in on us. He was all, 'Touch me and you're dead, motherfuckers.' I mean, he weighs like a buck-fifty soaking wet—he's not fucking anyone up—but when he was in that crazy drunken rage, he *was* difficult to wrangle." He chuckles but then sobers. "There were so many nights when I just wanted to beat the crap out of him. He said some things to her that were…" Shaking his head, he pauses. "Forget it, I'm gonna get you all crazy."

"Dan filled me in on most of it, so I know. But now that I'm with her, knowing that he was threatening her and saying things about her that weren't true? It makes it hard to be in the same room with him."

Chris looks to me with a raised eyebrow before shifting his gaze back to the road. "Do you think anyone believed what he was saying? Everyone knew he was committing perjury."

"Darcy knows exactly what he's told everyone, but she doesn't seem to care. I can't figure that out."

"She's confident enough not to care if anyone believes him or not. That's a good thing."

"Yeah, I suppose it is."

It's only been a few weeks, so I'm surprised it even registers that this is the first Saturday I won't be seeing her. I smile thinking about the fact that I'm missing her. It's good to have a connection again, to care.

I'm looking out the passenger-side window, absently taking in the scenery, my thoughts focused on her. I picture her from the day before, laughing at something stupid I said. The sound of her laughter makes my chest feel like it's being pumped full of fresh air— elated. And the vision of her lying beneath me, her hair fanned out on the pillow, looking up to me with trust and desire? It makes me feel a tenderness I've never known.

I am, without a doubt, falling in love with her.

Chapter 8

DARCY

"I don't recall asking for a makeover," Rene snaps.

Beth and I decreed a mandatory girls' night out. Our side mission is to snag a guy for the most serious and subdued of our roommates, Rene.

Maybe my own newfound happiness is my inspiration. I'm on cloud nine and want everyone around me to feel the same.

Jenna studies her reluctant subject's face before lining her lids in black to create a subtle but striking cat-eye. "Hold still."

"I am." Rene is scowling, but then the ghost of a smile appears when Jenna steps away and she gets a look at herself in the mirror. "Wow."

"Go get 'em, killer," Beth chimes in.

Rene turns to face me, Beth and Caitlin, the three of us crammed onto her twin bed. She sighs, shaking her head. "I don't see what the big deal is. I'm just too busy to be in a relationship right now."

"Who said anything about a relationship? We just want you to get boned."

Rene laughs, because you can't do much besides laugh when you're around Beth. "That's a hard no."

Beth points back at her. "Have you learned nothing from me, child? If it's hard, then the answer is yes."

Jenna squeezes her butt onto the one unoccupied square inch of the bed. "You do work too hard, Rene. I think you need to let your hair down a little more often."

I nod in total agreement. "It's senior year."

Caitlin inspects her fingernails, quietly adding, "Maybe it's time."

Rene had her heart broken by a football player with a serious case of roid rage and an inflated ego at the end of sophomore year. Ryder, with another babe on his arm, approached her to say hello in the library a few days ago. To me it seemed harmless, even though I never particularly liked the guy, but Rene has been in a funk ever since. Is she still sulking over Ryder a full year later? That's just crazy pants.

I remember she dated someone else briefly last year when I was abroad, but he's now obviously out of the picture too. Rene's had no interest in meeting anyone lately, and it's not like she doesn't have opportunities. She's an exotic beauty, and there's no shortage of guys looking to get with her.

The four of us were talking about it last night while Rene was at work. When Beth brought up Ryder, Jenna shook her head emphatically. "This is *not* because of Ryder. Something has been up with Rene since last year. Caitlin, I'm sure you noticed. I mean, last spring the girl was doing more than her fair share of crying. I knew she had you to lean on and I wasn't going to pry, but it was obvious that she was going through something pretty serious."

Caitlin looked away from us and shrugged her shoulders. "You know she's always dealing with family shit. Rene doesn't have it easy."

Caitlin and Rene are tight, just like me and Jenna, so I know Caitlin would never spill any of Rene's secrets.

With a killer outfit and the four of us serving as her own personal glam squad, Rene's snarky attitude won't be enough to scare the guys away tonight. She looks hot.

The first party we hit is at our friend Cara's place. We're already a little fired up when we get there, thanks to Beth insisting on a little pre-gaming with shots of tequila.

Rene starts the night out reluctant and pissy, complaining she isn't some charity case, but as the night wears on, she seems more like her old self. Within an hour she's in the midst of some heavy flirting with Tanner, a very handsome lacrosse player. Mission accomplished.

Jenna, Beth and I are dancing in a big group of people when someone bumps into me, knocking the drink out of my hand. I turn to see some girl staring right at me. When I say she's cheap-looking, I'm not being mean, just calling it as I see it. She has long red hair, an upturned nose, wears her jeans too tight and definitely has a penchant for push-up bras. Her boobs are practically spilling out of her low-cut top.

She gives me a snarky smile. "Oops."

I don't know who she is, but Jenna does. "Liz, what's your problem?"

"Relax, Jenna. Who's your friend?"

"I'm Darcy."

"Darcy." She eyes me from head to toe, taking her sweet time. "I'm Liz."

A bad feeling settles over me. I'm not about to return her fake smile because I can smell bitch from a mile away.

"I think we have a good friend in common."

My back is up. "I doubt it."

She smiles and nods. "Oh, I know we do. Are you still seeing Tommy?"

Tommy? Guess that's her pet name for him. "You obviously know that I am."

She tosses her hair to the side and laughs. "Well, you can never be sure with him. He runs through his girls like that," she says, snapping her fingers. "I wonder, what's it like? I mean look around, he's done about half the girls at this party. I guess I should welcome you to the club.'"

"You're in this club, too?"

She puts her hand to her chest, eyes wide with horror. "What? No! He's like, in love with one of my closest friends." She looks over her shoulder to where a small group of girls are standing. "Everyone knows he's still not over Morgan."

Yes, she uses the present tense. And the words feel like a hard slap.

She leans in, whispering, "But while they've been on a break, yeah," she pauses to lick her lips, "maybe we have had some harmless fun."

I roll my eyes. "And you're proud of that? You're a pig."

That's about as harsh as I've ever been with another woman, but my words don't wound her the slightest bit. As Liz turns to go, she looks back over her shoulder. "Don't get too comfortable, sweetheart."

Are you kidding me?

Jenna comes over with drinks. "Isn't she a skank?"

My hand shakes as I take the cup from Jenna's hand and force down a gulp. "Yes, perfect description."

"What did she say to you?"

"Nothing much. I guess she has a thing for *Tommy*. The way she said his name was vomit-inducing."

Jenna makes a face. "Probably does, even though she's friends with Morgan."

"Which one is she?"

"Green shirt." Jenna grips my hand before I can turn to get a look, saves me from embarrassing myself. "Those other girls aren't half-bad, but Liz is nasty." Leaning in, she laughs as she yells over the music, "If we were the type of girls who fought other girls, I'd hit her for you!"

I'm still dancing, but now I feel stiff and robotic. Liz had gotten in my head, and not because of the blow job talk. Didn't like *that*, but the reference to Morgan is what gutted me. The thought of Tom having feelings for someone else, past or present, makes me physically ache. Is he over her? Am I just a fill-in for her, the real thing?

Those girls are also at the next party we go to at my friend Sean's place. Sean and his girlfriend, Grace, are pre-med with me. We've been in most classes together since freshman year. We're catching up when Sean walks over. "Is there any reason those girls over there are looking you up and down? I'd say they're down for some hot girl-on-girl action, but they sort of look like they want you dead."

I laugh it off as best I can. "I guess this is the downside of dating someone with a colorful past."

When I glance back, Liz is staring right at me, so I take a page from her book and give her a big, fake smile. Morgan is a bystander to what's going on, and she just looks, I don't know, a little sad maybe.

I am way past ready to bail. I don't rehash the Liz incident on the walk home with the girls, even though I want to hear my friends' take on that weird exchange. I tell myself that the more I think or talk about it, the more credence I give to her nonsense.

* * *

This is the first Sunday in a while that I have no desire to go running. Tequila will do that to you. I still wake up at the crack of dawn, though. I don't think my body is capable of sleeping past seven.

I make my way downstairs and curl up on the couch thinking about last night. I can't shake the uneasy feeling that's settled over me. It was better when I could at least pretend that Morgan didn't exist. But the reality of Morgan and Tom, former star-crossed lovers, was shoved in my face last night.

I look up when I hear people laughing. Through the sliding glass door I see Rene and Tanner making their way towards our place. He's holding her hand and they're both smiling. *Way to go, Rene*. I don't want to be a creeper, but I can't help but watch when he gives her a sweet kiss. She comes in, collapses onto the couch next to me and smiles.

"Rene, that was some kiss!"

She lets out a contented sigh. "You are *not* cooking today. I'm treating us to takeout later to thank all of you for dragging my sorry ass back out into the world. I had so much fun! Tanner and I danced all night. We talked for hours after everyone left, and then we just curled up on the couch together and slept."

"Really? From the look on your faces I thought there was some earth-shattering baby making involved."

She looks pained for a moment, but quickly shakes it off and laughs. "Uh, no. I would never do that day-one with a guy I'm into." She reaches both arms up to stretch. "Seriously, though, I like him. We're going out Thursday night. He's taking me to dinner."

"I'm so happy for you." I force a smile that I do not feel. "Tanner seems like a great guy."

Not someone who gets blow jobs from dirty skanks.

I have to stop the negative thoughts running on a continuous loop through my fried brain.

Rene makes her way upstairs, dreamy-eyed. "Thanks, Darcy. All right, I will see *you* in a few hours. I'm going to go dream about Tanner Westerly."

My phone buzzes with an incoming text.

Did u miss me last nite? I missed u.

I'm just going to have to get over it because *this* is reality, not the garbage Liz is spewing. Why am I letting this girl get to me?

I missed u. Beth makes me drink tekillya when ur not around.

Hope I didn't miss u dirty dancing or anything.

I wasn't going to tell him what he'd missed.

Hmm, I do remember dancing….
A second later:
I'm coming over to interrogate. Coffee?
Now you're talking.
Hell yes. Cream no sugar.

"You owe me, woman," Tom teases as he places the cup into my grabby, greedy hands.

I take a few healthy sips before letting out a groan of pleasure. Coffee is my magic cure for a hangover. "I needed this."

"Glad to be of service," he says, smiling as he plops down on the couch next to me.

"You look a little under the weather yourself."

"I'm kinda happy to admit that my tolerance isn't what it used to be. When you go out two nights a week as opposed to a minimum of four, you get out of practice."

"What time did you get back?"

He rubs his forehead. "I'm not exactly sure. A few of Mac's boys are on UNH, so they went all out for us. I remember Chris corralling us back onto the bus at some point, but I was pretty much down for the count by then."

I gloss over the highlights of my night, omitting the part about meeting Liz and my pathetic jealousy over Morgan. We spend a lazy morning on the couch, watching TV and talking. At some point I fall asleep next to him, my head resting in the crook of his arm, and wake to the sensation of Tom breathing me in. When I open my eyes, his face is nestled against the tender skin of my neck.

"Do you know how good you smell? I miss it when you're not around me."

Everything he says and does makes me want him more. I shift, stretching to lay my body right on top of his. "Well then, I'll just have to make sure you're with me all the time."

I can feel myself falling.

He skims his hands down the small of my back, squeezing my ass in his hands before pulling me into a tight bear hug. "You'll get tired of me." I go to protest, but Tom silences me, pressing his full lips to mine in a slow and gentle kiss. Turning us both so that we're facing each other on our sides, he pulls back, tucks some hair behind my ear and whispers, "I'll never get tired of you, Darce."

Does he mean it? Sometimes I can't stand feeling the way I do. I feel desperate, needy and unsure. It's like we're in this limbo state—we're together, but not quite connected in that all-in kind of way. I want to blurt out that dreaded question: *Where is this relationship going?* I stay quiet, though, snuggle in closer, hope that my body can tell him the things I'm too timid to say.

* * *

The call I've been waiting on finally comes late in the afternoon. Luke and Kate are both on the line when they tell me their news. Tom looks worried when he sees the tears rolling down my cheeks, so I give him a thumbs-up to let him know it's all good.

It's better than good. I'm going to be an aunt in little over three months, and I'm so overwhelmed with the idea of it that I can hardly speak. Because of Kate's last miscarriage, which came late-term in the middle of the second trimester, they waited a long time to tell everyone this time around. Tom seems nearly as excited as I am when I relay the news, and he can read my thoughts a moment later when I come down off the high.

"You're thinking about everything that can possibly go wrong. Don't do that to yourself. Have faith that it's going to be ok."

"The last time was just so..."

"Must have been devastating. I imagine by that point in a pregnancy you're picking out names—"

"Buying a new house to accommodate a baby..."

"Jeez."

"Yeah, she miscarried a few days after the closing. Imagine having to constantly pass by the room you both agreed would have made the perfect nursery? They already had a crib and an antique rocking chair set up in there."

"That's rough."

I nod. "But you're right, this is good news. They're excited, so I'm going to keep thinking positive thoughts."

"That's my girl."

Beth and her boyfriend come in dressed like they just came from a workout. Marcus sniffs the air, looking both disappointed and confused. Beth whines, "No Sunday dinner?"

I stretch and get up off the couch with Tom following. "Nope. Takeout tonight, girls only. Rene's buying."

Tom kisses my forehead and reminds me to get a good night's sleep. "Remember, tomorrow's your big day."

In all the excitement I'd forgotten about my road test. The lessons have been going on twice a week for three weeks now, but it's been a total ruse on my part. Caleb and Luke take me driving all the time. I'm used to maneuvering around the streets of New York City, dodging bike commuters and reckless cabbies. In comparison, these Boston suburb roads are a breeze.

I've been holding out on Tom because I like the lessons, each and every one of them a sweet, flirty game.

Chapter 9

DARCY

He's waiting for me in the parking lot after class. The wave crashes into me again, this searing pain that washes over me sometimes when I look at him. I care about him so much, want this so much that it scares me.

Tom looks like a dream, leaning against his truck with his legs crossed at the ankles and his sculpted arms crossed over his broad chest. He's wearing his baseball cap backwards along with a mischievous grin.

"What's that look for? You're not betting against me today, are you?"

"You can't read my mind, sugar. You have no *idea* what I was just thinking. And for the record, I would never bet against my pupil. That would make me a bad teacher and," he pushes off the truck and moves to within an inch of me, holding me by my hips and leaning down to whisper in my ear, "I'm a very, very *good* teacher."

I touch my lips to his collarbone and whisper back, "So if I can't read your mind, then tell me, what *were* you just thinking?"

"I was thinking that the guy at motor vehicles is going to have a hard time concentrating once he gets a look at you."

"Don't be so sexist. Maybe he'll be dazzled by my driving."

He chuckles. "Sure he will."

The test is over within ten minutes and then I'm filling out the paperwork for my license. I jump into Tom's arms dramatically and shower him with kisses, gushing, "You are the *best* driving instructor on the planet, Tom Farrell!"

He laughs. "I think I've been played. You parallel parked the truck better than I could have."

"I'm an excellent parallel parker."

He kisses me slow and then purrs in my ear, "Really? I thought that was my line."

I pull away, teasing, "I wouldn't know. I don't know about your old parallel parking days."

As we hop back into the truck with me in the driver's seat, he nods his head slowly. "So you *do* want to know after all, huh? Sure you can handle it?"

That playful feeling evaporates. "No, Tom, I probably can't. But you can tell me about just one. Tell me about your first."

He takes my hand and kisses my palm tenderly. "Come on, let me take you to lunch. This story is pretty entertaining, but I don't think I can tell it on an empty stomach."

Tom orders enough food to feed five people, then dives in once the waitress sets our plates down, barely coming up for air.

"Are you stalling?"

"Nope," he says as he pops another fry into his mouth. He catches my doubtful look. "I'm not!" he argues, but then shakes his head and laughs. "I've only told this story once before, so if I tell you it stays in the vault, all right? It's embarrassing."

I cross my heart, unable to contain the grin spreading across my face.

"So, after Charlie I really wasn't into the whole high school social scene until the beginning of my junior year. But then all of a sudden, it was like a light turned on...I noticed the girls and I noticed that the girls were into me. Oh, and I can empathize with your boy, Matt. I kind of felt like I was going to die if I didn't get me some soon. So there was the making out, groping and all, but I only knew good girls like Darcy Donovan." He smiles as he leans over to feed me a fry. "No one was giving it up. So my junior prom is coming up and I decide to ask this girl, Amy Price. You know why I asked her, right?"

"Easy?"

He smiles then cringes. "That's what my seventeen-year-old pea brain assumed. She'd just broken up with her boyfriend who was a freshman in *college*." He raises his eyebrows and nods knowingly. "Figured she was definitely putting out."

"And did she?"

"*Oh* yeah, and I got a little more than I bargained for."

He stops, leaves me hanging, and doesn't go on until I gently kick his shin under the table. "Come on, spill it!"

"Okay, okay. After the dance, Dylan is throwing this crazy house party. You'll meet him soon. He's great. He's that guy, the one who has the tricked-out house with every bell and whistle—hot tubs, pool table, screening room, you name it. And his parents always seem to be out of town at these very opportune times. So he's having this party, everyone's there. All I want to do, though, is get Amy upstairs."

"What a dog."

"I know, I'm not proud of myself."

"So?"

"So she's willing and able. She was my age, but you know those people who just seem light years older and wiser than everyone else? Amy was like that. I was a boy, she was a woman. So basically, I'm doing everything I can to concentrate and not," he smiles as he looks back down at the table, "uh, shoot my load before things even get started."

I can't help but laugh and squeeze his hand for moral support. I can picture him as a nervous, fumbling kid with this worldly chick. "So how was it? Everything you dreamed of and more?"

"Hard to describe. It felt incredible on the one hand, just incredible, but also a little stressful. Like I said, it was taking an awful lot of mental effort for me to last. I didn't want Amy laughing at me. I knew I was being compared to a college guy, and Amy didn't know she was my first." He's smiling wistfully, fully back in the memory. "So just when I think I've got this great rhythm going and I'm feeling confident, you know, like I'm the man, Amy goes and…" His eyes shut tight and he shakes his head. "I can't."

I grab his hands again, laughing. "What. Did. She. Do?"

He leans in close to me and whispers, "She pokes her finger right into my ass. I mean, she really got *in* there. I didn't know what hit me!"

I'm laughing uncontrollably now, can barely get the words out. "I don't know why I feel like comforting you and saying, 'poor baby.' It was probably the best night of your life."

"No, I was kind of traumatized. I mean, there was no ass play or anything, no warning. Amy just went for it. So anyway, as soon as that happened, I had no prayer of holding back. And once I came I could barely look at her, let alone freaking talk to her or cuddle. We make our way back downstairs and she starts talking to some other guy. I didn't even care. I got piss drunk. I don't even know how she got home."

"Were you two an item after that? I'm thinking probably not."

"No. I was happy to hit rewind for a little while and go back to girls who wouldn't go past second or third base."

"And what happened to Amy?"

"She and I actually had a good laugh about the whole thing last summer. But right after? I've never been a kiss-and-tell kinda guy, but I did tell Dylan. He was way more experienced than me. I told him just to…maybe see if that's how it was? You know? Like maybe what she did was normal for high school kids and I'd missed the memo? Long story short, once Dylan was certain I wasn't interested in Amy, he got with her. They had a passionate, three-week long romance. She was right up his alley."

"Well, thank you for sharing, Tom. I do feel like I know you *much* better now."

"I can't believe telling that story makes me feel embarrassed now, so many years later."

"They say you never forget your first time."

He lays one hand over his heart dramatically. "I know I'll never forget my Amy."

* * *

TOM

The more time I spend with her, the more I need to be around her. When the guys are going out as a group, I go—and I'm not saying I don't have fun—but I'm always surprised to find myself wishing that I was with her instead. I've got Darcy on the brain twenty-four-seven, and I'm good with that.

But tonight the Sox are in the playoffs, and Chris's father, an exec with a big tech corporation, has a private box. Chris invited a few of us to tag along with him. I know Nick will be one of the guys going, but I decide to overlook it. The seats are great and we're in a VIP section with free beer and food. Basically, Charles Manson could have been coming along and I still wouldn't have turned down the invite.

We all meet at Chris's. I'm fairly good friends with Chris, Denny and Vic, but haven't been inside their place once so far this year. Nick lives with them, and I've been avoiding him like the plague. When I walk in, I'm thankful that it's not awkward. There are enough other people packed into their place so that we don't have to interact directly. Also, most of the guys here play rugby with me, so in some ways I'm more at home here than he is.

It has the potential of being a rough night. Someone starts passing shots early, but Chris puts a stop to it after the second round, reminding us that his father's colleagues will be there so we can't "act like a bunch of assholes."

We make our way to Fenway on the T, and Nick is already fired up. He's laughing too loud, being flirty in an obnoxious way with some girls on the train—nothing terrible, just stupid. And maybe I'm imagining it, but I can feel Nick's nasty vibe directed my way. It's almost as if he's doing things to provoke me into starting with him.

Chris is standing behind me. "You're catching this act, right?"

"Yeah. I'll give him a not so gentle reminder. Don't get involved."

"Wasn't planning on it."

Chris waits a few minutes, but when another loud, moronic comment is made, I see him grab Nick by his upper arm and whisper to him. Nick looks like a pissed-off, scolded child for the rest of the ride.

Chris's father goes all out for us. The seats are incredible, the food is awesome, and we have waitstaff handing us beers before you can finish the one in your hand. Mr. Dolan's business associates range in age from late twenties to fifties, and they're all fun to party with.

Midway through the game, I see Chris pull Nick aside after he corners one of the waitresses in a way that's borderline aggressive. Chris then goes to smooth things over with her, apologizing on Nick's behalf because he's too arrogant and inconsiderate to realize he's done anything wrong. Although Nick doesn't make a total spectacle of himself, the boy is a nuisance.

Everyone is going wild towards the end of the game, and then the Sox win it with a walk-off in the ninth. The night's been great so far, but as we're leaving I sense it's going to turn ugly. I know I should just go straight back to campus to see Darcy, but I jump off with everyone else to have a few beers at the little place in Allston where Mac just started bartending.

It doesn't take long—knew it wouldn't. Nick is standing off to the side, talking to Vic and getting progressively louder. I hear Vic say at one point, "I'd dial it down if I were you." Nick barks back, "Oh, so he can fuck my girlfriend and I can't say shit about it?"

I take a deep breath and turn to Dan. "Here we go."

Dan shakes his head and motions for the door, but I'm not pacifying this baby anymore. Truth be told, the things he's been saying about Darcy have been eating me up, and I feel a strong need to call him on it.

"Nick, when someone breaks up with you more than a year and a half ago, I don't think you can still refer to that person as your girlfriend."

"And you *can* call her your girlfriend? I never thought of her as a dumb bitch," coward jumps back a step when he sees that Dan is now holding me back, "but she has to be if she'd get with you. What does that make, Tom? I don't know, thirty girls in one year, fifty?"

"Shut your fucking mouth."

Chris comes over and stands between us. He looks to me as if to say, *Really?* and then turns to him and says, "Nick, leave it alone."

He shrugs. "No problem. I've had her, many times, and now I'm done with her."

I bark out a laugh. "Yeah right, Nick." I break Dan's hold, shove Chris aside and jab my finger into Nick's chest. That lame gesture alone knocks him backwards before I can land the punch I've been itching to deliver. "Listen up, asshole...If I *ever* hear you talking shit about her again, saying shit that's clearly false, I'll fuck you up. You got that?"

Dan and Denny pull me back, leaving Chris to deal with Nick. I text Chris to thank him for the night and to apologize for my part in what just happened, but I don't regret it. I wanted, no, *needed* to defend Darcy and needed every guy standing there to know what a dishonest piece of shit he is.

I wake up the next morning to a crack of dawn text from her: **Thanks for defending my honor.**

She answers on the first ring. "Hello, handsome."

"Hey, about last night…I couldn't help myself, Darce. He was being a total asshole."

"It's ok, really. I just think with him…I don't know, it's like you're kicking the hornet's nest. It just gets him more riled up."

"I'm of the belief that you need to call people out on their bad behavior. I'm never going to stand by like a chump and let him talk about you."

"He's just…Nick's had a rough life."

"You feel bad for him?" Before she can answer, I add, "I've had shitty things happen to me and so have you. It's no excuse."

"You're right, there's no excuse for the way he behaves. When I think of my parents, though, I have no doubt that I was wanted and that I'm loved. I'm sure you'd say the same about your parents, they love you. But Nick is like some poor, lost little rich kid. His parents really did a number on him."

"You sound like Chris."

"What do you mean?"

"Nothing." I take a moment, let my frustration ebb. "Darcy, the way you see him, the fact that you can still feel compassion towards a person like Nick? It's one of the many reasons I'm crazy about you."

"You're crazy about me, huh?"

"Lunatic level crazy."

Sadly, it's the truth. I felt outside of myself last night. Pretty sure that if given the chance, I would have beaten Nick bloody for running his mouth like that. I feel my anger rising up again just thinking about it.

"Same here." And the way she practically sighs when she speaks, dreamlike and happy, instantly calms me. A moment later she adds,

"Can you do me a favor and just ignore Nick? Believe me, it will make my life a whole lot easier."

"Let me handle him, he's nothing for you to worry about."

How I feel right now? If he so much as looks at her sideways, I'll put him into the ground.

TOM

Look at her.

I'm not the only one staring. She's dancing with her friends, and while no one would peg her as the most coordinated girl on the planet, there's something about her that draws the attention of every male in the room—a few of the females too. She's laughing and smiling, belting out the lyrics so loud that you can hear how off-key she is. But Darcy's not self-conscious or timid. No, she's having fun and her joy is infectious.

"You're always smiling like a lovesick fool lately."

I look over to Dan and nod, knowing he doesn't mean anything by it. "Can't deny it."

"She's happy too. It's good to see her like this, like the way she used to be."

"Can you see yourself in the future? I mean, see a future for you and Jenna?"

He takes a sip of his beer, thinks on it. "I can't see myself with anyone else. There are times I wonder, I guess, if being with the same person all through college is a smart move. Jenna is the first real girl-friend I've ever had. I've been in situations where I've had opportuni-ties, and I won't say the temptation isn't real, but when it comes down to it, I just don't want any other girl the way I want her."

I'm taking in everything he's saying, listening as my eyes stay fixed on her. There's some old Goo Goo Dolls song playing, and the lyrics, about a guy wanting to run away with his girl, marry her, wake up next to her—yeah, I don't want anyone the way I want Darcy, and I can't imagine that ever changing.

When Mac comes over to bullshit with Dan, I take my leave. The only place I want to be is alone with her.

"This song makes me think of you." I'm behind her now, both hands wrapped around her waist and pulling her in close. When her body is flush against mine, I feel her tense, feel her sharp intake of breath. I'm hard as steel, and she's now fully aware of the state I'm in. "You ok?"

"Do I do that to you?" Her words are spoken softly, meant only for me.

"You have no idea, do you?" I'm rocking her slowly from side to side, my front still pressing into her back. "You make me want to drop everything in my life, take you away, say those vows, watch my child grow inside of you." I laugh then, not because I don't mean every single word I've just said, but because I'm aware that I sound slightly deranged and I'm wary of scaring her off. "Don't worry, though, I'll let you graduate first."

She ignores the joke, leaning her head back against my chest and lifting her arms to lace her fingers behind my neck. The move pushes her chest out, and while I'm not one of those guys who gets territo-rial when another man checks my girl out, in this moment I want her all to myself.

"Take me home, Tom." She lowers her arms and turns to face me. "I want you."

How many times have I dreamed of this, of the moment I'd be

with her, be inside of her? It hasn't been just these past two months. I've been fantasizing about this night for over a year now. Thinking about it since that day in the cafeteria, feeling close to homicidal that she was sitting beside someone who had absolutely no right to claim her. But still I'm careful, still I want to be certain that it's me she wants, me she loves.

She's said the words to me. Just last weekend she whispered those three words when we woke up together. Nothing had ever felt better. But now this, watching her undress for me as I sit on my bed? I can't put the feeling into words. Darcy wants to be in control, wants me sitting here with my hands at my sides, and it's so damn hot in this room now that I'm sweating. *Look, don't touch,* she's telling me. But I'm like a starving man who can't hold out any longer.

"Come here," I tell her as she unclasps the front of her bra and lets the straps slide down her arms. She steps closer, standing between my legs wearing nothing but lace. I look up to her as I slide the fabric down over her hips, but I don't see any hesitation there, any sign of uncertainty.

"You want me." I don't ask, I state it as fact. She nods her head, eyes glazed over, heady with lust just like me. She's wet for me, same way I'm leaking for her. I want to take her like an animal, rut inside of her, ease this desire that's become a physical ache.

"Please," she says as she lowers herself to straddle one of my thighs.

Before we're done, I'll taste her, suck every sensitive spot on her body, run my hands over every square inch. But that moment when she leads me and eases me inside, I swear it's then that I see and feel everything: pure, unadulterated bliss. To move with her, to hear her whimper and sigh because I'm making it good for her, to feel her come with me buried inside of her—there's nothing in the world that compares to being with her.

* * *

DARCY

If he holds out on me now, when he's got me this hot and aching for him, I just might scream.

He's careful with me. And while I know I should be grateful that he respects me and treats me like I'm in some different category than every other girl he's been with, the fact that he's always applying the brakes on us makes me feel insecure. How does he see me compared to the others, compared to Morgan? Why does he treat me with kid gloves? I want him to care for me, to love me, but I also want him to be wild with desire for me.

Tonight I'm not taking no for an answer.

So when he sits on the edge of his bed and beckons me towards him, I stay out of reach. I take off my shirt, taking my time with each button, shimmy out of my jeans shaking my hips from side to side, and watch his mouth hang open like one of Pavlov's dogs when I unclasp my bra and bare myself to him.

"You want me."

It's a taunt, a dare, a command the way he says it. I feel victorious knowing I've unleashed the dark side of Tom Farrell. I can see how hard he is, and when he takes me by the hips and guides me to stand between his open thighs, he looks down to where his cock is trapped and then looks back up to me with eyes that ask, *What are you going to do about that?*

I go slow, reaching down to undo his belt and lower his zipper. He lifts himself off the bed slightly, commanding me to get his jeans down without saying a word. I kneel at his feet, strip him out of his pants as he's tugging his shirt over his head, then lean in to take him in my mouth.

I've done it before, but I've never wanted a man the way I want Tom, never craved the powerful feeling you get from rendering a man helpless with pleasure.

He's pumping his hips up, sucking in breaths between curses, and then pleading for me to stop. "So fucking good, but I need to come inside of you tonight."

I stand on shaky limbs, holding onto his shoulders as he lowers the lace down over my hips. His hand goes straight to me, and I hear him let out a satisfied groan when he feels how wet I am. I could rock my hips just a few times and come against his hand, I'm already so close, but he pulls me down to his lap so that he can touch and suck on my breasts, biting me gently when I grind against his thigh, helpless and desperate for relief.

When he lays back and pulls me with him, I know I'm more than ready. I feel powerful and greedy as I sit up, the base of his cock pressing against me. "You're sure?" he asks. When I nod, he reaches over and grabs the condom he left on the nightstand. As he fumbles with the wrapper, I move back and forth along the base of his shaft, so unlike the person I think I am, so eager to get off.

"Look at you," he says, eyes fixed on my tits as they move with each and every thrust. He whispers and curses, dirty words mixed in with words of reverence and devotion. I've never felt so beautiful, so desirable. And when he touches me, meets the place where he's moving in and out of me, I am lost, in the best, most unfamiliar way.

In that moment I realize that sex is something I've had before, something I've participated in, but it's been done *to* me. This time, my first time with Tom, it feels so different. I own this moment. And when I feel him shudder, feel him pulse inside of me, I feel so deeply loved I'm afraid I'll cry and ruin the moment.

He's clueless to this emotional free fall I'm in. With his eyes fluttering open and closed, breaths evening out and a contented smile on his face, I wonder if it's always like this for him. Is it just me alone having this crazy epiphany?

When I shift to move off him, he holds me to him, pinning me in place. "Don't move." He moves his hands from my hips, skimming up both sides until he reaches my breasts and cups one in each palm. Smiling, he says, "I think I've died and gone to heaven."

"Was that—"

"Mind-blowingly good? Yes, it was." His smile falters when he takes in my expression. "Tell me what's wrong."

"I'm happy, I swear. I'm just scared for some reason." Shaking my head, I add, "I know that sounds stupid."

He rolls me off him, tucking me into his side before taking the condom off and wrapping it in a tissue. Holding me in his arms, he kisses me, slow and sweet and deep. "You think you don't scare me, Darce? I'm just waiting for the day when you wake up and realize you can do a whole lot better than me."

"Don't say that."

He kisses me again, rolling me over onto my back to cover my body with his. "I love you." When I feel him getting hard again, my legs fall open on command. "And I won't hurt you," he says as he grinds against me, pausing to bite down on one nipple, "so don't be scared."

Chapter 11

DARCY

"How much shit is crammed into that bag?" Caitlin comes in as I'm sitting on my suitcase, struggling with the zipper. "It's a five-day break. I'm taking a backpack and my wallet, that's all."

"Aren't you going to your aunt's in Dallas?"

"Yeah, but I'll buy whatever I need when I get there. Day one I'm hitting Wild Bill's...I love the shopping down there."

"You love the shopping everywhere."

"True." Caitlin kneels down and crams one shoe in so that the zipper can close. "Seriously, though, why so much stuff?"

"I need options."

"Ah, meet the parents."

"I've met them before, but not as his girlfriend. So yeah, it's meet the parents, meet the brothers, and meet every member of his high school graduating class." In response to her confused expression, I add, "His best friend throws a party every Thanksgiving Eve that's like an annual high school reunion."

"Fun!"

"Right, I just love going to parties where I don't know a soul."

Caitlin unzips the suitcase, dumps everything out onto my bed and announces, "Move over, you need a stylist."

Within ten minutes I'm leaving with a much smaller, perfectly organized bag that has a killer outfit for the party, as well as three nice but casual outfits for Tom's house.

I'm focusing on the fact that Thanksgiving is my favorite holiday, and it does work to ease my nervous energy some. I focus on fall in Central Park, the good vibes that are contagious as the city gears up for Christmas, and spending time in my kitchen with family, baking and cooking the best meal of the year.

This year we have so much to be thankful for. Our newest family member will be here soon after the new year, and I'm thankful Tom will be a part of the excitement. Even though Matt spent a lot of time at my house, this feels different. It's like I'm bringing a real boyfriend home for the first time.

Tom's feeling the same way, if his constant chatter and tapping on the steering wheel are any indication. He squeezes my hand as we turn down a long driveway lined with giant oak trees, their leaves bursting with fall color. And there's no hiding the fact that this is a house full of boys. There are soccer nets on one side of the lawn, a basketball hoop above the garage door, lacrosse sticks strewn on the grass, and too many bikes to count.

"Does your family own a sporting goods store or a bike repair business or something?"

"Looks like Brendan and Terrence have friends over. They're probably here to check you out."

"What are you trying to do to me? I'm nervous enough as it is!"

As we get out of his truck, he grabs both of our duffels. With his free hand he grabs my hand, presses it to his lips and then holds it against his chest. He always touches me in a way that makes me feel cherished. And maybe it's just that I'm feeling extra sappy around the holidays, but the simple gesture makes me emotional.

Tom takes a whiff of freshly baked chocolaty something as we walk in the door. "Ah, she's going all out for you, Darce."

The smell of his mom's cooking and the sound of kids' voices make me feel at ease. This is a home like mine: nothing stuffy, nothing pretentious. And when Mrs. Farrell lays eyes on us and immediately takes me into a tight embrace, I feel all the tension bleed out of me.

"Mom, don't I get a hug? She's not even family."

"I'm getting to you! Darcy, it's so good to see you again."

As Tom grabs his mom into a bear hug, I see one clone of Tom and a slightly younger boy with dark brown hair and blue eyes bounding up the stairs from the basement. They're practically climbing over one another as they make their way towards us, all smiles and seemingly as confident as their older brother.

"Hi Darcy, I'm Brendan," the older one says, and then, as he pushes his hand square into the younger one's face, adds, "and this turd is Terrence."

Terrence shrugs him off, comes right over and hugs me tight, startling me for half a second. "Nice to meet you, Darcy."

Before I can get out a "hello" I'm belly laughing, because they've jumped Tom and taken him down. Mrs. Farrell pulls me into the kitchen with her away from the mayhem. "So first things first, do you want tea?"

And it's natural, sitting at the kitchen island with her drinking tea. It feels like home. I tell her all about Spain, my side trips, and the last part of the summer spent in Greece with my cousin and brothers. She's so easy to talk to. Matt's mom was kind of stiff in comparison. I always felt like I was on trial when she was drilling me with questions.

And the boys' friends do seem to be taking turns, coming up from the basement one by one to say hello to Tom, peering into the kitchen on their way back downstairs.

"You're making me wish I was twenty again. I think I need to go back to Paris."

Tom comes back into the kitchen, out of breath from wrestling. "Back to Paris? I'm twenty-one and I've never been to Europe."

"You go to Europe on your own dime," his Dad says, following Tom inside. He also takes me in for a hug. "Darcy, we're so glad you're here."

The Farrells are huggers.

"Hi, Mr. Farrell. It's good to see you again too."

"Ted, Darcy was just telling me all about her trip. You need to take me back to Paris."

Mr. Farrell laughs and throws his hands up in surrender. "Whatever you want, Clare. Book it!"

When they ask about our plans, Tom tells them we're staying in with them tonight and going to the party tomorrow night at his friend Dylan's house. I know Ben will be there, so I'll have at least two people to hang out with. I wonder if Amy will be there. I'd actually love to have a face to go with that story.

I don't have any younger siblings, so it's adorable to watch the way Brendan and Terrence look up to Tom. They seem so happy to have their big brother home. At dinner, they beg to take the next day off from school. It's only a half-day and they want to skip so they can hang out with Tom. When Mr. and Mrs. Farrell throw cold water on that plan, Tom promises to pick them up after school and then he'll be theirs for the day. When he looks to me and starts talking about the places we can take them, I beg off. I get the feeling the boys need some time alone with him. It's bad enough that I'm stealing him away for the second half of the weekend.

"I can stay back and help you get some cooking done."

"That would be great. I usually have no help in the kitchen beyond peeling potatoes. I wish you were staying for Thanksgiving, Darcy. We have a total of twelve more coming to join us, and from the way Tom raves about your cooking, I would have just let you take over."

"Oh, I don't know about that. Tom just thinks my cooking is good because he's comparing it to the cafeteria."

"No, I think his exact words were something along the lines of that he loves me, but your meatballs are hands down better."

I look to Tom. "I'm gonna kill you!"

He squeezes my hand and laughs. "But I also told her she makes better gravy than you do. I'm just an honest guy."

* * *

TOM

When you love someone there's no nicer feeling than knowing your family loves them too. This is what I'm thinking as I watch Darcy whip Brendan, then Terrance, and then my dad in ping pong.

Mom corners me when I come up from the basement with the rest of the dessert dishes. "She's *so* lovely and you seem very happy, baby."

"I am, Mom."

I know that seeing me happy is the best present I could ever give my parents. I told Darcy a lot about Charlie, about the years he was sick and the dark year or so after he died. But I don't know if you can accurately describe despair, fully express the depth of the pain I felt after I lost him.

After Charlie died, I spent all of my free time at home with the boys and my parents. I'd go to school and come home, nothing else. Friends would call and I'd blow them off. I was always an athlete, but freshman year I didn't want to go out for any of the high school teams. Time passed but I showed no signs of healing, of moving on. My parents were worried sick.

A few days before sophomore year of high school started up, my father took me to Charlie's favorite fishing spot. It was a beautiful day, sun bouncing off the water and all that. We spent a long time there that afternoon, fishing and talking about him, remembering how he loved this place. As I reeled in nothing but a stripped hook for the umpteenth time, it was almost as if I could hear him laughing alongside me, could feel his presence, and that's when something clicked. My brother would have given anything to beat his cancer, given anything to be here with us. I wasn't honoring his memory by sitting home, broken and miserable.

A week later I told my parents I needed new gear for football try-outs, and they looked so damn relieved. And the looks on the faces of Ben, Dylan and the other friends I'd all but dropped in middle school told me how long I'd been in my funk. They looked at me as if I was a ghost when I first walked out onto the field, but Ben and Dylan, truer friends I'll never know, took me right back in like I'd never left. The sun finally started to shine again that year.

Darcy is in the living room now, studying the pictures that hang on the wall. She turns and smiles when my arms snake around her waist, then gestures to a picture. The four of us are standing in size order, arms crossed in front of our chests in our bathing suits on the beach. "This one is my favorite. You and Charlie look like twins, and I love how the little guys are imitating you two, right down to the tough-guy look on your faces."

I stay quiet, planting kisses along the column of her neck and breathing her in. Tonight she's staying in my room and I'm sleeping in the guest room downstairs. The idea of her in my bed, where I've spent so many nights dreaming about a girl like her—let's just say I'll be sneaking upstairs at some point tonight.

Or maybe not.

* * *

She's sitting in the kitchen having coffee with my mother. When I sit down next to her, she whispers under her breath, "Nice try, lover boy."

I nod, acknowledging defeat as I think back to the locked door-knob and the taps on my bedroom door that went unanswered.

God, I love this girl.

I'm glad when Terrence comes downstairs in his pajamas with his hair sticking up in ten different directions. When I'm away at school I'm loving life, don't get me wrong, but I miss them, so I'm happy my parents caved in and gave them the day off.

After Brendan rolls out of bed, I take them to get outfitted with ski rentals for the season, pop over to Ben's for a few minutes so they can try out his new retro pinball machine, and then it's out for lunch at a chain restaurant one town over where the waitstaff wear skimpy referee uniforms—this is why they love me. We cap off the day throwing a football around at my high school field.

Watching and listening to them as they goof off, I remind myself that I've got to carve out more time for them. Next year Brendan will be starting school here and going out for the team, and Terrence will be in seventh grade, not far behind. It's hard to believe.

They ask question after question, hanging on my every word when I answer. How many wins do we have in fall rugby so far? Who should the Sox go for in the draft this year? Who would have domi-nated if they had played at the same time, LeBron or Jordan? They can talk sports for hours and so can I. But then Brendan shifts the conversation, leads us into uncharted territory. He actually wants to know the "exact words" I used when I asked Darcy to be my girl-friend. I have to remind myself that he's getting older, then I make up some generic line on the fly. The real story would have been confusing as hell—*I swear, Darcy, I'm not a manwhore*—and not something he'd be able to recycle for a girl in the eighth grade.

They're both under her spell. Terrence, still a little kid in his own way, tells me Darcy is prettier than Tallie in *Last of the Jedi*. He's a

Star Wars geek to the core. Brendan cracks up at that and then adds, "I think she looks more like Tom Brady's wife." Pretending to smooch his palm, he adds, "Oh, oh, Gisele." For that he gets a football thrown, not hard, but right to the face.

* * *

"Want me to get you after the party?"

My mother is driving us to Dylan's house, picking Ben up along the way just like we're back in middle school. And no, we'll be walking the quarter-mile home later on. I'm thinking my mother isn't down for staying up until three or four in the morning just to fetch us.

And when we walk into Dylan's, it's a scene. Packed wall-to-wall, the music is blasting and the smell of weed is thick in one corner of the house. I look to Darcy to make sure she's ok. She's no shrinking violet, but coming to a party where you don't know a soul, and add to that a bunch of long-lost friends acting like fools—I'm thinking it might be overwhelming.

I squeeze her hand. "Want a beer?"

She laughs as she takes it all in. "Desperately!"

I leave her with Ben while I hunt down the keg. I don't want to be rude to people, but I'm being accosted every two seconds by someone saying hello. I do want to catch up with everyone, but I'm more concerned with leaving her. It's probably no more than ten minutes when I get back to the spot where I left them. Ben is chatting up Kim and Steph, but there's no sign of Darcy.

"Where is she?"

Ben shoots me a look, darting his eyes from one girl to the other. Yeah, I get it, he's busy. "I don't know. She was just next to me a minute ago."

With that, both girls turn to me. One is eyeing me head to toe while the other is leaning in for a full body hug. I'm tuned out, ignoring them as they try for my attention. Same time last year I would have been all over this, but now the scene grates on me like nails on a chalkboard.

For the next ten minutes, which feels like an hour, I'm on a mission. I just keep saying, "I'll be right back," as I push right past people who stop to say hello. I finally find her in the den in an animated conversation with another girl. Dylan is sitting on the arm of the couch next to them.

"Jesus, I've been looking all over for you!" I'm sure I sound annoyed, but what I'm feeling is a combination of stress and relief.

She laughs and then smiles in a way that tells me my concern makes her happy in some way. "You were worried?"

Dylan jumps up and grabs me in a hug. "So glad you're here, man. Small world, right? This is *my* girl, Kasia Mazur, who happens to have gone to high school with your Darcy. Can you believe that?"

"Wow." I take in the beauty sitting next to Darcy, hoping this one has what it takes to rein my wild friend in. From the look on his face, I'm thinking she does. "It's so good to meet you, Kasia. And this is a crazy good coincidence."

My mind is already jumping ahead to next year, imagining the four of us in New York together starting out. A ridiculous thought, because who knows where on the map any one of us will be. Where will Darcy be?

Knowing Darcy is having a good time catching up with Kasia, I'm able to go back and make the rounds. My close friends are good people, so they make the effort to approach Darcy, introduce themselves and make her feel at home. And everyone knows me here, so I don't have to worry about any guys hitting on her. There are one or two times when girls are a little too determined with me, but I know how to handle that better now. I just start talking about Darcy, point her out, and then—magic—they politely back off. Works like a charm.

* * *

The next morning, I come downstairs to find Darcy and my mother in the kitchen again. Darcy is already showered and dressed, ready for the drive down to New York early this morning. They're busy dicing celery and carrots while chatting away.

I hang back for a minute, have a damn lump in my throat watching the two of them together. I want this future.

* * *

DARCY

We pull up outside of my house too soon. He tugs me back when I go to unlock my door and then grabs my other hand. "I love you."

"Where did that come from?"

"Sounds corny, but I was just overcome with the feeling. Thought I'd share."

I joke, "Right back atcha," but I've also been overcome with that feeling a lot lately.

Sarah is the first to greet us, and when she gets within arm's reach, Tom pulls her in for a hug. It's the Farrell way.

Caleb follows her out of the kitchen, wiping his hands on a very feminine, frilly apron. "Glad you're home. I've been on kitchen duty all morning."

Mom rolls her eyes. "He's lying. He got here half an hour ago, tops."

I'm smiling to myself, knowing Caleb only showed up early so that he could eyeball Tom. He's overprotective, that's the main reason, but I also recommended Tom when Caleb mentioned they needed someone to fill in for Luke in the tournament this weekend. Caleb and Tom shake hands. "So this is the first time I've let Darcy give me scouting advice. She said you're fast and fierce on the wing."

"Hope I don't disappoint."

"You won't. Darcy speaks highly of you, and I have to admit, she generally knows her stuff. When are you heading back down?"

"I was planning on coming Friday night, but my little brothers want to watch the tournament, so I'm heading down early with them on Saturday. I'll be here by eight."

Caleb takes Tom aside for a few minutes to give him the rundown on the competition, and then Tom, too soon, is saying his goodbyes. He kisses me once we're alone, holding me tight before we break apart. It's just two days, but I'm so bummed watching him drive away.

* * *

So it really is a thing, pregnancy does make you glow.

Kate isn't huge yet, but her bump is very noticeable. She looks beautiful and so happy. Both of them look over the moon. The way they hold hands, the way Luke places a hand on Kate's belly and then looks up at her with wonder and such absolute love in his eyes—it's moving.

I try to imagine me and Tom in their shoes, but the thought of devoting myself to a life growing inside of me makes me choke up and fret at the same time. Kids? I always imagined children so far into my future, or not at all to be honest. It's just another thing piling up, another thought making me itch when I take a moment to think about the decisions I need to make in the coming months.

During dinner, talk moves from Mom's latest photography project, to our upcoming trip to Puerto Rico, to possible baby names. Caleb suggests some doosies. No surprise, talk moves on to my love life next. Luke asks Caleb to fill him in on Tom, as if I'm a little kid sitting at the adult table for the very first time.

"Hello? You can ask *me* about *my* boyfriend, Luke."

"I will, but first I want to know what Caleb has to say."

107

Caleb shrugs. "So far so good, but I was mainly concerned with how he measured up for Saturday."

Luke speaks in between bites. "Don't be so touchy, Darcy. I love you. What kind of big brother would I be if I didn't check up on your boyfriends? I'm still mad Caleb didn't keep me in the loop about that last douchebag."

Mom shoots him a look. "Language."

"Sorry, that last *tool*."

Kate places a hand on his forearm. "In the past, Luke, remember?"

Caleb adds, "I had it under control, obviously."

"About that," I chime in. "Did Jenna tell you to pay Nick a visit?" Before he can tell me no, I see the word on his lips. "Forget it, I know you won't tell me the truth anyway."

Caleb leans in so that he's not talking to the entire table. "I know you can take care of yourself, but in that kind of situation keeping quiet isn't smart. When someone's making you miserable and being flat-out abusive," he pauses to take a calming breath, "that's when you reach out, understand?"

Kate smiles at me, eyes twinkling. "I can't wait to meet Tom on Saturday."

Luke gives me a look that's more like a warning. "I'm looking forward to meeting him too."

He finally stops when I peg him in the head with a dinner roll.

* * *

It's a sunny, crisp fall Saturday—the best kind of day to be in Central Park.

"Need help?" Luke asks, looking over the operation I'm running in the kitchen.

I'm up early to pack up our gear for the day. I've got thermoses of hot chocolate, a sack full of sandwiches, and bananas and oranges for the guys playing.

Luke is a spectator for the first time this year. With a baby on the way and a business to run, he's officially retired from rugby. I thought he'd be bummed standing on the sidelines today, but watching him explain the rules to Brendan and Terrence as he shows them how to pass the rugby ball, he looks content.

Caleb looks happy too, but I knew he would be. I've watched enough rugby to know that Tom is a better than average player. My dad is impressed with Tom's play also. I think he's even more pleased when the tournament ends without having to treat anyone on the sidelines for injuries.

Caleb and Tom's team is knocked out in the semi-finals, and while Brendan and Terrence take the loss hard, I think they're really disappointed because Tom's parents came to pick them up. Tom is staying with my family for the rest of the weekend, so this is goodbye for them until Christmas break.

Making our way to a bar on the Upper East Side, I pump my fist when I tell Tom that finally, after all these years, I'm finally allowed to tag along to the tournament after-party. Beers are definitely flowing, we're dancing, and Tom is probably a little too touchy-feely for Luke's taste. I hear him yell to Caleb over the music, "What's with the excessive PDA?"

Caleb answers, not realizing I'm straining to hear him. "It's all good. He seems solid, and I'm happy that for once I don't have to run interference for Darcy. With him here, no one's hitting on her and I can relax. And Tom is a major step up from that other piece of shit. I still wish I broke that guy's jaw when I had the chance."

Caleb really can't say anything about me and Tom anyway. He's been huddled in a corner most of the night making out like a fifteen-year-old with some girl who bears a strong resemblance to Jessica Rabbit. She's all curves. He introduced her before as a co-worker. She's pretty, and she seems nice enough, I guess, but because of Liz I now have a strong aversion to redheads. Also, she doesn't seem like the real deal. I want Caleb happy and in love the way Luke is.

The weekend has been everything I'd hoped for and more, but I'm itching to get back on the road and get back to campus. I'm with Tom, but still, I miss him.

I miss him in my bed.

Chapter 12

TOM

I'm working nonstop. That's what it feels like anyway. I'm catching up on all those assigned readings I didn't read, putting together study guides and writing paper after paper. For Darcy it's the same, except I'd wager that unlike me, her assignments were all completed in a timely manner.

Every night I look forward to eating dinner with her, especially when she cooks. We're staying together on the weekends, but weeknights lately have been crazy. Dinnertime is when I get to relax and just talk to her. I never get tired of just being with her.

In addition to getting ready for finals, I'm also preparing my resume for the on-site interviews the big firms will be conducting on campus. It's becoming more obvious with each passing day that our time here is coming to an end.

Darcy has been wavering on going straight to medical school in the fall. Last week she was talking about doing an interning stint with a medical mission and deferring school until the following year. I don't weigh in. For one, she knows better than I do on that topic, and secondly, I don't want to influence her decision with my selfish need to be close to her. It wouldn't be fair. If I did speak my truth, I'd tell her I don't want her on some aid mission in a poverty-stricken, far-off country. My panicked imagination conjures up highly erratic cell phone reception and a five mile walk along a dusty, deserted village road in a war-torn region to reach the nearest computer. I'd be worried twenty-four-seven. It would do me in.

What I want is for Darcy to be back in Manhattan next year when I'll be working on Wall Street. I know she won't move in with me, but we'll be able to play some version of house when I get my own apartment in the city. But like I said, I'm keeping my opinions to myself.

There aren't many big parties the last two weeks before winter break, but there are a few low key get-togethers. People need to let off some steam in between all the studying, and one such soiree is at our place. It's the usuals: Darcy and her roommates, Chris, Mac, Nick and their housemates, as well as the rest of the rugby guys and few other females. Low key by our standards, but it's still pretty crowded.

Nick and I are no longer friends. Since that night at the Sox game we generally keep our distance from one another, but we can't always avoid being in the same place at the same time. We have too many friends in common for that to be possible. And after some time has passed, if we're in the same room we don't totally ignore one another. A head nod might happen *if* one of us is feeling particularly benevolent, and 'tis the season. He's being well behaved tonight, chatting up Liz and Carrie, two of Morgan's roommates. He's currently off with his on-and-off again girlfriend. Even I'm hoping he finds someone who makes him happy, but that's selfish on my part. I want his thoughts focused on someone other than Darcy.

Darcy packs it in earlier than everyone else. After I take her back to her place and spend a few quality minutes groping and kissing, I walk back into my house to a considerably wilder scene. The music is louder, and Carrie is lying on the kitchen counter with her shirt riding up as Nick licks the leftovers from the shot he just took off her belly. So much for him finding true love.

When Liz spots me at the door she makes a bee-line for me. "Tom, there you are. Where's your beautiful girlfriend?" she teases.

"She hit the hay."

Liz shrugs. "That's too bad. I never thought you'd be one for the Patty Perfect type."

"I don't know if going home at eleven right before finals week qualifies her as a wet blanket, Liz."

"Whatever you say," she breezes in a sing-song voice, pressing a beer into my hand. "What's new with you?" She doesn't wait for an answer. "Since she's been in the picture I hardly ever see you. I feel like I've lost one of my closest friends."

What's with the pouty face? And closest friends? Yeah, I don't know about that.

She's the last person I want to be talking to right now, but I can't escape without making it totally obvious. She's standing too damn close, and I know this conversation is about to head in a direction I'd rather avoid.

"I've been around, Liz. Who's been in your life this year? I know you're not spending your time at home knitting scarves."

She lowers her head and then licks her lips when she looks back up at me. "No, not exactly, but every other guy pales in comparison."

I take a long pull off my beer and look away in shame. "That was a lifetime ago."

One slender finger coaxes me back and I yield, even though the last thing I want to see is the hurt expression on this girl's face.

"Yeah, tell me about it."

"And you know I feel like a total shit over it."

"You have nothing to feel guilty about. You weren't with Morgan anymore. I wanted you and you wanted me."

More like: I was drunk and horny and you were all over me.

"It just shouldn't have happened and I'm sorry, it wasn't fair to you."

Liz shifts her gaze to the floor and bites her lip before saying, "You know, you called me Morgan that first time." I want to vaporize, to run, to just get the fuck out of this miserably awkward moment by any means possible. She shakes her head when she adds, "And I just didn't care. I didn't care if you were thinking of her when you were with me. That's how much I wanted you. Some kind of friend I am, right?"

When she looks back to me, her eyes are glassy.

"C'mere." I hug her tight, feeling lower than dog shit. "It's all on me. I wasn't good to you."

When she nestles in even closer, I take a small step back on instinct. I see disappointment flash in her eyes, but she recovers quickly and cracks a shy smile.

Liz needs to see herself in a better light. No woman should be happy to be the back-up, to be second string.

"You're beautiful, you know that? And I'm really sorry that I took advantage of your kindness that night. You deserve so much better."

What she says next knocks the wind out of me.

"Are you still in love with her?"

"Who, Morgan?"

"I know she still creams over you."

Yeah, Liz has a vulgar side that I've always laughed off. She talks shit just like one of the guys, but tonight I find it repulsive.

"She always wanted it, still wants it both ways...Her man at home and you while she's here at school. I heard her tell Carrie she'd get back with you in a heartbeat."

Her man at home.

Why does hearing about that guy still make me want to punch a hole through the wall? I can see Morgan smiling at him as she walks out of the dorm, but then her happiness quickly gives way panic when she takes in the two of us standing side by side. But why the fuck am I hurting? I don't even so much as think about Morgan anymore, let alone love her.

Liz keeps it up. "You're the one who deserves better, Tom, but I never could compete with her. You were always wrapped up in Morgan, even after she fucked you over."

Fucked me over. I can feel the figurative kick to my nuts as if I'm physically back there, standing in that parking lot.

I peer into the depths of my now empty beer bottle, wishing I could squeeze through the neck to escape this brutal exchange. "No such thing as competing. You'll find someone who's right for you, Liz. Just make sure he's good to you."

She's struggling, about to say something I most definitely do not want to hear, when Ben comes over and pulls Liz in for a friendly hug. I'll have to thank him later for the save. I take the opportunity to sneak upstairs, locking my door behind me, so damn relieved to get away from her.

I don't like reminders of that year, of who I was. How could I do that when I was never even remotely attracted to Liz? *You know, you called me Morgan that first time.* First time? I don't recall there being a second time, or God forbid, a third. I can barely recall the details of that one unfortunate hook-up. Liz might have been willing, or even pushing for it, but I used her, plain and simple.

No one deserves that.

* * *

I'm trying, but in the days that follow, that conversation sticks with me like a shitty song playing on repeat. Every time I'm with Darcy I have this nagging voice in the back of my head asking: What would she think of me if she knew about it? Should I tell her what I did?

"You're sure you can't come to Puerto Rico?"

"Huh?"

Darcy snuggles in closer, tickles me in the ribs. "Puerto Rico?"

"Oh," I recover. "You know I'm dying to come, but Brendan and Terrence would be crushed if I didn't head to Florida with the family."

"I know. I'm just feeling bad for myself. I've been fantasizing about feeling you up in the pool, maybe doing a little naked night swimming in the ocean."

"You're killing me."

"Just teasing. Beth, Rene and Caitlin are coming, so with them and my parents, there wouldn't be any room in the house to sneak off and be together anyway."

"Caleb isn't going?"

"No, he said he can't get away from work. He's been...I don't know, quiet lately and hard to read. Overall, I'd say Caleb is kind of a dog when it comes to women, but I have noticed there's a girl down there he seems particularly friendly with, so I'm really surprised he's not coming. Her dad owns a local restaurant on the beach. He hasn't told me about her, but I know he flies down there at least every other month and it's not just for the surfing."

"Next time you go I want to tag along."

"Definitely. I know I sound like a whiner, but I'm already feeling crabby knowing I'll be missing you over the break."

My chest swells hearing those words, so I hold back from telling her, afraid to do or say anything that might change the way she feels about me.

And by the time we leave for break, I've put Liz out of my mind. Darcy's coming home with me for a few days before Christmas, and I'm focusing on the fact that she and I can just relax now, enjoy time without the pressure of school, finals, or decisions about the future.

My family is practically waiting at the door to greet her when we arrive. They love her, love how happy she obviously makes me. And Darcy seems more than content to hang out with my parents and brothers, even insists on taking Brendan and Terrence along with us when I suggest dinner and a movie one night. She spends time helping the boys pick out gifts for my mom and dad in the mall afterwards, and watching her with them just reinforces what I already know: she's it for me.

The boys and Darcy high-five when they come across a pair of matching berets for my parents. We're all in on the secret that my dad is planning to surprise my mother on Christmas morning with a trip to Paris this spring, so the gift, like Darcy, is perfect.

When she opens my present on Christmas, I hope she feels the love and thought that went into picking it out too.

A few weeks ago I called my mom for some advice, and twenty questions ensued.

"Well, that depends, honey. What do you want the present to say? Do you want to just get Darcy something that she likes, or is she a person you want to really *tell* something to?"

"I'm not following, Mom."

"Well, if it's not that serious yet and you just want her to be happy with what she opens, you could buy her concert tickets, a nice handbag or something else she'd like. But if it's meaningful that you're looking for, then you have to rack your brain."

"Rack my brain?"

After a pause she said, "You know that old teapot I keep displayed in the living room on the mantle…The one that's so old that the finish on it looks cracked?"

"Vaguely."

"Your father gave that to me on my birthday when we just started dating."

I laughed. "Man, who knew he was so romantic. A teapot?"

She snapped, "It *was* romantic, Tom. I was a big tea drinker, even back then, and your dad was fascinated that I brewed my tea and didn't use a teabag. He told me afterwards that he loved watching me make tea because it reminded him of being in his grandmother's kitchen as a child." Then she laughed when she added, "Listening to this story myself I'm thinking it doesn't sound like the start of a passionate affair," her voice went all nostalgic then, "but the point is, he was telling me with that gift that I was like home, familiar, somewhere he was very happy. Get it?"

"Yeah, I get it. Now this just got a whole lot more complicated."

"You'll think of something, Tom."

I tuck that something into my glove compartment before we head down to New York to spend a few days with the Donovans. I've met them all before, but never really spent a stretch of time with them. I feel like I've won her parents and Caleb over to some extent, but Luke is another story. He was definitely in protective big brother-mode over Thanksgiving weekend. I'd even go as far as to say he wasn't particularly welcoming towards me. But it's Christmas, so I'm hoping he'll be feeling that peace on earth, good will towards men vibe.

My house is a scene during the holidays, but Darcy's is next-level. It's decorated to the nines, and neighbors, Mr. Donovan's colleagues, friends and family come and go, popping into their all-hours open house nonstop. I don't know most of the visitors, so there are times when I'm just sitting back, taking it all in.

Darcy's family is warm, and affection is natural between them. I think to myself that Mr. and Mrs. Donovan are how I'd like to be with my wife after being married for almost twenty years. They hold hands and touch whenever they're near one another, so I don't feel weird pulling Darcy into my lap and hugging her whenever the urge strikes. No one here bats an eye. And as the visit goes on, I may be wrong, but even Luke seems to be warming up to me.

He invites us along to tour one of their current projects, a property in the West Village they're renovating and flipping. I notice Luke checking us out, watching as I hold a door open for Darcy and listening in when we speak to one another. I'm good with it. When it comes down to it, I'm glad that in addition to me, Darcy has Caleb and Luke looking out for her.

"Wait up, Tom," he says as he slows his gait. Darcy and Kate are a few feet ahead of us, but Darcy turns and rolls her eyes before shooting me a sympathetic smile as she opens the door and gets back into the truck. *Here we go.* "Darcy is important to us, you got me?" When I nod, he clears his throat. "I can tell that you care about her, and you seem like a decent guy, but sometimes I think she's too trusting. Don't hurt her."

"I don't intend to."

I seem like a decent guy. Maybe he's warming up, but I certainly haven't won him over.

"And promise me you'll reach out if that asshole of an ex-boyfriend even so much as looks her way. Promise me that."

"He's taken care of, believe me."

"I'm gonna hold you to that."

Nick, as far as I know, hasn't so much as said hello to Darcy in the past couple of months. He's still doing his drunk and disorderly act, but he steers clear of us for the most part. He knows I'll be out for blood if he messes with her.

"Are you all right?" Darcy seems nervous after Luke drops us off.

"I'm fine."

"Luke can be—"

"Intimidating?"

She laughs. "I was going to go with ridiculously overprotective, but yeah, that too."

"I don't have any sisters, but I imagine I'd be the same way if I did."

"Caleb's worse." She shakes her head. "I wish he never found out about Nick. Now he thinks I can't look out for myself. He insisted on weekly video chats the entire time I was abroad. It was infuriating."

"From what Chris told me, Caleb's visit was the only thing that had an impact on Nick, so I'm glad he got involved." She rubs at her eyes, and anytime she seems sad it makes me panic for some reason, like I'm afraid the axe is going to drop. "Tell me what's wrong, Darce."

We're in Caleb's old room, where I've been staying, and I'm glad for the privacy when her tears start to fall. "Everything. It's just happening so fast."

I pull her in when those few tears turn to sobs. Rubbing her back, I'm praying with everything I have that this isn't the beginning of the end: *It's all happening so fast, I'm not ready for this, I think we should take a break.* But how could that be? Maybe I was blindsided by Morgan, but I'm not completely clueless. Things are good between me and Darcy, we're happy.

"I feel this constant pressure because I've always had a plan. Now I'm panicking about what I'm going to do come September. I feel so...directionless. What am I going to do if I don't get into a good program? Wait around, study for the admissions exams again, reapply and hope for the best? And the thought of four years of med school, a residency, a fellowship...I don't know anymore. It's hard to admit it to myself and to everyone else, but maybe I don't really want it."

Does she notice the giant sigh of relief I just let out? *No break-up speech, this is good.* I pull back, look into her eyes. "I've been keeping my opinions to myself."

She rolls her eyes. "I know. Thanks for all the help and support."

"Seriously?" I cover my face with both hands when she whips a pillow my way. "I can't chime in."

"Why not? I want your input."

"I've been keeping my trap shut because I'm selfish. I just want you near me."

"I don't want to disappoint anyone, you know?"

"I guarantee that no matter what you choose, you won't be letting me or anyone else down. Wherever next year takes you, just know I'll be here, waiting for you. I want you with me, but I won't put any chains on you."

On this, our last night together, we exchange gifts in front of the tree. It's late, the guests are gone and her parents have gone upstairs to bed. I'm nervous handing over that little box. I'm starting to doubt my mother's advice, afraid Darcy isn't going to get what I'm trying to tell her.

Her eyes go wide when she sees the watch. It's a pretty cool design with a large retro-looking face and a leather strap that wraps around the wrist twice. Just a little funky, like Darcy.

"I love it!"

"Turn the face over."

She does, and then dips her head down for a moment before looking back up to me with an expression I can't easily read. Does she understand I'm telling her that it's okay, that she has all the time in the world? And that I want that time, all the time ahead of her, with me? Maybe it's too much, too soon.

"All the time in the world. Thank you, Tom." She smiles as she moves in closer to kiss me, and then whispers, "You never make me feel rushed or worried about the future. When I'm with you I don't feel so much pressure. I *do* feel like I have all the time in the world."

Score one for Mom. And I'm glad I followed her advice and put some serious thought into this because if I hadn't, Darcy's gift would have put me to shame. We both laugh when I open the box to reveal a watch.

"Great minds think alike, huh?"

"Turn yours over, Tom."

I'm no linguist. I took French in high school and it was my weakest subject, so she helps me out when she sees me struggling. "Siempre. It means always." She looks embarrassed, maybe a little uncertain. "Or it can mean forever. I wrote it in Spanish because you were on my mind a lot that year when I was away."

I pull her into my lap and kiss her gently. Can she possibly understand how much I love her? Those words are all I have, but they feel inadequate. I want to make her understand that she's everything, she's all I'll ever need.

Chapter 13

DARCY

"I'm bummed Tom can't come, but at least I'll have my girls to keep me company. You're sure you can't make it work? I know you'd just love Rene, Caitlin and Jenna."

When Kasia shakes her head and says, "I've seriously got too much to do," Dylan chimes in to add, "Mama and Tata like their baby at home. She turned me down too."

She smiles and pinches his side. "Maybe I just don't feel like yukking it up with all of those snobs in Palm Beach."

Watching the two of them together makes me miss Tom, but I'm happy as I fast forward to next year, when we'll all be back in the city starting out together. Dylan will be here working for his family's company, Kasia's parents will pretty much insist she be based in New York, and Tom is fielding offers from two different firms in the city as we speak. And with each passing day, I'm more certain that I'll be here with him, no matter which career path I choose.

I'm so grateful Kasia and I reconnected over Thanksgiving break. We were good friends in high school, but lost touch after leaving for college. I think I was drawn to her back then because she was so different from the other girls I went to school with. Most were nice, don't get me wrong, but we were all privileged, and most were overindulged. Kasia was at my school on scholarship, and some of the bitchier girls got off on reminding her of the fact. They were jealous, plain and simple, and I told her as much the first day we were paired up as doubles partners during gym class. We were friends from that day forward.

I've been to her home a few times over the years. Her parents are Polish, and back then her mother would make these delicious pierogis and entertain us at the kitchen table by telling us about her childhood in a small coastal town on the Baltic Sea. And her three older, smokin' hot brothers? My Lord, they were a sight to behold. One of them would always come along when Kasia walked me to the subway on my way back home to Manhattan. They were protective, and that alone gave us a whole lot in common.

Her parents kept a neat, tidy row house in Greenpoint, Brooklyn, but they also owned several other properties in the area. Greenpoint was a little gritty back then, but now it's one of the trendier outpost neighborhoods in the city. As landlords in that part of Brooklyn, Kasia's family is now probably well off. But while her circumstances may have changed, she's still the same down to earth girl I remember.

Looking to her man, she teases, "Who will I kiss when the clock strikes twelve on New Year's Eve?"

Dylan groans. "Are you trying to kill me, woman?"

"Yeah," I chime in, "I have no one to kiss on New Year's Eve either. Thanks for reminding me."

"You'll have your girls with you, that's better than nothing."

Toasting Kasia, I nod my head. "It wasn't easy to make this trip happen. I mean, Jenna was easy. She's always up for a getaway. But Caitlin and Rene practically made me swear on the Bible that they wouldn't be inconveniencing my family if they came along. I had to reassure them several times that Caleb has too much going on at work to make it, and that Kate and Luke aren't flying because it's too close to her due date."

Kasia is busy folding her napkin into pleats when she says, "I wish she'd find out what she's having."

But Dylan shakes his head. "And ruin the surprise? That's no fun."

"I know, but I'd love to make a cute little baby girl outfit for her."

"Or him," Dylan and I crack at the same time.

Yes, next year in New York, the four of us together. It's going to be epic.

* * *

I flew down with my parents the day before, so I'm in full-on island mode when I pick the girls up from the airport in our rented Jeep. Within five minutes of unloading their bags from the car, the girls do a quick change and we're on the beach with cold Medallas in hand.

"All right, I know I was a pain when you were planning this trip, Darcy, but let me just say this is *so* much better than Boston in January."

I hug Rene, so glad that she broke loose and did something spontaneous. "So happy you're here."

The girl does not have it easy. I work all summer as a lifeguard because I believe it's my responsibility to earn my own money instead of hitting my dad up for spending cash, but for Rene it's entirely different. I don't know the whole story, but it's clear that she doesn't have a lot of support from her family, financial or otherwise. Rene carries a full course load, an internship at a local television station, and works as many waitressing shifts each week as humanly possible. I admire her for it, and for the fact that she never complains.

So I'm glad when we spend the next day like the first, soaking up rays on the beach, reading trashy magazines, talking and talking some more, followed by drinks and dinner on the deck overlooking the ocean. Rincon is mellow and low key. The perfect place when you want to just get away and relax.

Caitlin shares the pictures she's taken so far, including Beth on the group text so she knows that we miss her, but after a few she writes back:

Stop it, bitches! I'm about to cry I'm so jealous!

By day three we're all tanned and totally on island time. I wake up at around ten, which is beyond late for me. I start a pot of coffee, knowing the other girls probably won't be rolling out of bed until noon. I'm pouring myself a mug of liquid gold when in walks Caleb.

"Hey, miss me?"

I practically race over to hug him. "Oh my God! I thought you couldn't make it?"

"The weather in New York was crappy, and when I checked the conditions here it seemed like I might be missing out on some good surfing."

"Really?" I eye him curiously because there are no waves to speak of. Dad took us out yesterday, and the ocean was so tame even I was able to stand up on the board. I felt like Kelly Slater out there. "Sure you didn't come down because you're missing a certain waitress?"

He looks confused for a split-second, but then practically bites my head off when he leans in close and whisper-yells, "What the hell are you talking about?"

"Jeez, a little sensitive, are we? I'm referring to that girl, the one whose family owns the restaurant down by the beach. Ring a bell?"

I've obviously touched a nerve, and touchy has been Caleb's middle name these past several months. I love my brother, but dealing with him lately has been exasperating. I cannot figure out what's crawled up his ass.

He lets out a breath. "Sorry I snapped, but really, you don't know what you're talking about."

"All right, forget I said anything." I try to paste on a smile, but his bad mood has rubbed off on me. Watching him struggle has always been hard.

With that, Caitlin and Jenna stroll out, looking sleepy. Jenna perks up right away and runs to hug Caleb when she spots him. Caitlin, on the other hand, takes a step back when she sees him, as if she's shocked or something. I've seen girls act flighty and awkward around Caleb, he's good looking and all, but Caitlin knows him. It's weird for a moment there before she recovers, shaking off the startled look. "Hey, Caleb, thought you were swamped at work?"

He reaches for the coffee pot and starts pouring for the girls. He looks to her when he hands her a mug. "I couldn't resist." Looking away, he adds, "Hope I'm not ruining your girls' getaway. I promise I'll stay out of the way. I'll even sleep on the beach."

Jenna teases, "You might get mauled by a pack of wild dogs in your sleep, but I have my own bed as it is now, so yeah, you stay on the beach."

"So that's how it's gonna be? All right, I know when I'm not wanted. See you later, chicas, the waves are calling my name."

Rene walks in at that moment and does Caitlin one better—she looks horrified. What is up with these girls?

"Rene...How are you?"

"I...I didn't think you were coming."

"I wasn't planning on it, but I couldn't stay away."

With that, Caleb grabs his things and heads downstairs to change.

Jenna sighs. "I love my Dan, but I will definitely be out on the deck watching Caleb run down the beach half-naked with his surfboard in a few minutes."

They're all irritating me now. "Would you please stop? That's my brother!"

* * *

TOM

Two very long weeks.

That's how long it will be until I see her again. Every year my family spends part of Christmas break on the Florida coast with my grandparents. I couldn't skip out on the trip because I won't be spending this kind of time with the boys in the years to come. I'll be working full-time once I graduate.

I call Darcy every morning and then we text back and forth all day. Instead of a message, this afternoon I get a cute selfie of my sweet Darcy in a skimpy bikini with:

Do u miss me?

She lays this on me as I'm playing cards with my father and grandfather. Talk about losing my focus. Forget the cards, I can't hold a basic conversation right now.

R u trying to kill me?

Lol. Now that you've seen that, delete it. I don't want ur family thinking I'm some ho that sends half-naked selfies.

No way.

Delete it? It's my screen saver.

I can picture her now, tapping away at her phone in full-on panic mode. You wouldn't know it from those two teeny scraps of material she calls a bathing suit, but Darcy has a modest side.

Not joking, T. Delete it NOW.

For the first time in my life, I'm anxious to leave the Florida sun for the gloomy gray skies and bitter cold of New England.

Chapter 14

DARCY

I usually have one glass of wine while I cook Sunday dinner, but I've just drained the very last drop from my second glass. And I generally wait until the dish is finishing in the oven, but this afternoon I decided to uncork a bottle before I even took the ingredients out of the refrigerator.

The stress is making me batty. Schools will be sending out their decision letters within a few weeks, and I'm scheduled to retake the MCATs next month so that if I don't get into any of my top choices, I'll be able to reapply for the following year.

The night before I flew back up to Boston, Sarah invited a few of the first-year residents over for dinner. Before they arrived, I shored myself up, told myself: *This is great, this will help you make your decision*, but by the time the last one left, I was more mixed up and confused than ever.

For as long as I can remember, I've wanted to spend my life doing something important. Imagine following your father around a hospital when you're a kid, listening in as people ask him questions like he's the ultimate authority on the subject, watching as hospital staff greet him with smiles and admiration, and seeing gratitude on the faces of the patients he's saved and their families. I grew up not only loving my father, but admiring him to the point where it seemed natural to walk in his footsteps. Becoming a doctor used to feel like a calling, a vocation. But nothing feels right anymore.

So here I stand at the crossroads—turn one way and I'm on the path to a career in medicine as planned, turn the other way and what? I've never had a backup plan. I don't know who I am without being on the track I've planned and laid out before me.

And he doesn't understand. *Follow your heart, Darce.* If he says it one more time I just might scream. Easy for him to say. The biggest decision Tom has to make is fairly simple: which of the now *four* firms that have offered him a job does he go with? Same job, same city, and thanks to his father, he has the inside scoop on all of his potential employers.

And it's not just Tom. From my vantage point, it seems like everyone else has it all figured out. Jenna will be teaching in Rhode Island, Rene has a job lined up with a television network in New York, Beth is taking a position in her family business, and Caitlin— well, Caitlin doesn't have to work. She may or may not be going to grad school in the fall, and for what subject she has no idea.

When I was explaining my dilemma to the girls this morning, Caitlin basically told me I was being ridiculous and to lighten up. She's a little more straightforward in her delivery, but her advice is along the same lines as what Luke, Kate and Caleb have been saying. *Don't worry, things have a way of falling into place. Dig deep and ask yourself what it is you love to do. Take some time to figure it out.* And Caleb's parting words to me: *Why are you always so damn hard on yourself?*

The one and only thing I'm certain about is that I don't want to leave Tom, and that pisses off my inner feminist. I've always believed it should be me first—my goals, my ambitions, my dreams. But the truth is, he's my good place. When I'm with him, I don't spend time over-thinking every little thing. I'm in the moment. I'm happy.

All the Time in the World. Sometimes I do feel that way. When I'm in his arms, I can see a different future for myself, one that's simpler. The other night I actually blurted out the words I've been holding inside for more than a year now: *I don't want to be a doctor.* But instead of acknowledging me, he made a joke. Pointing to my wineglass, he laughed when he said, "That stuff is as good as truth serum for you," and then changed the subject. And it's not like he doesn't listen to me, or that he makes me feel like my needs are subservient to his or anything like that. It's just that Tom generally doesn't sweat the small stuff. It's a good way to live, I know that, but his laid-back attitude sometimes leaves me feeling like we're from two different planets.

Hence the Sunday dinner that has gone from just us girls to a party for around twenty. I always cook extra, but I've been inviting people over all day because I need the distraction.

My third glass of wine puts me fully into avoidance mode. I focus on having fun with my friends. It's our last semester, the last few months we'll be in this nice bubble together.

The house is full. Tom, Dan and the rest of their housemates are here, Cara and some of her girls, and Chris with what turns out to be most of the rugby team. I see Tanner huddled up in a corner with Rene. I feel just the slightest bit guilty about extending that invite, but screw it, sometimes I don't think Rene knows what's good for her.

Beth nudges my elbow when she sees me looking their way. "Looks to me like there's trouble in paradise."

"What is she thinking? I mean, he's soooo nice." The way I stretch and slur my words sort of registers, makes me realize too late that the wine is now doing my talking and thinking for me.

Beth gently pries the wine glass from my fingers and comes back a minute later with a glass of water. "Drink this."

"Yes, Mom."

"I predict a break up within the month."

"No way." I start to say more but wisely keep my trap shut.

Beth cocks a brow. "She's been acting off lately, very distant. I'm telling you, they're toast."

I want to tell Beth that Rene's been acting weird since Puerto Rico. And I really hope—pray even—that it's not because of what I may or may not have walked in on between her and Caleb. It could have been totally innocent, and I might be imagining it all, but my intuition is screaming that something has gone down between them. If so, I feel bad for Rene. My brother is a great guy, I absolutely adore him, but he's no hopeless romantic and he leaves a lot of heartache in his wake. So maybe I make a point of mentioning the fact that Jessica Rabbit was over for Christmas Eve this year—Rene doesn't need to know that Caleb was checking his watch every ten minutes until the poor girl finally took the hint and left. But Rene doesn't even react when I drop that piece of information. Caitlin's eyes, though, go as wide as saucers. Interesting.

"Where's Marcus?" I'm definitely looking to change the subject. I mean, thinking of my brother with any of my friends is nauseating.

"He's flying in tomorrow." Looking back in Rene and Tanner's direction, Beth adds, "It's just as well."

* * *

Maybe it's something in the water.

I'm wishy washy, Beth and Marcus are fighting like cats and dogs, and Rene has been a guilt-ridden, weepy mess since she broke up with Tanner. And Jenna is also off. She left Rincon relaxed and happy, but came back from break after two weeks at home a very different girl. She's been distant and quiet, retreating to her room and closing the door a lot. She hasn't met us for lunch once since we've been back. When I ask Dan what's up, he doesn't seem to have a clue.

He chalks it up to Jenna being busy juggling student teaching and her classes, but I don't buy it. Something isn't right.

My fears are confirmed the next night when I get up to use the bathroom and hear her crying through our paper-thin walls. She tells me she's fine, tells me to go back to sleep when I knock on her door, but screw that. I walk in to see her curled up on her bed, eyes red from crying.

"Please tell me what's going on."

She raises her head and levels me with a look. "Just you and me?" That's what we say to one other, code for: *you tell no one else*. When I nod, she chokes out, "I'm pregnant."

I sit at the foot of her bed, momentarily stunned, and then say the stupidest thing ever. "How did that happen?"

She shakes her head. "I *do* take my pill every day, but...I mean, I guess I've been careless. A few times when I stayed over at Dan's I guess I didn't remember to take it when I got back. My routine is that I take it first thing when I wake up." She looks down into her lap, shaking her head again. "I can't tell him. He's going to think I've ruined his life."

"Don't worry about that now. Do you know for sure?"

She rests her head back and looks up at the ceiling. "Yeah, I'm sure. I rode the train for an hour so that I wouldn't run into anyone I knew in the pharmacy. I bought four different tests. I almost lost it in there because the cashier was some really sweet older woman and she looked like she wanted to lean over the counter and hug me." She wipes her eyes like she's angry at herself for crying. "I took them in the ladies' room at Neiman Marcus." She barks out a laugh when she says, "And by the way, you *are* right, those are the nicest bathrooms. Anyway, that pink plus sign came up within a minute on each one. But I knew it would. I feel so exhausted, my tits are beyond sensitive, and I'm craving tuna sandwiches for breakfast. I never eat tuna salad, it's gross." Jenna looks like a lost little girl when she asks, "What am I going to do?"

I take her hands in mine. "We'll get through this. Take a few days to think it through and then we'll take it from there. I mean, soon you'll have to go see a doctor to get vitamins and make sure everything is all right with the baby, but you don't have to do that today."

Way to go, Darcy. My dose of reality has brought on a new round of sobs. But the doctor in me—if there still is one—is already worried about folic acid deficiencies and the margaritas that were flowing in Puerto Rico before she knew she was pregnant.

"Jenna, I'm sorry. Don't think about any of that. There's plenty of time. I'll be here for you day and night. And you tell Dan when you're ready. We've got this."

We hug for the longest time and I don't dare leave her room until I'm sure she's drifted off to sleep. I go downstairs then, make some coffee and sit in the dark by myself. I can't believe that I've just heard the same news from both Jenna and my sister-in-law Kate, but the circumstances couldn't be more different. I'm so scared for my friend.

I want to call Tom. I want to hear what he thinks, want to talk about what we would do if it was us. But obviously, I can't.

Jenna is out the door and gone for her student teaching gig by the time I get out of the shower. I was hoping we could talk some more today, but when she doesn't come home after class, choosing to grab dinner alone before heading to the library, I get the feeling she's avoiding me.

✲ ✲ ✲

Two weeks.

She still won't tell him, and she still hasn't made an appointment to go see a doctor.

Jenna's acting like this isn't happening, like even talking about it will make it more real somehow.

I feel like shaking her and telling her to get her head out of her ass, but I don't think that would go over big. I'm truly afraid she'll stop speaking to me entirely, and I'm basically all she's got right now.

When Dan came to me last week, practically in tears asking what's come over her, I didn't tell him, didn't betray my friend even though I really, really wanted to. I'm shutting Tom out too. I've been ducking out of everything early, if I even show up at all, and when we're together I know I must come off as faraway and restless.

Twice this week I've told him I'd meet him for lunch and then bailed. He's waiting outside my afternoon class now, and he looks hurt. "What's going on with you?"

"What do you mean?"

"If it's me…" He shoves his hands in his pockets and looks away. "If it's me, Darcy, just say it."

I'm running on next to no sleep. I'm not used to keeping secrets and it's taking a toll on me. Am I protecting Jenna or ultimately hurting her by doing what she asks of me? It's too heavy a burden to bear.

"This has *nothing* to do with you. Please, I just need a little time."

He shakes his head, mutters something under his breath before saying, "I just don't get it. Out of the blue, all of a sudden you're avoiding me? And since when can't you talk to me about things?"

I'm speechless, miserable and so, so tired. "I'm not avoiding you. I just can't talk about it. Can you please just be patient with me?"

He picks up his backpack. "I'm trying, Darce." He's already turning and walking away when he says, "Gotta head to class. I have an exam."

Dan loves you. You know he'll man up. Tell him, please. I'm like a broken record. What I want to add goes something like this: *You're probably seven to ten weeks along by now. You're being so irresponsible. You need to see a doctor.* I'm getting impatient.

I'm impatient, I'm frustrated, and I also feel terrible about the way I'm treating Tom. I wake up determined to go to him today.

Maybe I can't tell him exactly what's going on, but I can do a better job of reassuring him. And the truth is, I need him.

I walk into the cafeteria and see Dan, Chris, Denny, Mac and Tom at our usual table. My stomach drops when I see Liz and a few of her friends sitting at the far end of the table closest to Tom, leaning in and chatting him up. One of the girls has her back to me, but I know right away that it's Morgan. I'm having a hard time processing this spectacle before me. Nothing about their interaction is subtle or polite. His shoulders are shaking as he cracks himself up, his smile spanning the width of his face. He's obviously enjoying their company. Her company. I try to swallow but my throat is bone dry. I can't walk over there feeling like this, like I've been kicked in the gut.

Having fun?

As soon as I fire off that text, I turn my phone off, go home, lace up my sneakers and run.

* * *

After knocking on her door once and getting no response, I don't make any further attempts to talk with Jenna. I just don't have it in me, can't be her shoulder to cry on tonight. I literally ran to the point of exhaustion, but still when I lay down, sleep doesn't come easily. I go heavy on the under-eye concealer when I wake up and take a good look in the mirror.

I'm making my way across the quad like a zombie when Tom grabs my arm and spins me to face him, nearly knocking me off balance. I want to burst into tears when I take in his expression, a mix of pain and rage.

"Having fun? You write some shit like that and then disappear and won't take my calls? What the hell is up with you lately?"

Just as I open my mouth to choke out what's bubbling up inside

—a tangled mix of apologies and accusations—Liz, like the bad penny she is, literally bounces herself in between us.

"Hey!" She looks to me and then Tom, taking in the scene. Then in that fake, sweet, pleading voice that I notice she only breaks out when guys are around, she chirps, "Sorry, hope I'm not interrupting anything. I just wanted to tell you we're having a party on Saturday. You both *have* to come."

I know she's just loving the obvious discord between me and Tom. And really, now we're friends? Now you want me to come to your party? What was it she said to me the last time she cornered me alone? Right, that Morgan and her boyfriend were on the rocks so I'd better watch my back.

Tom keeps his hard eyes fixed on me when he answers, "Can't, Liz, I have a rugby thing."

Anyone else would take the hint, but she just keeps at it, playfully poking Tom in the chest, no less. "Well then our party is going to be rescheduled because I'm *not* doing it if you're not there."

He breaks his stare-down with me for a second to give her a faint smile. "Yeah, all right."

Am I in some grotesque alternate reality? Is he really engaging in conversation with her about parties while the two of us are standing here, practically imploding? He's showing Liz his good 'ol boy public persona while I'm being manhandled and barked at? Now I'm burning. This is Liz, the girl who's been planting the ugliest seeds of doubt in my head all year long. I replay yesterday in my mind, see Tom with those girls, joking and living it up. *Screw them all.* I want to laugh out loud and tell Liz she can have his sorry ass. But I say nothing, I stand frozen.

In the ensuing silence, as the moment drags out and grows even more awkward, Liz looks back and forth between us, the ghost of a smile on her lips. When she finally speaks, she pours the drama on heavy. "Well, I can see this is *not* a good time. Um, call me if you need me, Tommy."

Can you get arrested for choking the life out of someone? Yeah, I know, but right now I so do not care about consequences. I watch her walk off and then turn back to Tom, who's shooting me a look that's borderline hateful.

You're mad at me?

"Well, Darcy?"

I jerk my head in Liz's direction. "Well what? If you're looking for a shoulder to cry on, *Tommy*, she just walked that way."

"What's that supposed to mean?"

"For someone who's intelligent, you're pretty stupid. I don't know what else to tell you."

It's a lame comeback, I know, but I'm not running on all four cylinders. When I walk away, he doesn't follow.

How did this happen?

The rest of the day is a blur. I know I've played a major part in how this has all gone down, but I am beyond pissed at him. Things are a little rough for less than three weeks and he can't hang in? He's looking friendlier and friendlier with Morgan and her besties? Does he still have a thing for her? My heart tells me no, that no one's that good of a liar. He loves me, I believe that, but what does it matter if we can't shoulder through tough times together? Knowing that Tom can turn his back on me so easily adds heaps onto to my hopeless state.

Before I face plant onto my bed crying and fall into a coma-like sleep, I get handed back a C-minus on my Molecular Genetics test and realize I forgot to hand in an assignment in Philosophy. It's been a banner day.

When my phone lights up with an incoming text in the middle of the night, my first thought is a hopeful one: Tom. But it's Jenna, and the urgency of her text has me springing out of bed and running down the hall to her room in seconds.

She's pressed up against the wall on the far corner of her bed. Her face is ghostly pale, and while her sheets are patterned and bright pink, there's no mistaking the blood on them.

"I'm calling Dan."

She hisses, "No!"

I'm crying, not just because I'm scared for her, but because I feel like I don't even know this girl anymore. But I snap out of it, knowing that right now I have a job to do. My hands shake as I rifle through her drawers for a shirt, sweats, clean underwear, and a pad from the bathroom. She lets me put the clothes on for her, following my instructions to lift her arms and legs, making no motion to dress herself.

I take Beth's keys and make the twenty-minute drive to the emergency room at St. Anne's in ten minutes. It's two-thirty when we check in, and thankfully, the waiting room is empty. I hand the triage nurse my credit card along with the paperwork I filled out on the fly, figuring Jenna doesn't want her parents finding out about this. By the time they take her in a few minutes later, she's bleeding through the pad and I'm frantic.

Jenna might never speak to me again, but I decide to take the risk and dial Dan's number. No answer, and with no other alternative, I ring Tom. He answers in a sleepy voice, but still manages to come off as icy and distant when he says, "Yup."

"Sorry to wake you, but can you put Dan on the phone? He's not answering."

He has his fuck-off voice going now. "You want *Dan*?"

"Please, I don't have time to get into it with you right now."

"You gotta be kidding me."

I want to fall into his arms crying and slap his face at the same time.

Dan's voice is scratchy with sleep. "Is everything ok?"

"I'm at St. Anne's with Jenna. You have to get down here but please don't tell anyone where you're going. She's going to kill me as it is."

"What the fuck is going on?"

"Just get here, ok? She's going to be all right."

I think.

Jenna asks for me to be in the room when the doctor comes to speak with her. She's had a miscarriage. She was probably nine to ten weeks along from what he could estimate. She's crying when she squeezes my hand and half-croaks, half-whispers, "Ask him. Ask him if I made this—"

"Doctor, she wants to know if this happened because she didn't get prenatal care soon enough."

He's kind and fatherly, the way I imagine my dad would be if he was the one delivering the news. "No, dear, that had nothing to do with it. It's not as uncommon as you would think. And it should have no bearing on whether or not you'll be able to conceive in the future."

Jenna squeezes her eyes shut and nods.

He's talking to her now about the process of miscarriage, and how he doesn't see a need for a D&C. I'm listening intently because I can see that she's not. When he moves onto more basic information, like keeping hydrated, getting adequate rest, and more effective birth control options for the future, I look over to see Dan standing in the doorway, tears streaming down his face. I squeeze Jenna's hand, and without speaking, Dan takes my place on the bed next to her. He wraps her up in his arms and kisses the top of her head as they grieve the loss together.

The moment feels too personal, too sad, so I need to go. Jenna has the person she needs with her now, and I need to get Beth's car back before anyone notices. The sky is just starting to turn light purple when the automatic doors deposit me back out onto the sidewalk. It's pretty cold outside, and I shiver against the wind wearing only a thin sweater.

"I followed Dan here." He looks crushed. "Are you ok?"

"I'm fine. I would have told you if it was me."

"Is Jenna all right?"

"She will be."

"I'm sorry if you think I've been an ass, but I have no idea what's going on with you, and I get the feeling you're still not going to tell me anything. I just don't understand why."

"And I don't understand why having a little faith and being patient with me is too much to ask. It's like you've turned your back on me, moved on."

"Moved on?"

Tears prick at my eyes, but I won't allow myself to break down right now.

He comes closer and reaches out to hold me tentatively. "Please tell me how to fix this. I miss you."

You miss me? I feel no tenderness towards him right now. There's nothing but hurt and pain.

I shake my head, take a step back so that I'm out of his arms. "The last few weeks have been so hard. And I don't know, the way you've been? You don't miss a beat. I'm out of the picture for a few days and you're having lunch with Morgan and her friends? What is that? And yesterday when you and I were talking..." I can barely get the words out, the fire in me now boiling over. "I mean, when you were *berating* me in public, you just dropped everything to talk parties with your buddy Liz. I keep wondering, do I really even know you?"

My words knock the wind out of him. He's wide-eyed, shaking his head. "What are you talking about? How am I supposed to know what you've been dealing with, Darcy?" His voice is getting louder with each accusation. "You don't tell me shit. You've basically just dropped me. You're driving me fucking insane!"

"I don't want this!" I yell back at him. "I don't want to feel the way I do!"

"What does that even mean?"

Good question, and I look to the sky because I've got absolutely nothing. All I do know is that I'm currently some messed up combination of confused, jealous, angry, broken-hearted and physically exhausted.

"I've got to go. I have to get the car back before Beth wakes up."

I leave him standing there, knowing that everything is falling apart. How could I love someone so intensely one day and then feel something so close to hatred for him the next? And that's what I feel, white hot rage, every time I picture his smiling face, sitting at that table laughing with the girl he once loved.

I let myself back in quietly, return the keys to their spot then gather some fresh sheets, bleach and a garbage bag to get Jenna's room back to normal. That's when the tears really start to fall. Wiping bleach over the mattress and gathering the bloodied sheets and pajamas into the trash, I think about Jenna and know she must be suffering. I imagine I'd be feeling a mixture of relief and guilt if I were in her shoes. I hope she's not mad at me, but I know getting Dan there was the right thing to do. He loves her so much. I picture the two of them in the hospital, Dan cradling her in his arms. Once he knew, he was there for her. It makes me feel the loss of Tom so heavily.

I know I'm at fault. I've gone from spending nearly every free moment with him to barely returning his calls. I'm the one who's left him confused and hurting. I owe him more of an explanation, but still don't know if I can communicate without feeling the angry stab of jealousy that rises up whenever I look at him. It comes down to dreading the very question I need to ask. I need to know about her, need to know how he feels about her. I'm afraid he'll confirm my greatest fear.

I wake to my phone ringing. Dan tells me they're releasing Jenna in about an hour, so he's swinging by to get a change of clothes for her. No one else is home, which is a relief, because I can't hold back from collapsing into Dan and crying when I see him. When he gets back with Jenna an hour later, she looks pale and wiped out. There are more hugs and tears in her room as Dan parks the car.

"Are you mad at me?"

"Mad at myself. I should have told him right away. I feel terrible. And I want to apologize to you."

"Don't."

"No, I've been impossible, and you've been so good to me."

"You'd do the same for me. It's going to be all right, Jenna."

Dan walks back in, gives me a kiss on the cheek, climbs right into bed with Jenna and strokes her hair. I watch them together for a second before turning to go. "See you later, guys. I love you."

It's time. I send up a silent prayer as the call connects, seeking, I don't know, wisdom, understanding, courage? But it rings only once and doesn't go to voicemail. His phone is off. *Great.* I'll just have to suck it up and go to him.

"How are you doing, Darcy?"

I look up to see Nick, and if I'm not mistaken, he seems to be giving me a wide berth on purpose, standing back several feet and out of arm's reach. It's like he's trying to reassure me that he doesn't intend to bother me or make me feel uneasy, and for some reason it makes me feel bad for him, or guilty in some way.

"I'm fine. You?"

He looks like he's not buying my claim that it's all good, but nods his head anyway and says, "I'm doing well." He offers a sad smile when he says, "See you around."

"Hey, what's up? You ok?"

Chris is the third person who's asked me the same question, so I'm guessing I look like the walking dead.

"I'm fine, just heading over to see if Tom's around."

"He's at the rugby house. I just came back to get an extra tap for the keg. I'll take you there."

I'm not in the mood for a party. "I don't think so, Chris."

"Oh, come on. He'll be happy if you're there. That boy's been walking around like a kid who just dropped his ice cream cone for the past few weeks. Not taking no for an answer. You're coming."

You know that age old advice of listening to your inner voice? Well, mine was screaming: *Don't go!* but I didn't listen. No, I went walking right into a red-headed spider's web.

* * *

TOM

Moved on?

I know women and men don't always view the world through the same lens, but what would lead her to believe that I'm looking to get back together with Morgan? Darcy is either losing it, or using this bizarre theory as some lame excuse to push me away.

I'm going to give her the benefit of the doubt given the events of this morning. I'm still in the dark, but in the very least I know that something heavy has gone down. I decide to give her some time but not much. Today is Saturday. If she doesn't come to me by tomorrow, I'm busting her door down and making her see things my way.

I'm not letting her go. No chance.

I've been awake since my 3 a.m. car chase to the emergency room, so I can therefore now honestly say that I feel like shit. How I let Mac drag my sorry ass to the rugby house is beyond comprehension, but I'm battling negative emotions along with fatigue, so I happily take the shot of Patron he lines up for me. I'm a few beers in when the party starts to get crowded. I see Liz and Carrie walk in, thankfully without Morgan. It's a big house, so I can avoid them, and that's what I aim to do.

I keep to my perch on the windowsill in the far corner of the main room. Life goes on around me, and I'm content to be a voyeur. I sit there observing, studying the hook-ups in progress. I'm transfixed, watching as some girl whispers into her man's ear while his hand slides down the length of her, from the nape of her neck to the curve of her lower back. God, I miss touching Darcy.

I keep wondering, do I really even know you?

My heart sinks thinking back to this morning. You know me, Darcy. You know just about every crappy thing I've ever done, every bad decision I've made. And you know you're my weakness.

I've had enough of this place. I motion to Mac that I'm heading out, ducking into the bathroom to take a leak before I bail.

I'm mid-leak when the door creaks open. I'm mid-*What the fuck?* when Liz walks in and closes the door behind her.

"What are you doing?"

She's wide-eyed and laughing, oh so surprised, as if she never in a million years expected to come upon me, dick out and pissing after she followed me into a bathroom. "Ohmygod!"

I put my junk away and turn to face her. "Hello? What are you doing in here?"

"Sorry, you just, I don't know, looked so miserable out there." She puts her right hand up in a pledge. "I swear, I just wanted to check on you. Are you ok?"

Hmm, maybe she could have asked me this, I don't know, after I exited the bathroom? I turn away from her to wash my hands. "I'm good, Liz."

"I couldn't help but notice that you're alone *again,* Tom. What's up with that?"

Once I take a step back, she wedges herself between me and the sink basin, leaning back with her hands braced behind her so that she's propping her chest out. She's always so damn obvious.

"Nothing's up, just working some things out."

She moves in closer, flashing me a wicked grin. "I can work some things out for you, remember?"

I'm definitely feeling my liquor, but I'm not totally out of it. As she reaches to get me back out of my pants, she whispers, "You used to love the way I made you feel."

Hooking up with my ex's roommate is definitely up there with my all-time most shameful moments. It wasn't premeditated, and definitely wasn't done in an effort to hurt Morgan. It was just a drunken, careless, thoughtless mistake. I'd swear it happened only once, but again Liz is making it sound plural.

"Liz, stop."

She keeps at it, and she's lightning fast, gliding one hand down into the narrow opening she's made by popping open my top button. And I guess I'm more impaired than I thought, because when she moves in, I stumble a bit, landing with my back against the tile wall. She now has one hand firmly around my shaft. I hear myself suck in a breath and she moans in response. "That's right, baby, I've got you."

I push her off, hard.

"What's wrong?" She's got her hands on her hips now, facing off with me like a petulant brat. "Don't worry, I'm not looking for a damn proposal. I just want to be with you, make you feel good, have some fun. Do you even *remember* how to have fun?"

With a firm grasp on both of her shoulders, I move her back to create some distance between us. "*This* isn't fun." Raking a hand over my face in frustration, I'm fumbling for words when I say, "Look, Liz, you're a nice person. Any guy would be lucky to claim you as his own. You don't need to be like this."

She lowers her head. "You always say that...Any guy would be lucky to have me. Any guy, but not you, right?"

What can I say to that?

Liz looks to me, pained. "It never works out for me. I get it, I'm not the girl you take home."

"Yes you are. Don't sell yourself short."

"Ever since I met you freshman year, you've always been good to me. No guy has ever treated me better. So even though I knew you belonged to someone else, I didn't care. It's pretty pathetic, just waiting for you all this time, but I just keep hoping."

"You're building me up, seeing me as someone I'm not."

"I wish you weren't worth it, Tom, but you are. You're a good person."

No, I tell myself, *good people don't do the things I've done*.

It feels like the walls of this bathroom are closing in on us, suffocating me, and I need out. How many times can we have the same conversation? And here I am, standing in a goddamn bathroom dealing with Liz, when what I really need to be dealing with is the growing distance between me and Darcy. I have to end this.

"I'm sorry, and I don't want to hurt you, but if we're still going to be friends you have to understand that this," I gesture between us, "can't happen again. I'm with Darcy."

Her eyes plead with mine for a moment before she sighs. "All right, I get the message." She wipes at her eyes and then cracks a shy smile. "Still friends?"

"Absolutely. Come on, let's go."

I turn her around so she's facing front and I'm walking behind her, guiding her out of the bathroom with my hands on her shoulders. As she opens the door, she turns around and rises up on her toes to give me a peck. "Thanks, Tom."

I smile back down at her, hopeful that I've made myself clear and we can put this behind us for good.

But in that moment I know something is very, very wrong. My pulse begins to hammer even before I look up to see Darcy standing in front of us, her eyes locked on Liz.

Fuck my life right now.

Darcy turns and storms out the front door. Before I can get to her, I'm thrown back by a pair of giant hands.

"What the fuck, Chris?"

"You're not going near her." He glares at me before turning on Liz. "And you, you're fucking pathetic."

And then it's on. Is he kidding me, acting all protective over Darcy? Protecting Darcy from *me*? She's *mine*. Chris pins me after we both land several punches, his forearm lodged against my throat.

"You done?" When I don't answer, he roars, "I brought her here for you, and you let me walk her right into that? You're the stupidest motherfucker on the planet."

I push him up to alleviate the pressure on my throat. "You don't know what you're talking about."

He gets up off me and pushes me hard into the floor again before leaving. It takes me a minute to pull myself together, and I get to lick my wounds with an audience, as the music has stopped and the room's gone silent. When I make my way to stand, I've got Liz hovering over me, wiping the blood from over my eye. Yeah, my very own Florence fucking Nightingale.

"Thank you, Tommy. He was *so* out of line."

Great, now this one thinks I was fighting for her honor? And what's with the *Tommy* crap? No one in my family even calls me that. A flashback to Darcy hissing my name that way in the quad the other day hits me hard. She was mocking me, mocking the way I let Liz talk to me. Pointing out how I've let her come between us.

"Go away, Liz." When she opens her mouth to speak again, I can't hold back. "I'm warning you, stop fucking talking and GO AWAY."

Battered and bruised, I make my way back to campus.

Ben starts in on me first. "Rough day?"

"You could say that."

"You want to tell me what happened? I gotta tell you, the version I just heard doesn't sound like you. At least, not the you I've known this year."

"Why don't you tell me then, because I was there and I have no clue what just happened."

Ben shakes his head like he's already casting judgement on me, then proceeds to state the facts. "Chris ran into Darcy when she was on her way here, looking to meet up with you. He took her to the party. When they walked into the house they saw you and Liz coming out of the bathroom together. Apparently, you kissed her on the lips. And then when Liz saw Darcy, she winked and made some crude gesture, licking her lips like she was savoring the last drops of cum on them. Oh, and I almost forgot the icing on the cake...Your pants were undone."

"That's not what happened. I've gotta go talk to her."

Dan bolts up off the couch and makes as if he's going to block me when I move towards the door.

"She's not there, and even if she was, you're not going anywhere near her right now."

"What the hell is the matter with you two? Do you really think I'd do that?" I sink back onto the couch, running my hands over my head in frustration. "It's like I'm losing her and I can't stop it. *She* did this. Darcy shut *me* out. Everything was good and now..."

And now what? Now everything just sucks.

Ben gets a call and walks outside to talk in hushed tones. Hundred percent certain the call pertains to me. Whatever. I'm so fucking tired that all the anger has bled out of me.

When we're alone, Dan lets out a deep breath then speaks slowly. "Hey, look at me. You need to hear this, and I know this shit is safe with you." He glances up to make sure Ben isn't coming back inside. "Jenna was pregnant. She didn't tell me, which...I can't even describe how that makes me feel. For some reason Jenna didn't trust me, but she did tell Darcy. She had a miscarriage the other night." He's choked up, on the verge of tears. When I go to put my hand on his shoulder, he shrugs me off. "My point is that for three weeks Darcy didn't leave her side. Darcy dropped everything for her."

"I followed you the night you went to the hospital. I saw Darcy that next morning when she was leaving, but she still wouldn't tell me anything. I'm just sorry. Must hurt like hell."

"Yeah it does. It hurts because one day I want that with Jenna.

And it hurts because I'm relieved it's not happening now, and that makes me feel like a total shit."

"I'm sorry, Dan."

When Ben comes back in, Dan changes the subject. "What really happened tonight?"

"Liz followed me into the bathroom and tried to get with me, but I turned her down."

Dan shakes his head. "Jenna told me she's been trying to stick it to Darcy off and on all year. She's a bitch, Tom."

"What do you mean?"

"Basically talking shit about how you are between the sheets, how you love *her* blow jobs, how you've done half the campus, and not to get too comfortable because you aren't just going to be with one girl. So I can see why Darcy has been starting to think you're not worth it. She sees this girl chatting you up, obviously flirting with you, and you do nothing to discourage her. And then this today—"

"Nothing to discourage her?"

"You heard me. Why are they starting to sit with us at lunch? Come to our parties again? If you're not discouraging her, then with a girl like Liz, you're encouraging her. I'm even thinking back to that first night this fall at the rugby party. You acted like an ass. I knew you were into Darcy, but you didn't push those other girls away. You didn't make it absolutely clear to them that the attention was not welcome."

"Those girls mean nothing to me." My voice trails off when I add, "Liz is just a friend."

Ben is standing a few feet away, arms crossed, looking down on me. "Do you hear yourself right now? Liz is your friend?" I know what's coming and it's deserved, so I just sit there ready to take the blow. "First off, that girl's a walking nightmare, so calling her a friend doesn't say much about your judgement. And after you sleep with someone, they're no longer just a friend."

"I didn't sleep—"

Ben holds up his hand, cutting me off. "Don't want to hear it."

He won't believe anything that comes out of my mouth right now, and really, what can I say in my defense? *I didn't sleep with her, I just let her suck me off once or twice?* I jump up off the couch, making it to the bathroom just in time.

When I sit back down, I notice Ben has left the room. Dan is sitting across from me and lets a minute pass in total silence.

"Maybe…" He pauses as I brace for impact. "Did you ever think that maybe Darcy's the right girl, but she didn't come along at the right time? Maybe you're not ready."

Not ready to be in a serious relationship. Not ready to be responsible. Not ready to man up.

I know Dan's intention isn't to hurt me, but his words feel like a bullet in the back.

I don't look his way, but imagine he's shaking his head when he says, "Go to sleep, Tom. Tomorrow's another day. I'll talk to Darcy if I see her tonight. I'll tell her what happened."

Won't change a damn thing at this point.

She's done with me.

I'm not worth it.

DARCY

"I can't believe there's not some weird story behind this. I just can't believe he'd do it."

A bottle of wine sits on the table between us, but I'm the only one drinking. I had to get out of there. He's probably banging on my door right now, looking to plead his case, and I don't want to hear it.

"Jenna, you didn't see what I did. It is what it is. I'm over it. He deserves her. I hope they get married and have red-headed bucktoothed babies together."

Jenna eyes me curiously. Tom has an overbite that's barely discernible, but imagining a station wagon full of children who look like Alfred E. Neuman gives me pleasure.

Now I'm just being mean.

"I feel like I caused this in some way."

"No, stop it." I can't listen to her blame herself. "I know what you're thinking and it's ridiculous. Better I learned early on that if the going gets tough, he's not in it for the long haul."

"I hate her so much, Darcy. She's a plotting, manipulative bitch."

"I hate that word."

"Seriously? I was being nice."

"He didn't look like he was suffering. I guess plotting, manipulative bitch is his type." My head drops into my hands. "I can't believe it either. I can't believe he'd end things between us for her. I don't know what actually happened, but it really doesn't change anything, does it?"

"Please don't make any final decisions. I want to kick Tom in the balls right now, but you love him, and I know, I *know* he loves you."

"Do you think there's a reason? Is there something about me that makes things not work out right? I know I sound like an idiot, but really, I want you to tell me if you think it's me."

"Darcy, no! That's all I'm saying on that subject, no."

I answer when I see Chris's name flash on my screen. "See, I told you I shouldn't have gone to that party."

"Holy shit. Are you ok? I feel so bad for bringing you there."

"It's not your fault."

"I really don't know what we walked in on. I don't dislike many people, but I think that girl is trash." Chris clears his throat, sounding angry when he says, "He claims that we got it all wrong, that nothing happened. I don't know what I believe, but I just want you to know what Tom said. Hey, you want me to come over? We can watch *Bridesmaids* or something, get shitfaced and just laugh."

"You like that movie?"

"Yeah, the bridal shop scene is classic."

He manages to get a laugh out of me, which is monumental, but I want to wallow in my own sorrow tonight. "Thanks, but I think I'm just going to crash."

Jenna texts Dan before we drive back. He's wanted to be with her, to stay with her and hold her every night since everything happened. He's there waiting when we walk in. He kisses Jenna's cheek and then comes to me and tussles my hair.

"I'd ask if you're all right, but I know you're not. Look, he said nothing happened and I believe him. He's not that much of an ass." I say nothing, choking on my damn tears again. "He said she followed him into the bathroom, and she tried, hence the undone pants, but he pushed her off."

"Poor defenseless Tom. I think I'm going to be sick with the visual on that."

Dan looks down at the floor. "Yeah, I know. He's not looking too innocent right now."

"I hate him."

"Hey, I know you're hurting now, but he loves you. I've known him for a long time. He's never been into anyone, Morgan or anyone else, the way he is with you. He's all kinds of messed up right now."

Hearing her name doesn't have the same impact it did before. I feel empty now, like I have nothing left.

He turns back when he's halfway up the stairs. "Just hear him out, Darcy. Seriously, you're like a sister to me. I wouldn't tell you to give him another chance if I thought he'd intentionally hurt you."

* * *

Tom didn't come by that night. No sign of him on Sunday either. I can't *hear him out* because he's not talking. And after yesterday, there's no way in hell I'm going to him.

Beth, Caitlin and Rene are walking on eggshells around me. If every dark cloud does have a silver lining, I suppose my misery has distracted the rest of the girls from what's been going on with Jenna, and that's for the best.

I give in when they stage an intervention Sunday night, dragging me out to the movies and dinner. Rene is scolding Caitlin for picking out a movie with so many sappy love scenes as I push my food around the plate. I can't stomach more than half of one onion ring.

"It's all right, Rene." I make an effort to smile, but I don't pull it off. "I know you girls are trying to keep my mind off of everything, and really, I appreciate it."

Beth grabs my hand. "I'm sick over this. I feel bad saying this to you, but we all love Tom. We love you and Tom together."

Caitlin nudges her. "Just tell her."

I raise my eyebrows when she doesn't say anything. "Might as well spit it out, Beth."

"I saw Liz last night. Marcus heard from Ben, so I knew right after it happened. Can you believe after all that drama she had the nerve to show up at Cara's party? It was a small get together, and those girls don't even like Liz. It's not like she was welcome there to begin with. Anyway, when I saw her I kind of lost it. I'm actually pretty ashamed of how I acted even though I do hate her."

"Did she say anything?"

Beth can't even look me in the eye. "Yeah, she came right back at me, screaming in my face. She said we think we know Tom, but we don't. She said Tom had been sneaking off to get with her while he was with Morgan, and nothing has changed now that he's with you."

Rene jumps in. "I don't believe her. She's a low life and Tom wouldn't do that to you."

Caitlin leans in. "Think about it, Darcy. When would he have been able to sneak off and be with her? He's been glued to your side twenty-four-seven."

"It looked *so* bad." I shake my head in an effort to erase that sickening image of her licking her lips from my mind's eye, but it doesn't work. "But even if he is innocent, I don't know, things have been going downhill between us. There's a part of me that just wants to walk away. I have other things I need to focus on."

Rene takes my other hand. "You don't mean that. He loves you. Don't throw that away."

I look to her and admit what I've been ashamed to say out loud. "He hasn't made one attempt to contact me. Not one call, not one text or message. He's left me twisting in the wind. If he loves me so much, where is he?"

* * *

TOM

She walked away from me in the quad last week. She walked away from me at the hospital that morning. I'll bet the farm that nothing I say is going to change her mind now.

She's walking away.

The sane part of me wants to go to her, but the urge to withdraw, to wallow alone in this is taking over. I'm pretty much avoiding everyone, and people are avoiding me. Chris breezed past me like we were complete strangers on his way to class Monday. Rene and Caitlin nearly slammed into me on their way out of the cafeteria this afternoon, and then looked away and hurried off without even acknowledging me. I don't answer when Ben or Dan reach out, and we live together. I've been steering clear of our place, just wandering around campus and town so that I won't have to face them. I go to class, but don't hear a word the professors say. I go to the gym, but it's just to kill time. I'm eating, but it's like I can't even taste the food.

I have an overwhelming urge to go home, but I don't want my parents to see me like this. I've put them through enough, and with them I won't be able to hide what's going on. It feels like I have a crushing weight on my chest, and one quick look in the mirror confirms what I already suspected: I look like crap.

Caught a glimpse of her walking into the library on Thursday. She didn't notice me, but I was close enough to see her slumped shoulders, her blank expression and the fact that her clothes looked like they were loose on her. I felt torn, both angry and sad when I saw her. Part of me wanted to run up, grab her and hold onto her for dear life, but at the same time, I'm furious with her. She's pushed me away how many times? Maybe my anger isn't justified given what she saw at the rugby house—what she *thinks* she saw—but why is it that when it comes to me, she so easily believes the worst?

And that line she practically spat at me, *do I really even know you?* I want to punch the nearest wall every time I think about it.

All of a sudden my past matters?

Having second thoughts now, are we?

Make no mistake, she knows me. So I understand now, I know that in her eyes I'm not good enough.

People side-eye me as they pass. I'm a few miles from campus, walking alone on Boylston Street and laughing like a deranged lunatic because I've just had an epiphany: I'm now officially in the same category as Nick Brunner. I am one of Darcy's good-for-nothing, undeserving ex-boyfriends.

Oh, the irony.

Liz texts me an invite for the party they're throwing Friday night, and even goes so far as to add that Morgan is hoping I'll be there. Liz is a head case. Now she's pushing Morgan on me? I think about texting back something like: *I'd rather contract gonorrhea*, but decide it's probably best to ignore her completely.

Yeah, I'm finally seeing the light where Liz is concerned. I know for that, Darcy has a reason to be angry, or in the very least, confused. But in my defense, I'd been in the dark. If I knew about the bullshit Liz was spreading, I never would have been the least bit friendly towards her. But positions reversed, even without all that, I know I wouldn't have been cool with Darcy sitting around chatting up an old flame or his buddies. And I wasn't sensitive to her feelings on that front.

I've been doing a lot of thinking—lots of time on my hands now that I don't engage in meaningful social interaction with other humans. I keep thinking back to one night soon after we got back from Christmas break. I was at one of Mac's parties while Darcy was out with her girls. Morgan approached me, asking if we could talk. I assumed Morgan wanted to apologize—yawn—yet again. I may have rolled my eyes, so bored and irritated and just so over it. I no longer gave a fuck. But Morgan stood her ground, leaning in for an awkward hug when she said she was happy for me. Darcy was made for me, she said, with nothing but kindness and friendship. The way we ended was ugly, what Morgan did was hurtful, but I still never thought of her as a bad person. I hugged her back, hugged her good-bye. I guess it was the closure she needed, and maybe I needed it too. I remember feeling grateful to her as I watched her walk away.

Did I tell Darcy what happened that night? No, and I can't even conjure up a reason as to why. But looking back now, it was a lie of omission. And the party was packed, maybe someone else told Darcy? If the shoe was on the other foot and she'd had a heart to heart with Nick without telling me, I may not have taken it as an outright betrayal, but I would have been curious, maybe even hurt. I'm sure of it.

But does she really think I'm capable of lying to her face, of cheating? That I could pledge my love to her one day while secretly looking to get with someone else the next? That's what's been eating me up.

I'm skulking around campus Friday night, doing my best to avoid everyone on the way to their respective drink-ups, when I run right into Nick. Last person I want to see.

"What's up, Tom?"

I raise my head but don't make eye contact. "Hey."

"You want to go grab a beer?"

"No offense, Nick, but we're not commiserating over this together."

"Hurts like a motherfucker, right?" When I don't answer, he spits on the ground at my feet. "She can't say I didn't warn her. Fuck you, brother."

There's absolutely no fight left in me. When I'm fairly certain Dan, Ben, and the rest of the guys will be gone, that's when I head back home, flop onto my bed and stare at the ceiling. Dan, of course, comes back for me at one point. When he knocks on my door, I don't answer. When he pokes his head inside, I drape my arm over my face, pretend to be asleep. He knows I'm awake—the same set of misery-laced songs is blasting from my speakers, playing on repeat. Dan lets me be.

I think about going to her at least a hundred times, but something—my pride, my anger, my shame—holds me back.

Chapter 15

DARCY

An entire week has passed and...nothing.

He hasn't reached out, and Dan has no insight into what's going on in Tom's head. Dan just keeps saying that Tom is a mess. I know better, though. I know Tom is angry with me. He has a valid reason to be upset, I'll give him that, but I think coming out of a room with your pants undone and kissing a girl with whom you've exchanged bodily fluids in the past trumps my transgressions by a mile.

Too much time has passed. The fault lines have split, leaving us on opposite sides of what feels like a canyon. I'm not confident we're going to come through this anymore. Fact is, I'm becoming more certain with each passing day that we're over.

I've never thought of myself as a stubborn person, but maybe I am. That word heartache? I literally ache in my chest. I know that if I was giving advice to someone else, I would tell them to stop being stubborn and just go to him. But I can't bring myself to do it. I'm hurt. Hurt that Tom let someone come between us. Hurt that he's not crawling on the ground, begging me, doing everything in his power to make things right with me. Hurt that he's cutting me loose, same as I'm doing to him.

The girls tried to convince me to go out with them tonight, but they didn't press too hard. They knew it wasn't happening. Dan and Jenna asked me go to dinner with them, but I said no. I know I'm bad company, just bringing everyone around me down.

I sit at my desk, reading over the rejection letter I received this week from NYU. I'm still waiting on three other schools, all of them far away from where Tom will be in September. Maybe it's for the best. I stick it back in my desk drawer before curling up on my bed and staring at the ceiling, thinking of him. Every song on my playlist reminds me of him. Some remind me of good times, and some fit better with times like this, when I'm battling the worst kind of sadness I've ever known. I'm pretty sure I'm crying as I drift off to sleep.

I just remember feeling good. He's behind me. It feels so right being back in his embrace, feeling his fingers trace the skin along my arms, and feeling him kiss the back of my neck. I nudge my body back into his and feel him hard against me. His hand skims over my bare breast and then moves down to the curve of my hip. I need him, so I arch back, pushing my bottom against him more urgently. He grips my hip and then his hand slides over, lower, until his fingers splay out beneath my navel.

He whispers, "Damn, you feel so good. Tell me you want this, baby."

No.

I take in the sour smell of beer on his breath, register the voice, and realization sets in. This is not Tom behind me. My body stiffens as the contents of my stomach begin to rise into my throat.

"Nick, what are you doing?"

He makes a lame attempt to soothe me. "I told you, baby. I told you he was a fuck-up. I knew he'd hurt you. I'll never do that to you."

He digs his fingers into my hip, trapping me against him when I try to move off the bed.

"Don't touch me, Nick. Don't do this, please."

He freezes for a second and then pushes me away from him with force. I'm at the edge of the mattress now, shaking.

"Don't touch you? Now you're telling me not to touch you? Two minutes ago you were begging me to fuck you!"

Someone knocks gently. Rene's voice is barely above a whisper. "Are you all right, Darcy?"

When I don't answer she begins rattling the doorknob. Nick planned ahead and locked it. I scramble off the bed and scoot away from him on the floor, dragging the sheet behind me, trying to pull it up around my body. I'm topless, the straps of my tank top down, the fabric bunched around my waist. I start crying when I ask him to leave again.

He sits up and rakes his hands through his hair. "Are you kidding me right now? I'm not going to hurt you. I would never...I just wanted to....I know...I...." He stands and punches the wall in frustration.

There's more than one person at my door now. The knocking has quickly turned to pounding.

"Go the fuck away! I'm just talking to her."

Beth yells, "Then open the door!"

I stand on shaky legs and move as if I'm going for the door. He stands to block me, but his hands are up in a silent plea for me to stop, to hear him out. Rene and Beth are kicking at the door now, trying to bust the lock.

I speak in the calmest voice I can manage. "Nick, it's ok. Just go now. Please, go before this gets ugly."

His tone is harsh when he laughs. "No second chances for me, right? I bet Tom will get a second chance with you, even though that piece of shit tossed you aside for some used up whore. That's how special you are to him."

I hear several sets of heavy footsteps bounding up the stairs. With one solid push the lock gives, and Tom is rushing into the room with Dan just a few steps behind. Tom sees me first, takes it all in, and the look of panic in his eyes turns murderous. He has Nick pressed up against the wall. There's yelling and screaming, but I'm still tuned in enough to hear Tom ask Nick if he put his hands on me. I want to vomit when Nick taunts Tom, saying he was on me and *in* me, that I begged him for it.

TOM

Here we go again. Dan is knocking on my door, his umpteenth attempt at a heart to heart.

"Please, can you just leave me the fuck alone?"

"Get up, asshole. Nick's locked himself in Darcy's room."

I don't remember getting there except for practically tossing Jenna aside and pushing past her as I took the stairs three at a time.

Darcy is crouched down, pressed up against the far wall. She's grasping the edges of a sheet that's pulled up and gathered around her. Are all her clothes off? Nick comes at me then, but he doesn't have a prayer. I'm running on pure adrenaline, out of my body, landing punch after punch after punch. I look down at my knuckles to see that they're split open, bloody and raw.

* * *

I don't know how much time has passed, five minutes or five hours. I'm sitting on a kitchen stool and Darcy is here with me, fumbling to get ice out of the tray with shaking hands.

What have I done? I left her, walked away. I am responsible. I did this. Darcy's been hurt in the worst possible way because of my actions.

"Did he..." I'm shaking with rage as I make a second attempt to get the words out. "Did he hurt you?"

She turns to face me slowly, but keeps her head low, fixing her eyes on my bloody hands. Her eyes are puffy and red-rimmed. Now her body is covered head to toe in a long-sleeved shirt and baggy sweats. When she goes to speak, she sucks in a breath and starts to cry.

"It's all right." I wrap my arms around her and pull her close, but Darcy's body is stiff. "Please. I need to know what happened. He's not walking away from this."

She lowers her head to my chest and whispers in between soft sobs, "I thought it was you. I thought you were in bed with me."

"I'm so sorry. I'm so sorry." And now I'm crying with her. What a fuck-up I am. I think back to Luke's words and the promise I made to protect her. Seeing her like this brings me to my knees. "I messed up."

She sinks into me then and holds me close like she's comforting me. I don't deserve her comfort or forgiveness, but I want it so badly. We stay like that, just holding one another up. And I want to keep holding her like this, so much, but I pull back, knowing there's serious business we can't avoid any longer.

"Do we need to call the police?"

She breaks away and looks up at me wide-eyed. "No, it didn't happen!" Her voice is back to a whisper when she adds, "He was lying. He...he touched me...but nowhere...I know he wouldn't have gone any further."

I pinch my eyes closed, don't want to see the image. "I'm gonna kill him."

With that, Dan walks into the kitchen. "You just about did. He's still there for observation with a concussion, a broken hand and a busted nose. And he needed a shitload of stitches. The cops were at the hospital, Tom." Darcy gasps and starts crying again. I shoot Dan a look to shut him up, but he goes on, trying to reassure Darcy. "It's gonna be fine. The nurses called the cops because he was pretty banged up, standard procedure. Nick isn't pressing charges."

Jenna huffs, "Yeah, because he's such a stand-up guy."

Dan pulls me aside, shaking his head. "You scared the shit outta me. If I didn't pull you off, I think you would have beaten him into a coma."

"I'm gonna fuck him up next time I see him."

He grabs my forearm, hard. "No, you're going to stay away from him. You nearly did kill him. It won't do Darcy any good if you're sitting in jail."

I shrug him off and make my way back over to her. The sun is just starting to come up, but it may as well be midnight. We're all exhausted, but I don't want her going back up to that room.

"I know things aren't good between us right now, nowhere close to good, but I can't leave you. I need to be near you. Can we get out of here? Will you please come and stay with me?"

She nods and I let out a relieved breath.

I take her to my room, lay her down on my bed, crawl in behind her and wrap my arms around her. We sleep like that for most of the day. I wake before she does and just watch her sleep. Her eyes are still puffy, her nose red. Her breaths are uneven at times, shuddering as if she's crying in her dreams. I'm consumed with guilt and regret. Yes, Nick was the catalyst, but I can't lay all of this at his feet. I know he's really the least of our problems.

* * *

"Lucky Charms? The breakfast of champions."

I nod my head towards the view of the darkening sky. "It's actually dinnertime."

"Right."

We both look like we've gone nine rounds with Tyson.

We're sitting up in my bed, eating our cereal in silence. The silence feels like a heavy blanket that's suffocating us. I finish first and put my bowl down. I'm nervous as hell, but can't put this conversation off any longer.

"I'm sorry, Darcy." When she goes to interrupt, I put my hand up. "Hear me out, please. I'm sorry for what happened to you, but I'm even more sorry for everything that led up to last night." I really don't want to bring her up, to say her name out loud, but I have to. "I just need you to know that when you came to see me that night and you found me with Liz, you'd gotten it all wrong. Nothing happened. I let time pass though, and the more time that passed, the angrier I got. Do you really think I'd ever cheat on you?"

"I didn't think you'd cheated on me with her." Her face contorts with the effort it's taking for her to go back to that ugly scene. "God, I despise that girl. But no matter how bad it looked, I didn't think you would do that...with her, but I didn't entirely trust you either." She scoots back against the headboard, putting some more distance between us. "We've never talked about Morgan, you know? You've never once mentioned her name. Why is that? I mean, you dated her for a very long time, and I've talked to you about *my* old boyfriends, but you never speak her name. Now she's been coming around more and more, and you seem down with it. I can't help but wonder if you still have a thing for her." When I go to protest, she stops me and says, "No, now it's my turn. Do you know how much it hurts to hear from other people that you're hanging out with her at parties? Or to walk into the cafeteria and see you laughing it up with Morgan and her friends? A part of me has just been waiting for you to tell me what I already know...That we're done, that you want her back."

"No! Do you know how far off the mark you are right now? There's no one but you." I scramble for words when I see that I'm not getting through to her. "There was a day, sophomore year...You, me and Nick were in the cafeteria. Do you remember?" Darcy nods, looking bored. "You thought I was shaken up when Morgan walked by me without saying a word, but the truth is I hadn't even noticed she was in the room. I was spaced out, hating on Nick, daydreaming about what it would be like to be with *you*. I don't want Morgan. I haven't wanted her in...forever."

I pause then, take note of the fact that I'm doing what I always do. I'm not telling her everything, not sharing anything real with her.

"I did love her." Right away I want to stop. It hurts to open up like this and it hurts to see Darcy holding back tears, but I know I have to put it all out there and take what comes. "I never said those words to anyone before her, so you can imagine that what she did gutted me. When someone important to you cheats and then lies to your face about it, it's about the shittiest feeling in the world. But you need to believe me when I say that what I felt for Morgan isn't even close to the love I feel for you. There's no comparison, never was."

"I'm so angry." Her bowl makes a thud when she drops it onto my nightstand. "Do you realize when you shut me out, when you tell me *nothing*, that I have nothing to go on besides what other people are saying? And they're saying you've never gotten over her. They're saying Morgan's boyfriend is history, so it's only a matter of time. They're saying that you screwed around on her—the love of your life —so what makes you think Tom isn't cheating on you?"

"I never cheated on Morgan and I never cheated on you. You *chose* to believe the shit Liz was spewing. Why didn't you come to me?"

"This is *my* fault? Why are you even friends with someone like her? You'd have to be a complete idiot not to see she was wedging her way in between us. Why didn't you acknowledge that and *handle* it? And how could you treat me the way you did in front of her? You humiliated me."

"That day in the quad?" She's so pissed she won't even look at me. "I'm so sorry for that, Darce, I really am. I should have had more faith in you. I was just angry and…I don't know, scared when you wouldn't let me in. You wouldn't tell me what was wrong, so I figured you didn't trust me the way I trust you. I couldn't imagine what could be so bad that you wouldn't share it with me. You were pushing me away and my mind just went to the worst places. I thought that in your eyes maybe I'd never measure up, maybe you were having second thoughts about being with me. But believe this, if I'd have known what Liz was saying, I would have put an end to it in a heartbeat. Not one thing she said was true."

She lets out a tired breath. "I'm not saying everything is your fault, Tom. I should have let you in, and I should have handled the situation with Jenna better."

"Nah, you were being a good friend to her."

"But I was still *your* girlfriend. I owed you more than what I gave you."

"Please tell me you're still my girlfriend."

The sad look in her eyes just about crushes me. "I think we both need some time."

* * *

The weeks that follow are rough.

Time apart? I give her one day. I know that a break, without talking and working through the tough shit, is what got us here in the first place. So I show up day after day, and thank God every time when she doesn't turn me away.

It feels like we're starting over again, but not in that happy, new love kind of way. It's like we're trying to bridge a big gap, getting to know each other all over again. I take her out every day after classes, either for dinner or just long walks. We don't stay at each other's places, but eventually we're back to holding hands and kissing when I drop her off.

When Darcy gets word that Kate is in labor, she calls me, so excited, and lets me know she's heading home for a few days. I was hoping she'd ask me to come with her, but I know we're not there yet. At the airport I hug her close to me and kiss her, desperate for her to know just how much I'm going to miss her.

When we break apart, she looks up to me and smiles. "I love you."

Those three words have never sounded so good.

* * *

DARCY

Rebecca Rose Donovan. She's named for my mother, Rebecca, and Kate's mother, Rose. She is twenty inches long and weighs in at six pounds, eight ounces. She is perfect—rosy red lips, blue eyes and a little blond fuzz on her head. Holding her is something close to magical. I've never experienced instantaneous, unconditional love like this. It's overwhelming for me, so I can only imagine how Kate and Luke are feeling.

Me, Caleb, Mom, Dad, Luke, Kate's parents and her sister are all crammed into the hospital room with mother and child. I am surrounded by love and happiness, but I feel Tom's absence. He should be here to experience this with me. I snap another picture of Rebecca and send it to him.

Looks like her beautiful aunt.

I miss u Tom.

You can't imagine how much I miss u.

My heart aches reading his words. The past month or so has been soul crushing, and the past two weeks, with us trying to get back on our feet, has been painful. I hate the awkward moments. And some of the things we've said to one another are tough to express and upsetting to hear. As each day passes, though, my outlook grows more positive. I'm starting to believe we'll come out of this stronger. But we're not there yet, we're both still reeling from the aftershocks.

Caleb nudges me playfully. "Texting your boyfriend?"

"Yeah."

When he puts his arm around my shoulder, his smile drops. "What the hell? You feel like skin and bone. Are you eating enough?"

"I probably haven't been. I had a pretty crappy month. I was helping Jenna through some stuff and Tom and I hit a rough patch. I wasn't sleeping much, and I haven't really been taking care of myself."

"Is he good for you? I mean, he should be making damn sure you're all right. I gotta say, Darcy, I don't like this."

"He's very good to me. Like I said, some things happened. I was kind of caught up in what was going on with Jenna, and then Tom and I lost our way. It's better, back to normal now."

"What's going on with Jenna?"

I look to him apologetically. "Sorry, Caleb, I can't say. But everything's good now."

"Whatever, as long as you're all right. Let's go, I'm taking us out to eat right now. I'm thinking shrimp scampi and fettucini Alfredo. Lots of butter. I've got to fatten you back up."

After Mom stuffs me with pancakes and bacon the next morning, we head out shopping. Kate was so worried about the pregnancy that she didn't want to tempt fate by having a baby shower. So we go to town picking out little outfits, tiny little socks, sleepers, hats and blankets. I decide shopping for a baby is loads more fun than shopping for myself.

Having a new baby in the family just infuses everyone with joy. My dad is walking around with a grin on his face twenty-four-seven, and Mom is thrilled as well. I'm giddy too, already thinking about all the places I'll take Rebecca. I envision us buying her first American Girl doll, bringing her to Alice's Tea Cup, the Central Park Zoo, and taking her ice skating at Wollman Rink.

I am over the moon, but as I fly back to school, I remind myself that I have to be mindful of Jenna. She's still emotional about what happened, and I know she will be for a long time.

Tom is leaning up against his truck when I come out of the terminal. When he spots me he jogs over, grabs my duffel and wraps his free arm around me. "That felt like the longest three days. I missed you."

"I missed you too."

"How's Rebecca doing, and Kate?"

I fill him in on everything. I feel so relieved to be sitting next to him again, with my hand in his. I feel like we're finally getting back to normal.

When I get back to our place, Jenna is sitting on the couch waiting for me.

"I can't believe you haven't sent me any pictures!"

I hand my phone over as soon as the photo app opens. There are already at least fifty shots. She smiles but there are tears at the corners of her eyes. "She's so beautiful, Darcy. So perfect."

I wrap my arms around her. She's trying to be positive for my sake, but I know how painful it can be to put on a brave face when you're not feeling it.

* * *

TOM

Lots on the agenda.

Now that I'm back on track making things right with Darcy, setting things straight with a few other people is tops on the to-do list.

When I see Chris at the rec center, I swallow hard before asking him if we can talk.

"Things didn't go down the way you think they did that night."

"I know that. And I think I knew it right away, but it just looked so bad from where me and Darcy were standing. And I was pissed, because even if what Liz was implying never happened, it was thoughtless on your part."

"I get that, and I'm aware that I fucked up big time. I also want to apologize for going after you."

"We're all good."

"I'm coming by your place tonight to talk to Nick."

He looks to the ceiling and lets out a tired breath. "You think that's a good idea?"

"It's gotta be done."

* * *

I'm not surprised when Chris opens the door. I'm sure he deliberately stayed home to prevent another beating. Even though I'm not here to finish what Nick started that night, it's probably for the best that Chris is around.

It's obvious that I've taken Nick off guard when I knock once and then walk into his room. A nasty scar is visible above his left eye, and a cast peeks out from underneath the cuff of the long sleeve shirt he's wearing.

After a few moments of staring at one other, I break the silence. "Do you want to explain to me why you did that? Why you climbed into bed with her and put your hands on her?"

He slumps into his desk chair and turns away from me. "I heard things were over between the two of you, courtesy of Liz. I couldn't believe you would hook up with her when you had Darcy." He turns back around and holds his hand up to silence me when I go to speak. "Yeah, yeah...I've since heard it wasn't true, but I was drunk and fucking ecstatic thinking you two were done."

I take another step closer and he stiffens. "Just warning you...If you do anything, if you so much as touch her or speak to her in a way that you shouldn't, no one is going to be there to pull me off you next time."

He doesn't look mad, just defeated. His jaw is tight when he gives a quick nod. "You done?"

"Yeah, I'm done with you."

* * *

Liz is the last one on my list. She's the last person I want to see, and that's saying a lot given that Nick was also in that pool. When she walks up to me, Mac and Ben in the quad, she looks wary.

"Hey, guys."

The boys give her a head nod in greeting but say nothing. Ben looks to Mac and then they both say some version of *later* before blowing off like paper the wind.

And then there were two.

She goes for the amnesia approach. You know, where we pretend that the oh so awful thing she did never happened. "Where you been hiding, stranger?"

But my vision is a whole lot clearer where Liz is concerned now, and I'm not having it. "I've been spending my time working to rebuild things with Darcy. But it's good we ran into each other, I've been wanting to talk to you."

Her eyes brighten with what looks like hope, but that's going to be short lived. I'm not going to go as far as to say I'd step over her body if I saw her bleeding out in a ditch, but I don't have any remorse for what I'm about to say.

When I open my mouth to lay into her, she speaks before I can get any words in.

"I'm sorry, Tom."

And she looks so repentant that I almost cave, but then I get a visual of what she did. I imagine what she looked like when she stepped out of the bathroom with me, licking her lips, intentionally trying to hurt Darcy.

"What exactly are you sorry for?"

"I...I'm sorry that our friendship gave your girlfriend the wrong idea. That she has a problem with us being friends." She doubles down when I start to laugh. "That's why I've been keeping a low profile. I don't want to cause any trouble between the two of you."

"You don't want to cause trouble? So when you told Darcy I'm not over my ex-girlfriend, when you told her I've been sneaking behind her back to get with you, when you told her I run through girls like toilet paper...You weren't looking to stir up trouble?" I don't give her a chance to respond, but from the way she's just standing here with her mouth hanging open, I'm thinking she's got nothing to counter with. "And what does that even mean, the toilet paper thing? That I shit on people and then toss them away? If you're referring to the way I treated you, I've apologized, and I meant it, but I'm done. You played your part in that disaster, same as me."

She grabs the sleeve of my jacket, but I shake her off, hard.

"Wait, you don't understand!"

"Listen up, because I want to make sure *you* understand. Forget you know me, because as far as I'm concerned, you no longer exist. Don't drop in to check on me, don't talk to me, don't even make eye contact. I don't want to see you at our parties or at the rugby house. If I'm there, you stay the fuck away." She visibly shrinks and her chin trembles, but I don't care if she cries. "I'm not interested in the bullshit you're peddling anymore, Liz."

Chapter 16

DARCY

We're in a really good place.

This winter was sucky, not gonna lie. January and February might go down as two of my worst months ever, and March, with Tom pleading his case around the clock, was trying in its own way. The fact that the damn snow would not stop falling just made everything even more blah.

Looking around as I take the scenic route to class, I laugh when I realize we'll be graduating at the end of May, in less than one month, and the remnants of those once massive snow drifts still stubbornly dot the campus. But the trees are spouting new buds, and new grass is pushing up through the damp soil, so suck on that, Massachusetts. Spring is here.

I sense his approach before I feel his hand on my shoulder. "You walk so damn fast." He's slightly out of breath, and he's in great shape, so I'll assume he ran full speed to catch up with me. "Why didn't you get me this morning?"

"I wanted to go to the mailroom on my way to class."

"What's the good word?"

He winces once he says it, so I pat his arm and smile. "No news is good news."

I told him about NYU and Johns Hopkins, both rejections, but haven't told him about the others. I want to tell him about Northwestern and UCLA, but for reasons I'm very well aware of, I've held back. I decide to go with less interesting, albeit tasty news. "Luke and Kate sent us a gift card for Assaggio. A thank you for babysitting."

"That was totally unnecessary, but very nice of them. And I'll never turn down osso buco. When do you want to go?"

"Tonight?"

"Works for me."

I close my eyes for a moment, remembering back to the last time I cuddled my sweet little bundle. I miss the way she smells, miss what it feels like to hold her.

"I miss her."

"Yeah, Rebecca's a cutie."

She's a dream. And last weekend in New York was a dream. We stayed at Luke and Kate's place, giving them a chance to get away for the night together. They acted like we were doing them some massive favor, but getting to spend the weekend playing house with Tom was so great that I felt sad when I heard the key turn in the lock on Sunday afternoon.

There was a specific moment, one that's stayed with me. Tom was tending to a fussy Rebecca as I warmed her bottle. Within a minute, he had a hungry, squawking baby looking up at his face, transfixed as he rocked her back and forth, butchering the lyrics to *Itsy Bitsy Spider*. I thought to myself: *This is what I want.*

Tom is the one I want, and I want to be where he is.

And maybe it's just some crazy kind of primal instinct to reproduce, but whatever, taking in that scene made me want to tear my clothes off and maul him.

We're back on track in that respect too. It was like starting over.

He's still careful with me, heavy on the tender and loving, but I'm good with it. He seems afraid sometimes, like he thinks if there's one more misstep we'll be irrevocably broken. And while I want to put his mind to rest and tell him to relax, I get it. I get his need to reassure me every step of the way, to make sure I know how he feels about me. When it's just us, he makes the effort to let me in, sharing more with me than he did in the past. When we're out, it's like he wants to make sure everyone knows I'm it for him. He's got an arm wrapped around me or he's holding my hand in his. And when we cross paths with anyone from his jaded past, he makes a point of ignoring them and showering extra attention on me. It's a little over the top at times, but deep down I appreciate it.

Liz no longer speaks to me or acknowledges me in any way. Nick's also been keeping his distance, and that's fine by me. He texted to apologize for that night, but I thought it best not to respond. It's not like I don't feel anything in the way of sympathy or forgiveness towards Nick. I still hope for the best where he's concerned, hope that he finds his way. But Nick has proven time and time again that he doesn't respect the boundaries I've set, so there's nothing left to do but cut ties.

"Are they making the trip up for graduation?"

"Who?"

"Luke and Kate. I was wondering if they're bringing Rebecca up with them."

"I don't know. I'll ask Luke the next time I talk to him."

Graduation.

It's not as if the word is giving me hives, but it does land like a gnat that I want to swat away. Shaking my head, I decide to focus on enjoying these last few weeks with my closest friends. My father is great in the guidance department, so I'll talk to him soon and hash out all my options.

Yeah, I'll get right on that.

Of course Tom, without breaking a sweat, has it all figured out.

He's decided not to join the firm where his dad is a managing partner, opting for a position at another big investment bank. He'll be based on Wall Street after attending two weeks of training in Chicago for all the new employees. I'm excited for him, but a little jealous of how effortless it all seems.

But I've got to focus on the upside. One such upside of his new job is that the training in Chicago doesn't start until mid-July, so he has six weeks to goof off before he dons a suit and gets down to business. Three of those weeks will be spent traipsing around Spain and Portugal with me, thanks to my frequent flier miles. I cannot wait.

We've spent hours plotting out our itinerary. We're going to backpack, splitting our nights between cheaper youth hostels and splurging some nights on nice hotels. We'll be flying into Barcelona, ferrying over to Mallorca, heading north to San Sebastian, down to Salamanca where I attended university, and then further south to Seville. Then we have a few days in Madrid. Thanks to Luke, I scored tickets to a sold-out concert on Tom's birthday. I can't wait to surprise him with that. Then we're flying to Lisbon and bumming along the Algarve coast for a week. Three whole weeks of walking the cobblestoned streets of some of my favorite cities, lounging around in bathing suits, eating seafood on the beach, and living day and night with Tom.

Heaven.

$$\mathcal{C}hapter\ 17$$

TOM

Friday morning is spent loading up both my truck and Chris's with beer, tents, air mattresses—anything and everything you need when you're expecting over fifty people to crash at your house.

Mac's third annual Cinco de Mayo party on Cape Cod is this weekend. I'm looking forward to it, his parties are legendary, but last year it took me a full week to recover afterwards.

Mac always does his best to put on an upscale event. This year he's hired a caterer to prep a lobster bake and has a guy manning a raw oyster bar. The only nod to Mexico is the tequila and the massive Aztec temple ice sculpture that doubles as a shot luge. It's over the top and wholly unnecessary. By the time everyone gets around to eating, they'll be half in the bag and would be more than satisfied with plain old burgers and dogs. That's Mac, though, always keeping it classy—the guy had been known to show up to class in a jacket and tie for no good reason.

The party isn't until tomorrow, but we always head up a day early to set up. Mac's friends from his hometown in New Hampshire will be helping out too. A few of them are UNH guys we square off against in rugby.

It's a low-key night after we finish setting up. The group of us are sitting around the fire pit, relaxing and having a few beers.

Mac turns his phone screen in my direction. "Another text." He shakes his head. "That girl is desperate."

When Ben says, "Put her out of her misery," I choke on the beer I'm sipping and shake my head.

Dan says, "Don't cave, Mac."

"I won't. I already told Liz it's not a good idea. When she kept at it, I flat-out told her not to come." Holding up the phone, he adds, "She doesn't take no for an answer." Dan gestures for the phone and Mac tosses it over. "Be my guest."

"I'm sorry, but you are not invited." Dan reads it out as he types. "Just have to make it crystal clear," he says as he tosses the phone back.

One of Mac's friends asks, "Is this chick mental or something?"

Chris nods. "Mental, difficult, obsessed…She's lots of things, and none of them good."

Do I feel bad she's not coming? I still have some lingering guilt over the way I treated Liz in the past, but no, I basically don't want to cross paths with the girl ever again. I have mixed feelings over Nick's absence, though. Chris tells me Nick has flown home to California twice since that infamous weekend, and suspects he's getting help for his drinking and other issues. So while I'm relieved he isn't coming this weekend, I feel bad for him at the same time because I know he has a problem. I hope he is making changes and trying to do better, and I do wish him the best, but I know we'll never reconnect. There's no going back after what's happened. We're done.

* * *

People begin rolling in at around two on Saturday. The sun is shining, there's not a cloud in the sky, and the pool is heated to a comfortable eighty degrees. There's a lot of skin on display, and Mac is smiling as he surveys the scene.

My shitty luck, one of the first to arrive is a girl I hooked up with last year from UNH. Sure enough, I can't remember her name. She comes over, hugs me and squeals, "Tom, I was hoping you'd be here," to which I reply, "Hey *you*, how've you been?"

Within the span of our five-minute conversation, I let Amanda know—silent thanks for the monogrammed duffel bag—that my girlfriend will be here soon. Amanda is a good person, backs off right away. Unfortunately, she's not the only former fling I'll have to maneuver around this weekend. Best case scenario, there will be another one or two girls here that I've *spent time* with. No escaping the past.

By the time lobster claws are being cracked, there are people spilling out of every part of the house. Mac hired a local indie band, there's a DJ playing during their breaks, and everyone is starting to go a little wild. The drinks are flowing, but I'm stressed when the clock reads five and there's still no sign of her. It's nearly an hour later when I get a return text telling me they're almost here. And I don't know if it's their looks, or the fact that I'm so impressed with the fact that they managed to change a flat tire without calling for back-up, but they look like the hot squad walking in, all long legs and long hair. A crew of UNH guys practically part like the Red Sea as the girls make their way through the crowd, and when I see one of Mac's friends handing Darcy a drink, I'm by her side within a minute.

"Brian, meet my girlfriend, Darcy."

He rolls his eyes. "I get the hint. Is he always this possessive, sweetheart?"

Darcy smiles and laughs. "Well, I can be pretty vicious when girls try to chat him up too."

I laugh because that statement is not even close to being true. I know she really doesn't sweat it when I talk to other girls. I know she trusts me now, despite my history, and that makes me love her even more. Same goes for me. Darcy never makes me feel like I have anything to be concerned about, which is a relief, because guys look, ogle or flat-out leer at her on a regular basis. She always lets guys down gently when they offer her drinks or are getting too chummy, and now I've got that act down to a science myself. I never want her to doubt my feelings for her again.

Rene and Darcy are by my side most of the night. Rene's ex is here, and he's looking particularly miserable. She mentions something about asking for Caitlin's car to head back early, but Darcy convinces her to stay. When those two, along with Caitlin, Cara and a few other girls head for the pool, I help Mac rotate the kegs. Looking up when I'm rolling a new keg onto the back deck, I see Darcy standing by the pool braiding her hair over one shoulder. She's talking to Amanda and another girl. *Shoot me now*. I decide to keep myself busy on the other side of the deck, but can't help looking over there every few seconds. Darcy is in a bikini, and drawing the attention of the men nearby. I watch as three guys approach with drinks and Amanda enthusiastically introduces them to Darcy. Guys are so obvious. I cringe thinking about how often I've done what they're doing right now, boldly eyeing her from her toes to her tits as they chat her up.

Enough is enough. I make my way over there and slide my arm around Darcy's waist. "Hey, Amanda, I see you've met Darcy." Then I look to the three guys, my message clear. "What's up? I'm Tom."

They all back off some and introduce themselves. No one here is looking for trouble. Amanda chirps, "Oh, *Darcy's* your girlfriend? I just met her, but I love her already! Now I don't blame you for dropping me, Tom."

Darcy gives me a raised eyebrow. "Long story," I whisper as I slide my hand down and squeeze her hip. When Amanda leaves, I explain that it was long ago. "I was trying not to come over while you were talking to her, but I had to run interference between you and those three douchebags."

"What?"

"I can't stand by and watch when someone's eyeing your body like you're some tasty treat. Please, go in the pool or put a shirt on, otherwise I may wind up starting an ugly brawl."

Darcy bats her eyes, all innocent, and then slips out of my grasp. "Well, let's see...I haven't gotten horizontal with anyone else at this party, while you, you've had your fun. Maybe you deserve to be tortured a little."

With that, she does a slow, sexy strut towards the bar with her shoulders back and chest out. She knocks back a shot with Caitlin, then hits me with a wink and a smile.

I follow close behind and come up to her, wrapping both arms around her waist. I want to torture her back, so I make my whispered words extra breathy. "Oh, no you don't. This hot body, this ass, these thighs, these beautiful tits, they're all mine. For my eyes only. Do you understand, Miss Donovan?"

She whispers back, "I wish no one else was here, Mister Farrell. I'd like you to untie the strings on this bikini and do dirty, wicked things to me in the pool."

Now I'm sporting a massive hard-on. "Shit," I practically groan. "Start talking about the weather or something so that I don't embarrass myself."

She presses her backside closer, turns her face to the side flashing me a sweet, shy smile. "I feel like some all-powerful warrior princess just knowing I can do that to you."

"You *always* do that to me. You always will."

But it's so much more than that. She calms me, wrecks me, owns every part of me.

Darcy turns around fully and wraps her arms around my neck. "I love you, Tom. I always will."

She's everything I need.

Chapter 18

DARCY

"Are you serious, Caitlin? You seemed so into Chris this weekend."

"No, Darcy, you just want me to be into Chris, so you turn what you see, which in this case was a basic conversation, into what you want to see." She rolls her eyes. "Which in this case I'm guessing is something along the lines of a marriage proposal. You're like a well-meaning, yet slightly deranged matchmaker."

Rene takes a break from filing her nails. "Poor Chris has it bad for Caitlin, but the feeling doesn't flow both ways. My girl doesn't know a good thing when she sees it."

I roll my eyes back at Caitlin. "Fine. I guess I'll just have to get used to what's-his-name."

She taps her chin, faking the lost in thought look. "Yeah, what *is* his name?"

"I guess I have one less dateless loser to hang out with the night of the Commencement Ball." Rene is pouting for real. "I hate you, Caitlin."

Is she nuts? "You don't need to be dateless. I could name ten guys right now who'd get down on their knees to go with you."

"Thanks, but no thanks. And I'm going to end this conversation right now. I love you, but I'm not up for twenty questions."

"No fun," I tease. "Why can't we meet your new guy? Do you think your boyfriend will hate us? Are we really that awful?"

Rene blows us a kiss. "I'm outta here."

Caitlin and I are both flopped on the couch. It's Monday morning, but we're both still beat from Mac's party. "I'm sorry, Caitlin. I just think Chris is great and I know he's crazy about you."

"I don't feel that way about Chris so I don't want to lead him on, you know?" She smiles. "Bill, which is his *name* by the way, is nothing but fun and that's all I want right now. I envy you and Tom, really, but I haven't found the one yet and I'm ok with that."

"All right, I'm officially resigning my post as house matchmaker. I know I can be a pain. I just want to see all of you happy."

"I know that, and I love you for it. Now onto more important topics...Did you get your dress yet? I need to go shopping."

"Yeah, I thought I showed you." We make our way upstairs. As I take the garment bag out of my closet, I tell her about Kasia and her fledgling business. "She's a really talented seamstress, or I should say, a talented designer."

She's crafted a strapless, knee-length cream-colored dress with a lace overlay and a slim, lavender grosgrain ribbon detail around the waist. Kasia made it just for me, so it hugs my curves. I can't wait for Tom to see me in it.

Caitlin moves in close, inspecting the seams and the stitching. "Wow. She's good, Darcy."

Caitlin knows clothes, knows designers and knows quality, so those simple words are high praise coming from her.

"Right? I know Kasia's going to do something great with all that talent. I wish there was still time for her to whip something up for you, but we'd be cutting it too close. I'm definitely up for a shopping trip, though."

We spend a lazy afternoon on Newbury Street, and Caitlin finds a great, super short dress that's mighty expensive, given the very little fabric used in its construction. Mission accomplished, but Caitlin's not a one-and-done kind of shopper. She makes a day of it. And Caitlin walks on the wild side compared to my other friends, so when out on an excursion with her, it's not unheard of to wind up in an adult entertainment store. Today I get off easy when she drags me into La Perla. I like beautiful lingerie, but I don't own anything more daring than what you'd find in your typical department store. For one, this store is seriously pricey, and it also feels risqué. The women in the store look way more sophisticated and worldly than me. Caitlin doesn't bat an eye in places like this, though, and her attitude rubs off on me. And now I can't wait to surprise Tom with the corset, garters, and beautiful everyday sets I bought. He's going to flip. I decide the corset and garter will be the present he unwraps after getting me out of my dress on the night of the dance, and I'll save the satin and lacy sets for our trip.

Tom makes me feel like some desirable, sexy goddess. Sometimes I don't even recognize the wanton chick I've become.

* * *

TOM

I feel like I should be lighting up and taking a drag right now, but I don't smoke.

I've just had an epic romp with Darcy, and lying here, side by side on our backs together, the sheets tangled around our waists, I don't know if I've ever felt so content.

"Is anyone else home?"

"No." I tickle her sides until she's squirming and giggling. "Is that why you were biting the pillow?"

"I don't want any of the guys to hear me."

I roll over on top of her, push her hair back so we're eye to eye. "I wouldn't have been letting loose with the dirty talk like that if anyone else was home. You and me?" I shake my head. "I'd never share this with anyone else, never expose you like that." Now that I'm so close, I can't help but run my lips over her breasts. "You're mine, and everything we share is ours."

"Again, Tom," she whispers as her legs fall open.

"No one is home," I tease as I move down her body, dropping kisses along her belly, nipping the fleshy curve of her hip. "Let me hear you beg for it."

"Yeah, I want you to fuck me," she whispers as she trades places with me, rolling us over so that I'm on my back and she's straddling my hips, "but you'll be the one doing the begging."

"I'm not too proud to beg for you, Darce. I'd get down on the ground," I lift her a few inches, "on my hands and knees." I look to her as I guide myself in bare, make sure she wants this too, and thank the powers that be when she nods her head once as her eyes drift closed. "I'd do anything to be with you," I rasp as I guide her back down onto me.

Her lids are hooded when she looks down to where we're joined. "You feel so good."

She's never felt this before, never felt a man inside of her without that barrier. And I feel bad for a second for wanting this so much, for wanting to have her the way I've been with other girls who meant nothing and left me feeling empty. But I was searching for something then, something I never found. I'd close my eyes, lose myself in the sensation, just try to feel good in that moment. But then it's over, and when you open your eyes again you feel lonelier than before.

It's not like that now. No, my eyes are open and I'm taking it all in—

her soft skin beneath my rough calluses, the pressure of her hips grinding against mine, the sight of her breasts moving in time to my movements, the divine pleasure of being skin on skin, inside of her. Gazing at this woman, I'm amazed that she wants to be with me, that she chose me.

* * *

"What's on your mind?"

"You. Just decided that I really like you."

She swats at my chest, laughs as she snuggles in closer. She is on my mind, but I don't share that my thoughts are ping-ponging back and forth between happiness and worry. It's good to have this time, just the two of us being lazy together without any pressure. We're at the finish line, though. Just two weeks until graduation. Those weeks together in Europe are going to be awesome, but I know soon after that we're going to have to figure some things out. I won't weigh in, suggest or push any ideas on her. All I can do is hope that Darcy will be with me next year.

"Aren't you going to answer that?"

"Unknown number...I've been getting so many bullshit telemarketing calls on my cell lately." It stops ringing and then starts up again. "So annoying."

I roll over and grab my phone off the nightstand. Unknown number from a local area code. I'm sure I sound annoyed when I answer the call. "Yes?"

"Hello, I'm looking for Thomas Farrell." It's an elderly woman's voice.

"Um, yeah, that's me."

She tells me she's calling on behalf of Breanne Riley. I don't say anything because the name doesn't ring a bell. Her breath is labored when she asks, "Thomas, can you hear me?"

"Yes, I can. What is this pertaining to?"

"Pertaining to?" She sounds flustered. "Well, pertaining to my granddaughter, Breanne. Did you know her?"

"I'm sorry ma'am. The name doesn't sound familiar."

"Young man," she says softly, "Breanne told me where you go to school and I live nearby. I know this is an odd request, but could I trouble you to meet with me this afternoon?"

"Uh, I guess. Can you tell me what this is about?"

"I'd rather speak with you in person. It's of great importance."

She gives me her address, and as we end the call, a feeling of cold dread washes over me.

* * *

DARCY

"Everything ok?"

Tom looks far away. "Yeah, fine. What were you just saying?"

I'm in the middle of telling Tom about a phone call I got last night from my high school's headmaster. He'd run into my father at a fundraiser, and when my dad told him about the possibility of me taking a year off before medical school, he asked if I might be interested in teaching some Advanced Placement biology sections. My father told me about it at the time, but I didn't take it as a serious offer until the headmaster reached out to me personally. During our call, he seemed anxious, as if he was selling me on the idea of taking the position. It was flattering, and honestly, I was feeling good about it. Not just because I'd be in New York with Tom, but the idea of teaching was exciting, especially teaching AP Bio at my alma mater. Those kids were bright and would keep me on my toes. Conducting labs and preparing them for the AP exam would take a lot of work, but I think it would be work I'd find fulfilling. I'm going on and on about it when I realize Tom hasn't heard one word I've said.

"So you're ok with me posing naked for that photographer?"

"Uh, that sounds good."

I wave my hand in front of his eyes. "C'mon, what's up? You're in space."

He closes his eyes tight. "That call was...weird."

"Who was it?"

"I'm not sure. It was some old woman asking if I'll meet her later today about something important. She mentioned a girl's name."

"And?"

His pained expression makes me nervous. "At first it didn't register, but I do know the name." A moment passes before he goes on. "I feel like a total shit, but I don't want any lies between us. I hooked up with a girl last year right after school let out, a bartender at some place in Newport. Her name is Breanne."

"Like a one night thing?"

"I wasn't lying when I told you I'd changed my ways. I just wasn't, uh, one hundred percent reformed at that point."

I roll onto my back, away from him. "God, I hate thinking about you with anyone else."

"It was a year ago. I'm not trying to make myself look innocent here, but at that point I was convinced you were never coming back." He puts a hand on my hip, holds onto me as if he's afraid I'll run. "I'm going to be honest with you, even when the truth hurts us both."

I nod but I still can't look at him. "What do you think this is about, Tom?"

"I don't know, but I don't have a good feeling."

"I want to come with you."

"Absolutely. I want you there with me."

With the dance just one week away, all of us girls have an afternoon planned to go shopping for shoes. I send a text, backing out. Coming face to face with one of Tom's old fuck buddies has disaster written all over it, but I want to meet the girl anyway. I tell myself that I want to be there for Tom, to support him, but the truth is more basic. I just need to know what's going on.

* * *

TOM

She reaches over without looking at me, stills the knee that's been hitting off the steering wheel every few seconds. I am hyped up on adrenaline and edgy as all get out. Why the hell didn't I keep my mouth shut before? I should have done this on my own, found out what's going on before I involved Darcy in this. Now she's sitting here next to me, staring absently out the passenger side window lost in thought. This is going to be bad. I mean, there's no way this lady called to inform me I've won the lottery.

At four o'clock sharp we pull up outside a modest house, small and older but neatly kept. I clear my throat before I knock on the door. I am so nervous my hand actually shakes. An older woman, like late-seventies maybe, opens the door. She takes me in and then looks to Darcy.

"Hello, I'm Thomas Farrell. This is my girlfriend, Darcy."

She smiles at Darcy as she takes in a deep, ragged breath. "Come in, please." We all stand in the living room, and it's awkward as hell until she breaks the silence. "My name is Marjorie McDaniel. My granddaughter, Breanne, was someone you were acquainted with, Thomas?"

"I believe so. Is she here?"

"No, but if you turn around, on the table there's a recent picture."

The high school graduation picture jogs my memory. I'm back in Newport, back to that wild night, flirting with the good looking girl tending bar. There's another picture, one of a newborn in the kind of hat and wrap they wear in the hospital. Next to it is a shot of Breanne with the infant on her lap.

Fuck me.

I look to Darcy, who is now sitting next to the old woman on the couch. She nods to reassure me, but I shake my head. I want to warn her, protect her from the atomic bomb that's about to drop and destroy us both.

I clear my throat, the anxiety making my voice sound strange to my own ears. "Where is Breanne?"

"She's...gone." Her eyes shift to the hallway like she's half expecting someone to come walking into the room. "Do you remember hearing about an accident between a charter bus and several cars on the Mass Pike last month?" When I shake my head, she continues, her voice now a whisper, "Of course you wouldn't. My Breanne was on her way home from working late and was involved in that accident. She died instantly."

The woman draws in another ragged breath. Darcy gasps and then instinctively moves in closer to take the woman's hand in hers.

"I'm so sorry."

She turns to Darcy and smiles. "Thank you, dear."

I stammer when I ask, "Is-is this her baby?"

Mrs. McDaniel clasps onto Darcy's hand tighter. "Yes, her baby and yours. I pled with Breanne to get in touch with you. She was unsure whether or not she would keep the baby or give him up for adoption. And when she was a few months along she did go to see you. It was not her wish to do so, but I convinced her that every man is entitled to know he's going to be a father. She came home that day, told me she didn't go through with the plan to tell you. She was adamant she could do it all on her own."

I keep my eyes closed, afraid of facing this, afraid to look at Darcy. When I do open my eyes, she's looking down at her shoes, still holding hands with this stranger. I want to ask if Breanne was one hundred percent sure it was mine, but I know enough to know that doing so would be a dick move.

I'm having a flashback to the cramped space she shared with her roommates. The air mattresses on the floor, a random dude crashing on the couch, clothes strewn everywhere—your typical summer house share. We ended up doing it leaning over the bathroom sink so that we had some measure of privacy. Yeah, make no mistake, I'm a real gentleman.

My head thumps against the wall as I look to the heavens in frustration. I'm such an asshole.

"I raised Breanne. She didn't have it easy. My own daughter was irresponsible, and Breanne's father...Let's just say he's not someone I ever wanted involved in my granddaughter's life. And he never bothered with her, which was for the best. Breanne was very smart, she worked hard, she was a good student and she had a future mapped out for her and for James."

Darcy says his name aloud, "James."

"Yes. James was born on February fifth."

Darcy looks to me. "He's three months old."

I want to lie down on Mrs. McDaniel's couch and just close my eyes. I have this sudden urge to sleep, to drift away, to escape.

I force out my next words. "Where is he?"

"I know this must be a shock for you, Thomas. No preparation and all. But life is like that, sometimes cruel and sometimes difficult. Breanne's life was cut short without any warning." Mrs. McDaniel wipes at her eyes and nose with the tissue Darcy hands her. "I don't know what her wishes would have been. I'm the only person she had on this Earth, and I don't know if she would have wanted me to contact you. I'm just doing the best I can. I'm an older woman." She gestures over her shoulder to where an oxygen tank stands in the corner. "I have emphysema. I'm not exactly able to go outside and teach the boy to throw a baseball."

"Is the baby...Is James here?"

She gestures towards the hall. "He's sleeping in the back room. Go ahead in."

When I don't move, Darcy gets up and takes both of my hands in hers to prompt me. She leads me in there and then puts a reassuring hand on my shoulder as we approach the crib. Yep, a little baby dressed in a blue one-piece thing is in there sleeping peacefully.

I want to say something to Darcy, but I only manage a sound that's more like a croak, and really, I have nothing to say. I just look at her and shake my head. There's nothing I can do or say to make this better.

"Hey, it's going to be all right. Come." She leads me back out of the room and I stumble behind. Darcy joins the old lady on the couch again. "He's a beautiful baby."

"He's a dream, but in my condition, you can imagine he's a handful."

Darcy presses on. "Yes, I can imagine. But where do we go from here? What are your wishes?"

"I'll be frank. I can't care for him. I can barely lift him from the crib without having a wheezing fit. I feel sick about setting him out in the world." She stops, wipes at her eyes as she tries to catch her breath. "Each night I go to bed praying that I won't become ill during the night because we're alone here. I worry frantically for him. My wishes? Well, my *hope*, Thomas, is that you're the type of man who will step up to care for him. That you'll keep him safe and raise him with good values. I also hope with all my heart..." She breaks off again, crying for a moment before pressing on in a voice choked with emotion. "I pray that you'll keep me in his life by bringing James to visit whenever you can."

Darcy looks to me expectantly, but I've got nothing. I turn around, stare at James's hospital portrait again.

Mrs. McDaniel asks, "Thomas, are you all right?"

I am pretty much out of it, but I manage to eke out a response.

"Yes ma'am. Of course I'll take care of him." I hear my voice crack over the words. Shit, I'm about to cry like a little girl.

Darcy, meanwhile, leaps into action. I want to ask her what the hell she's doing, but I'm currently busy having an out of body experience. As I sit there like a zombie, Darcy writes down my parents' address along with both of our cell phone numbers, explaining that we'll be taking the baby there for the next few days until we get our situation sorted out. Within ten minutes, and with no help from me, Darcy has a car seat fastened into the back row of the truck, and has a playpen, clothes, formula and diapers packed up. She has paperwork from the woman and is holding hands with her, reassuring her that we'll take excellent care of James.

"James will be well cared for and loved."

What is happening?

Mrs. McDaniel whispers as she hugs Darcy, "You can't imagine how hard this is for me, but I want James to have a chance at a good life. I've gotten progressively worse over the past two years. I know that I won't be on this earth for very long. My only peace is in knowing he'll have a good home and someone who loves him."

Darcy hugs her close. Mrs. McDaniel comes over to hug me then, coughing first before she's able to say, "Thomas, you'll do the right thing. I can tell that you're a good man."

"Yes ma'am."

Yes, ma'am. I'm like a robot, and I have no fucking clue what I'm agreeing to.

Darcy walks out of the back room with the sleeping baby in her arms, tells Mrs. McDaniel she'll call when we get to Connecticut tonight, and then goes outside to put him in the car.

At least I have the sense to say, "I'm so sorry about Breanne," before I walk out.

Chapter 19

DARCY

"Are you ok to drive, Tom?"

"What the hell are we doing? What am *I* doing?"

"Where are your parents? Did they leave already?"

"My mother is going to fucking faint." I grip the steering wheel tight. "They won't be back for another four days."

"Where are the boys?"

"They're staying with Aunt Mary and Uncle Rob."

I put my hand on his when I see that he's shaking. "Tom, whatever happens, I love you and I'm not going anywhere, ok?"

He shakes his head. "All I do is fuck up."

"Stop it. We'll go home and call your uncle Rob. He's a lawyer so he'll know what to do. And we'll take care of this little guy. It's going to be all right."

"How can you say that?"

"Look at him. He's a sweet little thing. He has no one. He *needs* us."

We stop at a store once we cross the state line into Connecticut.

Tom stays in the truck with James while I run in and manage to grab a basic crib, bedding, more diapers, formula, wipes, pacifiers and bottles, making it in and out of the store in twenty minutes.

By the time we get to Tom's house it's dark, and James is just starting to open his eyes and fuss. Tom spends over an hour putting the crib together without uttering a word. I give James a bath in the kitchen sink—little baby tub thing is on the shopping list I've posted on the fridge—then I diaper the little guy and feed him before checking back in on Tom. When I walk into the living room holding James, Tom is kneeling next to the finished crib with his face in his hands.

"Tom? Hey, are you all right?" I'm past the point of being worried about him; now he's starting to scare me. "It's going to be ok."

His face is twisted and bitter when he looks up at me and snaps, "Stop saying that! This is fucking terrible. Jesus, I'm not even twenty-two." He puts his head in his hands again and forces out his next words. "I'm sorry, Darcy."

I don't do pity parties, so this woe is me routine is starting to grate on my nerves. "Here, take James so I can put the sheets on the mattress and settle him in."

Tom sits on the couch and I place James into his arms. I'm happy to see that even though he looks shaky, his natural instinct is to kiss James's head and rock him. I take my time so Tom can get a feel for James, hold him close.

I can't explain why, but I don't feel angry or even disappointed. I guess I should be upset, but I just want to make it better for Tom. And I really believe news of a baby is a good thing. Cancer, car accidents—that's the kind of news you don't want. Babies are here to be loved. Tom will come around.

I pour myself a glass of much needed wine, then sit at the kitchen table and look through the papers Mrs. McDaniel gave me. I'm glad to see he's received pediatric care and that everything looks up to date. I study the birth certificate next. Thomas Farrell is listed as the father, and yes, that's sobering. The third paper is a death certificate for the mother. With that, I remember I have to call Mrs. McDaniel. After telling her that all is good and we'll stop in again next week as soon as we're back up by campus, I sit back down and look at the death certificate again. Breanne McDaniel. She doesn't have her father's surname. Maybe that's why it was important for her to make sure James had something from his own father, his name if nothing else.

Did she come to campus looking for him? Wait outside on the quad hoping for a chance encounter? An outsider standing in the background with her belly swollen, did she see him, see him with me?

That poor girl, just twenty-one when she was taken from her baby. From the little I know, it seems like Breanne was dedicated to raising her child with love and care. The circumstances weren't ideal, but she was doing the best she could.

Grief is a wretched thing, and I'm surprised at the feeling, grieving for someone I've never met.

I make a mental note to ask Mrs. McDaniel for some pictures of Breanne. James needs a remembrance, some bridge to his mother. I know from my own experience that pictures can give you that connection. The pictures of me in my mother's arms will always be among my most valuable possessions.

My heart sinks when I check my phone and see a notification about our upcoming travel itinerary. I shoot off a few emails, essentially cancelling the trip. Like I said, this is no time for a pity party.

Tom puts James into the crib, grabs himself a beer from the fridge and then sits across from me. He drains half the bottle in one go and then takes my hand. "I'm sorry I spoke to you like that. I should be kissing the ground you walk on right now. You're so calm, but I know you must be mad at me."

"I'm not mad. Shocked maybe, but I'm not angry. You weren't with me. It's not like you cheated on me."

"You can be mad at me for screwing up our plans, plans for a life together."

"That hasn't changed for me."

"Holy shit, Darcy." He shakes his head. "I can't believe this is happening."

I'm relieved when I call and get Jenna's voicemail. I put on a fake, cheery voice, tell her not to wait up, and that I'll talk to her tomorrow. I still haven't fully wrapped my head around what's happening, so for now this is just between me and Tom.

* * *

TOM

Darcy and I fall asleep on the couch next to the crib, only to be woken up at two and then again at six to feed and change James. We both fall back asleep when he settles in for a morning nap. Taking care of him is a workout, and really, Darcy's been doing most of the heavy lifting. Combine fatigue with stress and anxiety, and I'm hot mess. Darcy announces that she's planning on turning in no later than eight o'clock tonight, and it sounds like a solid plan to me.

My uncle Rob leaves his office when I call and comes straight over. He takes James in with wide eyes, gets over the initial shock and then he's right down to business. He's a tax attorney, family law is not in his wheelhouse, so he gets in touch with a colleague who gives us a referral for a paternity test. When that lawyer states my options in a matter-of-fact way—keeping the baby or contacting an adoption agency—Darcy gasps and then lays down the law. "Give him up for adoption? If James turns out to be Tom's child, no one is giving him up!"

Shit is getting real.

Darcy, Rob and I head to the lab with James. I feel so bad when they draw blood from the little guy and he wails like a banshee. And

Darcy, she's so damn good with him. She rocks him, speaks to him softly, and just like that, he's calm again. More than that, he's looking up at her like he's in a happy trance. And I'm awestruck too, but then guilt washes over me. What did she do to deserve this? And, oh God, what is her family going to think of this mess? Caleb and Luke are probably going to lay down an ass-kicking that I fully deserve.

As we're getting ready to go, the lab tech tells me that in forty-eight hours I'll know for sure, but I already know. James is mine, I feel it deep in my bones. I wish I had that same look I saw Luke sporting when he held Rebecca, but I'm just not there yet. Sure, I want to protect James and keep him safe, but I'm also scared shitless about what this means for my future.

Darcy, on the other hand, is maternal by nature. In the twenty-four hours she's known James, she's probably kissed him a hundred times. She speaks to him with love in her voice, and she feeds, bathes and changes him like he's her very own.

But he isn't.

My aunt Mary is at the house when we get back. She offers to stay and help, but I need to think, to process all of this, and the less chattering in my ear, the better. I beg Mary not to tell my parents when they call. I don't want to ruin the first real vacation they've had in years without kids tagging along, but I'm also not ready to break it to them. That's going to be a shitshow.

We move the crib upstairs to my room, and Darcy and I sleep in my bed. I crawl in behind her and drift off with her body nestled into mine. I sleep—no joke—like a baby. When I wake up, Darcy is standing by the window holding James. She looks so beautiful. My t-shirt falls halfway down her thighs, and I can make her curves out clearly as the sunlight turns the threadbare fabric almost translucent. I smile at the picture the two of them make, but then that same mournful feeling washes over me. It's Senior Week. She should be having fun at school, not here, saddled with me and some other girl's baby.

Lord, that sounds so bizarre.

"Darce, my parents won't be home for another two days. Do you want me to bring you back to school? I feel bad you're missing everything. Aunt Mary can help me with James."

She looks crushed. "You don't want me here?"

"No, it's not that. I just feel bad about...everything."

"Don't. I love you. I know James is most likely yours and I love him too. There's nowhere else I want to be."

I smile even though my heart is heavy. "You know you look really beautiful holding him."

I think about how happy the idea of her carrying my baby once made me. I want it to be five years later and I want James to be Darcy's child. Then this picture would be perfect.

"I called my parents this morning, Tom."

"Oh shit."

"They were okay. It was a little bit of a shock, but they took it pretty well. They even said we could drive down and stay there until your parents get home, but I told them we're fine."

"Your dad probably wants to kill me."

"Why? You didn't get *me* pregnant."

"Darcy, don't joke."

She shakes her head in frustration. "You have to get on with it. Stop feeling sorry for yourself. I know you hate when I say that it will be ok, but it will."

I force a smile that I do not feel. "I know, you're right. Come here, woman, and bring my son to me."

With that, she smiles and climbs into bed placing James between the two of us. I'm still feeling very sorry for myself, not gonna lie, but my heart feels like it's going to burst with the love I feel for Darcy. And looking down at James, he's so small and so helpless. There's a growing sense of awareness that he is my child, my flesh and blood. And then it's there, this warm feeling, an unconditional love for my son.

* * *

DARCY

Giving Tom the impression that my parents are just fine with all of this was misleading. Truth be told, it's an out and out lie. When I told Dad, he freaked me out when he didn't say anything in response for a full minute. You think a minute is a short period of time, but when you're anxiously waiting on someone to react, a minute can feel like an eternity.

"I want you to come home, Darcy. I mean, I want you to get yourself back up to school right now. You're graduating in a few days. This is crazy!"

"I can't! Daddy, take a breath. I can't leave him here with James. I'm in this with him."

My dad goes silent on the other end again, but when he does speak, he reminds me of one of his many good qualities. Unlike other people, who would go into full-on damage control mode, he's thoughtful.

"How is Tom doing?"

"I'm handling this better than he is. He's still kind of in a daze. I think he's seeing his entire future evaporate before his eyes. And Dad, I really don't see it that way. I mean, was this in the plan? No, but plans change."

"You sound like you're along for the ride, no matter how bumpy."

"I am. I know it sounds crazy, but I've been with this little baby for only forty-eight hours and I'm completely attached to him."

"Listen to me and hear me out. You're attached because you're a loving person, but this child is not yours and this is a lot of responsibility. Too much responsibility for a girl your age."

"Mom was only two years older than me when she had Luke."

"Luke was ours, he was planned and we were married."

"Are you suggesting we get married?"

My father rarely raises his voice, so I know I've touched a nerve. "What I'm suggesting is that you think! What, it's been one or two days and you're committed to this life? You're all in? No cares or worries about how this is going to affect your future? You're ready for diapers, midnight feedings, teething?"

"Please Dad, stop."

I can hear him breathing, deep and labored. The thought of hurting or disappointing him breaks me. "Dad, I'm sorry. I just...I know it's hard to understand, but I have to be here. I love this baby and I can't imagine leaving Tom over this."

Another long, tense moment passes before he speaks again. "No, I'm the one who's sorry. I shouldn't be laying into you, you've done nothing wrong. This is just a lot to take in. What's Tom's position?"

"I don't know. He's a mess and I know he feels guilty."

"I want you to lean on me and Mom. I have a feeling you're going to need us in the coming weeks. There's a lot going on here and there will be a lot of emotions. Why don't you and Tom bring James here until his parents get back?"

"Thanks, but they're getting home tomorrow so we're good here. And Dad?"

"What, baby?"

"I love you."

"Love you too."

* * *

TOM

Uncle Rob's news comes as no surprise. The lab results are in, and they show a ninety-nine point something percent probability that James is my baby.

Darcy and I already know this, it's already sunken in, but I tell her the official word anyway and she hugs me tight. She's being too good to me, showing me a tenderness and acceptance that I don't feel deserving of.

How is this going to work? I don't see any other alternative than moving back home after graduation, being that I'll need full-time help with childcare. Forget the downtown bachelor pad I've been dreaming of, the nights out after work with Darcy, my friends and my new colleagues, the lazy Sundays catching brunch and planning out our bright future together. I can't help but feel I'm going in reverse. In a few weeks I'll be another kid back under my parents' roof, reliant on my mommy and daddy like the goddamn fuck-up that I am.

I saw my future with her. Another year or two dating, marriage, kids, the whole thing. Talk picket fences and minivans to me and I don't feel suffocated, don't feel cheated. Marrying the girl of my dreams, making a home with her, having a family—it's what I wanted. Now everything is upside down and screwed up. Now if I ever proposed, it would look like I was doing it to trap her, to have her care for James. And forget about how it might look, she hasn't even turned twenty-two yet. She deserves to live life, to be reckless and have fun, not to be tied down because I've made yet another careless mistake.

And she thinks I don't know.

I saw the letters in her desk, the acceptance letters from UCLA and Northwestern. The woman has options. I won't tie her to New York. I won't be the deciding factor in whether or not she chases the dream she once had of becoming a doctor.

I'm sending her back to school today whether she wants to go or not.

I feel sick over what I'm about to do.

She's been quiet since I told her the news, same as me. I want to ask what she's thinking, but I'm not in the mood for her to tell me *It's all going to work out, James is a blessing*, or to repeat what she said last night: *I'm in this with you*. I cannot listen to Darcy pledge her devotion to this cause.

When she comes out of the bathroom, she peeks in on James sleeping in the crib and then smiles as she places a finger over her lips to let me know he's still fast asleep.

I whisper, "If I told you I needed you right now, would you hate me?"

She smiles, of course my sweet Darcy smiles. "I won't hate you, I'll love you."

With that, she crouches at the foot my bed and moves back up slowly as she kisses me on my toes, my calves, my thighs, my hips, my torso, my chest, my neck, and my jaw. When she gets to my lips, her body is spread out along the length of mine. I inhale sharply when I feel the soft skin of her abdomen against my erection. As her hands slip through my hair, I slide off what little she has on. She shifts up then, so that I'm pressing into her entrance. I think she's trying to prove something to me, telling me she wants me without protection the way we did it that one time the other day. She's on the pill, so it's not taking much of a risk, but I think in her mind it's symbolic. It's her way of expressing her commitment to me. I let out a choked gasp, knowing this may very well be it, that I may never be with her in this way again. God, it hurts deep in my chest.

I lift her up to break the connection, reach over to my nightstand and grab a condom. She motions to help me put it on, but I don't let her. I roll her onto her back and look away as I dig my hands into her shoulders and bury myself deep inside of her. My intention was to take her slowly, show her how much I love and care for her so she'll know I never meant to break her heart, but that's not how it goes. I'm like this unfeeling being, numb and mechanical as I push into her over and over again. I don't slow or ease up even when I hear her gasp. When I come, I cry out and collapse onto her chest, but still I don't look at her. I roll off her immediately and stare at the ceiling as

I catch my breath. From the corner of my eye I can make out her sad expression as she lays beside me not saying a word.

It feels final, like a death.

* * *

DARCY

He hasn't made eye contact with me in hours.

I put a plate of leftovers in front of him and take the seat across from him at the kitchen island. I didn't even ask if he was hungry. I don't feel like normal conversation is something we're capable of at the moment.

He looks up at me, goes to say something but then stops. After pushing the food around his plate for a few seconds, he looks up again, and my heart begins to sink before he speaks one word.

Here we go.

"I want you to drive back tonight. I'm picking my parents up at noon tomorrow and I really need to do this alone."

"Ok."

"It's not that I don't want you here…"

I'm trying to swallow past the lump in my throat. "I know. You want to deal with your parents on your own. It's all right, I understand. Are you taking James to the airport with you?"

"No, Aunt Mary is coming over to stay with him."

It's all been sorted out then. I wonder when he decided to send me packing.

"You're missing all of the senior events because of me."

I have to look away so he doesn't see the tears burning a hot path down my cheeks. "Do you really think I care about missing a clam bake?"

"I just don't know how this is going to play out right now. And, uh, we need to talk about the trip."

"I took care of it the night we came down here. I cancelled everything already."

He lets out a breath and shakes his head. "I wish you hadn't done that. You could have taken Jenna or one of the other girls with you."

Why doesn't he just go ahead and tell me he's down with another guy taking his place? He's pushing me away. I shrug to cover my hurt. "I've been there already. I was only into this trip because we were going together. I'm not upset about cancelling it."

"All right."

James is eyeing us both from the carseat that we moved inside and set on the floor. He's so little. I know it's stupid, but I can't help but wonder if he knows how dramatically his life has changed in the past month, or in the past two days even. Is he looking at us like, *Who are these people?* I go to him and lift him up, cuddle him close, try to tell him without words that he's safe here, that we'll take care of him.

"I'm not leaving right now. I'll help you with James tonight and then leave first thing in the morning."

"I can manage on my own if you want to get back tonight."

Can you now? You tried to serve him an ice cold bottle of formula straight from the fridge, and you've managed to put his diaper on backwards every single time.

"I know you can, but I'd rather stay if you don't mind."

He takes our plates to the sink, doesn't even look over his shoulder when he answers, "No, of course, it's fine."

The odd vibe hangs in the air.

It's a pretty shitty feeling when you realize the person you love doesn't want you around. And what *was* that this morning? I choke back tears when I think of it. It's like I can still feel it, the push push push into my body—treating me like a quick fuck and nothing more.

"I'm taking him up," I tell Tom, leaving him downstairs to stare at the television screen like he's been doing for the past hour. After I diaper and change James, I feed him. Sitting up in bed, I put him on my shoulder to burp him, rubbing soft circles on his back. He drifts off to sleep fast, but I don't want to put him in his crib yet. I lay him on my chest, whisper to him that I love him. And I do. I think I loved James the first time I held him. He's a part of Tom. Before laying James back in the crib, I say a prayer that I'll be with him again, that this isn't the end.

I pretend to be asleep when Tom tiptoes into the room an hour or two later, doing his best not to wake me. He gets into the bed making as little movement as possible, and keeps to the far side of the mattress. God forbid he touches me. Once his breathing evens out and deepens, I let the tears I've been holding back flow.

* * *

TOM

I heard her crying last night.

I pretended to be asleep, just like I'm pretending right now. She padded down the hallway before, so as not to wake James up by showering in my bathroom. Now she's back in here, and I can smell the shampoo my mother buys for the boys, can smell that soap. I crack one eye open and see her by the crib. Already dressed, hair left wet, she's picking James up and whispering something in his ear.

I know she's broken up, but she doesn't act that way when she's dealing with James. With him she's all love and happiness, whisper-singing a sweet song to him as she changes his diaper, wipes his little body down with a soft cloth, and gets him settled in a clean outfit.

I wait until she takes him downstairs before I get up and shower, coward that I am. It's too hard to face her. I take a deep breath as I head downstairs, and nearly break down when I see her small bag already packed up and waiting by the door. I find her standing in front of the wall full of family pictures, baby in her arms.

"Thanks for getting James all settled."

She doesn't turn to look at me. "Why are you doing this?"

"Darcy, you're acting like—" I'm about to say *acting like we're breaking up,* but I don't. I know where this is all heading, but I can't speak that truth. Not yet. "I just need some time to work this out with my parents and to plan for the next couple of months."

"I know you. Your *plan* for the next couple of months is to push me away thinking it's for my benefit. I'm asking you not to do it."

With that, she kisses James's little head, hands him to me without making eye contact, walks out the door and leaves in my truck. As I watch her drive away, I feel guilty and sad, no doubt, but I'm more relieved than anything else.

She's free of me, of my responsibilities and burdens.

I'll make sure of that, even if it kills me.

TOM

My father has tears in his eyes, and they're not tears of joy.

It's scary as shit to see your father cry, especially him. Ted Farrell is not a stoic, cold man—not even close—but he's not a crier. *Say something*, I plead silently

"I'm a grandmother," my mother whispers to no one in particular.

I played it off when I was there waiting for them at the airport instead of my uncle, asked about their trip and made small talk for the majority of the ride home. I waited until I turned onto our street to slow the car. That's when I dropped the bomb, and everything came out in a torrent. The call from Mrs. McDaniel, Breanne's accident, the lawyer and the paternity test—total diarrhea of the mouth.

"I'm sorry, Mom. I'm really sorry."

When we pull up in front of the house, I see Mary looking out the front window with James in her arms. I give her a thumbs up and remember those tired old words she said to me this morning: *Every-*

thing will work out, you'll see, to which I replied with no enthusiasm, "Yeah, everyone keeps saying that."

My mother gets out first, walks straight to Mary and gently takes James from her arms. My father looks shell shocked as he takes in the scene. We both get out of the car, but I stand back as he makes his way over. He lays his hand on James's little body and then leans down to kiss his forehead.

"Oh my Lord, he's so beautiful," Mom whispers.

Dad nods but then turns to me with hard eyes. He stays out on the porch when they walk inside, so I know it's time to face the music.

"How could you be so careless?" Before I can answer, he raises his voice. "This is on you, so you better man up quick. This child isn't my responsibility or your mother's. Do you understand?"

"I know. I brought this on myself and I'm going to shoulder the responsibility."

He looks at me shaking his head. "Yeah, you'll take care of it. Brand new full-time job, raising a baby...Piece of cake, right?"

He walks down the front steps and kicks at the gravel before starting off down the driveway.

I call after him, "I don't see that I have much of a choice here, do you?"

I take a seat on the steps and wait the minute or two it takes for him to walk the length of the driveway and back.

"Dad, I'm gonna work this out, I promise."

He takes a seat next to me, looking like he's aged ten years in the last ten minutes. "You don't have a choice."

"I need to figure it all out, but I'm hoping I can live here with James, and Mom can help me out with childcare for a little while."

He takes a deep breath, lets it out and looks to me. "You know I didn't mean that before, when I said we wouldn't help."

"I get it, though. You raised four babies already. I don't want you guys to feel like James is your responsibility."

"James." He repeats the name like he's processing his sudden existence, just like Darcy did that day in Mrs. McDaniel's living room.

"He's a good baby." I feel myself smiling when I tell him, "He doesn't cry much, just when I take too long heating his bottle or when I screw up and put his diaper on the wrong way."

"And Darcy, where does she factor into all this?"

I imagine my heartache must be written all over my face, so I look away. "She left this morning."

"How did she handle the news?"

"It's kind of crazy, but she's been handling it way better than me. She's like Mom just was, totally maternal with him from the moment she picked him up. I asked her to leave today and go back to school. I know I've hurt her, but I just can't...I can't put this on her."

* * *

DARCY

"Come in, come in." Her hand feels bony and frail on my arm as she guides me in and directs me towards the couch. "Do you want tea?"

"No, I'm fine. Just had a coffee on the drive back up."

"I want to thank you for calling me every day. Without you checking in I think I would have lost my mind. Your Thomas seemed like he was a bit overwhelmed."

That's an understatement. "He's doing just fine," I lie. "His parents are getting home today so they'll be there with him. They're a great family, Mrs. McDaniel. Really, James couldn't be in better hands."

"I'm so relieved to hear you say that. I've been feeling so much weaker since Breanne's accident, but setting that sweet little angel out into the world the way I did, on a wing and a prayer...I've been questioning my sanity all this week and I've been worried sick." She sits with me and takes both of my hands into her frail ones. "This has to have been a terrible shock for you, dear."

"Yeah, you could say that. I feel so bad for you, though, about Breanne. My mother died in a car accident. It's such a sudden, shocking way to lose someone."

"Oh dear, I'm sorry."

"It's actually why I'm here. I want to take a few pictures of Breanne, ones that you can bear to part with. I want James to have some idea of the person his mother was. I was young when my mom died, and I cherish the pictures I have of her, especially the ones where she's holding me."

"What a wonderful idea."

We spend the next half hour sifting through pictures, some of Breanne with James, some of her as a child herself. One picture that stands out is a terrific candid of Breanne holding James up to her face, practically touching noses. She has the most contented, loving look on her face. I feel the slightest bit jealous, knowing she has something of Tom's that I don't and may never have, but it's more sadness than anything else. Breanne was a beautiful girl, and it's tragic when someone so young is taken unexpectedly.

As I get ready to leave, Mrs. McDaniel clasps my hands in hers again, as if she can sense my melancholy. "I truly hope you're in James's life, too. You are a mother at heart, and not all women are."

I try not to cry but it's useless. It's been just a few hours and I already miss James. I cry for the loss of James, for the loss of Tom, and for the loss of the life I thought I'd have with him. It's clear to me that Tom is looking to eliminate me from the equation, and it hurts like hell.

I drive up and down the same stretch of Marlborough Street several times, looking for the framing place I found online. When I finally find the store and explain the situation, the sympathetic clerk arranges to have duplicates and enlargements made. The owner comes out then and helps me pick out frames and matting, assuring me the project will be done to make the pictures impervious to mois-ture, sunlight and the fading power of time. These have to last. Thinking of James as an older boy, I know how much he'll need this, to feel that he knew his mother in some way.

* * *

Jenna spots me and approaches with caution. "Are you all right?"

All right? If wanting to crawl into bed, bury myself under the covers and not come out for the foreseeable future is all right, then yes, I am.

"Did Dan fill you in?"

She nods. "Never a dull moment, right?" I can't help but laugh as Jenna pulls me in for a hug. "Come on, let's make a toast to the crazy, messed-up year we've both had."

With graduation looming, the senior area of campus is basically one giant party. You can't walk five feet without tripping over a keg, the beer pong games are going in full force, grills are fired up and shots are being passed around. It's easy to fall into it when you're feeling the way I am. So one drink turns into three or four, and I'm definitely feeling no pain as we make our way back to our place.

I curl up in bed and check my phone for the one hundredth time. Not one phone call or text from Tom since I left this morning.

Excellent.

* * *

TOM

As if breaking the news to my parents wasn't bad enough, I still have to tell Brendan and Terrence.

They come bounding in the door, excited to see my parents after staying at my aunt and uncle's for ten days, right in the middle of a full-on crying fit. I'm attempting to change James's diaper, and the kid has dropped one nasty load. My mother tries to jump in and take over, but I insist on doing it by myself. I'm making a mess of it, too.

Terrence, so innocent, comes right over and starts babbling to James in an effort to calm him. Brendan, though, instinctively knows something is not right with this picture.

"Whose is that?"

"Hey B, what's up? I'll be right with you."

I look to my mom, and without a word she takes over with James.

"Brendan, Terrence, sit down." I take a deep breath and force a smile. "I know this is totally weird, but this baby is mine. His name is James, and that makes you both uncles."

Brendan is getting so old. He hangs his head, knows the score. Terrence looks confused. "He's *your* baby, Tom? Since when?"

"Uh, Terrence, it's complicated. I didn't know about James until last—"

Brendan interrupts, the anger barely contained in his voice, "Is it going to live here, with us?"

With that, my mom breezes in and states things in a way that make certain there will be no follow-up commentary from Brendan. "James is a part of our family, of course he's going to live here with us."

Terrence is smiling but Brendan is looking at me like I'm the most disappointing piece of shit on the planet. I want to tell him that I agree with his assessment, one hundred percent. He takes off upstairs, goes to his room and slams the door behind him. I follow and walk in after I knock.

"I know this is tough. I'm still trying to wrap my head around it myself. I'm sorry."

He's sitting on his bed, facing the wall and shaking his head. "I just don't understand. Is this Darcy's baby or just some random girl's?"

Shit. "James isn't Darcy's baby. The girl is someone I knew before I started dating Darcy. It's a long story, but her family contacted me after she, uh, after she died last month in a car accident."

He turns to me, eyes wide and watering. After a moment, he asks, "Is Darcy mad at you?"

"No, she's been really understanding about the whole thing."

I can tell he's softening a little. "Where is she?"

"She went back to school. There's a lot going on this week before graduation. I don't want her to miss it."

"I can't believe she's not mad. You should probably be extra good to her, Tom."

My little brother is strategizing on my behalf. I know in that moment that my entire family is going to feel the loss of her. I manage a smile even though I don't feel the least bit happy.

"Yeah, I know that. Now come back downstairs, you need some practice changing dirty diapers."

Chapter 21

DARCY

I'm surprised when Tom's mother picks up on his cell.

"Darcy?"

"Hello?"

"Darcy, it's Clare. Tom is out for a run with his father. I'm glad you called. How are you, sweetheart?"

"I'm all right. How's Tom?"

Her pain is unmistakable when she answers, "A bit of a mess."

"And how are you? I mean, you came home to a shock."

"Yes, it certainly was. I haven't had a baby in the house for quite some time."

"He's so adorable though, isn't he?"

"Yes, I was in love the moment I held James."

I laugh, remembering the feeling, the happy warmth of holding him. "I know, me too."

"Darcy, I don't know what's happening between you two. I imagine things are very difficult."

I don't want to spill my guts to his mom, but I'm kind of desperate. I need someone in my corner, someone to make him see how wrong he is. "Tom doesn't want me there and he hasn't called. It hurts."

"Honey, just give it time."

"I know, I keep telling myself that. I'm just calling because I have to bring his truck back. I'll have Dan follow me there later on today and then he can drive me back to school. He told Dan about the baby, so I figured it would be ok with him."

"I'll give him the message and have him call you back."

I know he's not going to call, but what can I say? "All right, thanks."

"We all love you, sweetheart."

My voice cracks when I thank her again.

I do need to return the truck, but the real reason I broke down and called is that the Commencement Ball is tomorrow. It's not like I'm looking to rope him into going to the dance, I could care less about going myself. And I know everything has totally changed in the last week, but has he totally forgotten about it? Forgotten about me?

A few hours later Dan comes by. "Hey, I just spoke to Tom."

"You've got to be kidding me."

"Huh?"

I'm choking back tears again. "Nothing. It's just that he's calling you and not me."

He winces. "Oh."

"What did he say?"

"He asked me to grab the keys and have Ben follow me in my car. He just doesn't want you to have to leave school again during Senior Week."

"No. You're not getting the keys. Tell Tom if he wants his truck back, he can have the decency to call me."

"Shit, I'm so sorry."

"Why is he doing this?"

"I don't know. He loves you, Darcy. Maybe so much that he doesn't want you stuck with him and the baby. I know he believes that if you stay with him, you'll be giving up everything. He thinks a baby will be a burden on you."

"This isn't love, Dan. Every time something goes wrong, he cuts me out of his life."

"I don't know much, but I know he loves you."

I don't know what to think anymore, but I know that I need to talk to him, to see him.

"I'm coming with you."

Dan looks nervous but nods. "Uh, yeah, I think you should."

* * *

TOM

I come in through the garage, thirsty for a drink after my run. I've put more miles in this week than I have in the past few months. Just trying to clear my head, thinking of every possible scenario, every possible plan. It's also a way to physically punish myself. I know I'm making Darcy hurt, and the physical pain is a way to hurt myself back. After my runs I usually hit the heavy bag with so much force that the gloves don't do anything to protect my hands. I do sit ups until I can't breathe, and there's a part of me that has this recurring desire for someone to hit me—punch me right in the face. I know I'm being a bastard to her, and I know I'm going to keep it up. She's better off without me and that's the simple truth.

I stop cold half-way up the stairs when I hear her voice. She's laughing with Terrence. Then I hear Terrence ask if James is her baby —ouch—followed by Brendan screaming at Terrence, "Are you a goddamn idiot?"

Darcy doesn't miss a beat, sets right about smoothing it over.

"Brendan, it's ok. And no, Terrence, James isn't my baby, but I do think he's just about the cutest baby boy on the planet."

"He is pretty cute." Is that Ben chiming in? "Smells like he needs a diaper change, but he's cute."

Dan spots me on the stairs. "Tom?"

No choice, I have to face them. I put on a phony, cheerful voice. "Hey! I see you've met the little guy."

I go over to hug Darcy from behind as she's changing James's diaper. I don't go for the more intimate, arms wrapped tight just below her breasts like I used to. No, I keep it chaste, stiffly wrapping my arms around the outside of her arms, which would be totally awkward to begin with, but it's even more so being as she's in the middle of a diaper change.

"I'm glad you're here."

She hisses so that only I can hear, "Oh yeah, I'm sure you are."

Sweet Darcy is gone, replaced by stubborn, hostile Darcy.

With that, my mom and dad come down the stairs and greet the three of them like they've never been so happy to see my friends. My mother holds Darcy close, her hug probably meant to convey so much.

I wish I could make this better.

Sorry my son is such an ass.

So sorry you'll never be my daughter-in-law.

Dan lays into me. "Have you been up for all the midnight feedings, bro? You look like crap. When's the last time you shaved?"

"Ha-ha. Thanks."

Dan moves in closer, and when we're out of earshot he says, "I couldn't keep her from coming. Please talk to her. You're killing her with this silent treatment."

"Won't change anything, Dan."

He narrows his eyes and cocks his head to the side as if he truly doesn't understand. "But you don't have to abandon her. Look at what you're doing. I'm not the most sensitive guy in the world, and even I see how wrong this is."

I'm not good at this.

The selfish side of me wants Darcy to say yes to it all. Yes, she'll marry me. Yes, the three of us will make a cute little family right now, no need to wait. Yes, she'll give up everything for me. But I'd never do that to her. And cutting her loose, even though she'll hate me now, is what's best for her in the long run.

As I approach, she straightens, tenses up. I hate how she's bracing for the worst around me.

"Can we talk alone for a minute?"

I lead her down to the basement, so uncomfortable that whenever I try to look at her, I wind up shifting my gaze to the ceiling, the far wall, anywhere else but her eyes. Deep breath. *Just do this.*

"I know I'm hurting you, Darcy. I do. But one day you're going to thank me."

She pushes me, her two hands on my chest, and I stumble back a step. She looks more angry than hurt as she gets right up in my face. "When will I thank you? In five years, when I hear you're marrying someone else? Or when I settle for someone else out of loneliness?" She lowers her voice. "When I'm thinking of you as I'm *fucking* someone else? When exactly will I feel thankful?"

"You're twenty-one. I'm not having you play house with me. If you're with me, it's going to keep from you doing the things you *should* be doing right now. You should be going out, having fun and traveling. And if you're with me, what happens to medical school?"

"Don't use that. Med school may or may not be happening regardless of whether or not you're in my life." She goes to reach for my hand, but when I don't meet her halfway, her arm falls back to her side. "Tom, we can make this work." Those last words are a plea, but when I don't answer, her voice hardens and she takes my chin in her hand, forcing me to look directly at her. "You promised me that if things ever got difficult between us again, you wouldn't just pull away. We would talk to each other, no matter what. I'm not pulling away from you, Tom, I'm here. Where are *you*?"

I know she's struggling to keep from breaking down in front of me. I should pull her into me, comfort her, but I don't. It's killing me to do it, but I'm putting the final nail in this coffin.

"Darcy, what is it that you don't understand here? You've got to stop this. I'm doing this on my own. I *don't* want you with me."

I don't know where I dig that icy, indifferent attitude out from, but her expression tells me that I'm a damn good actor.

Score one for me.

She stares at me in disbelief, stunned. Her breath is shaky when she looks away. "Can you stay down here for a minute until I leave?"

I hit the heavy bag without gloves. Try to drown out the sound of her, but I can't. She manages to sound composed and cheerful with Brendan and Terrence. I hear her saying her goodbyes to my parents, taking James from my mom for a kiss. A moment later I hear the front door close.

When I come back up, Darcy and Dan are gone and everyone else is staring at me. Dan walks back in the house, red faced and mad enough to spit nails.

"She took the car back. I'll head back with Ben." A moment later he slaps his forehead. "Oh crap. Unless you're heading back with us, I'm going to need to take your truck again." Ben chuckles but Dan looks like he wants to punch me. I know his shitty mood has nothing to do with the transportation dilemma he now finds himself in. "This trip was pointless."

My mother excuses herself with James, looking as if she's about to cry. That leaves me, my dad, the boys, Dan and Ben standing around looking at each other in a massive awkward silence.

My dad shakes his head and then looks to the boys. "Come on, we're going to go pick up dinner. Let's give Tom some time with his friends."

Brendan and Terrence look back at me, bewildered and disappointed. I'm getting a lot of that lately. They love Darcy, and they know what just went down was not good.

I wish everyone would go the fuck away and just let me crawl into a hole like I want to.

Ben nudges my shoulder. "So what's your plan, Tom? Are you and the baby going to live here with your parents?"

"Yeah, for now that seems like the best idea," I answer absently. "Dan, what did she say outside?"

Dan shrugs. "Just said she had to leave right away. She wanted to get out of here before she broke down and bawled in front of everyone."

"I know you think I'm being a dick."

"Yeah, gotta say I do. Total dick."

Ben weighs in. "I don't know, it's a tough call. You think she really wants to be a mother at twenty-one? Darcy's bright, beautiful, young...She can do anything, be anything. Sitting home with James while Tom is off working all the time might get old real quick."

Dan shakes his head. "No, it doesn't have to be like that. You and Darcy could make a family for James. You're letting the best thing that's ever happened to you walk out the door."

"Shit, I can't do this anymore. Please stop telling me what's good for me, ok?"

Dan is clearly livid. "Whatever."

Ben asks, "You want us to hang out here with you tonight? I'm into it, you know, having a mellow night." He's looking at the door as he says this, so no, he is by no means into it. "I just have to be back in the morning. I forgot to pick up my tux, and I think I have to get it by noon tomorrow."

"I totally forgot about the dance."

Dan is deliberately looking away from me. "She told me she's not going. Even if you come back to school for it, she's not going with you. Don't sweat it, Tom."

Great, now I have to think about Darcy in her room miserable while all of her friends are getting dressed up and going to what was supposed to be the biggest event of our senior year.

"Go on back tonight. I appreciate you coming down here, I really do."

Dan looks at me with sympathy. "I'm sorry I'm giving you such a hard time. You know I just want to see you happy, and I think you're making some pretty shitty decisions right now."

I shake my head. "I've got to work this out myself."

Ben is ready to bolt. "All right, we're outta here. Are you coming up before graduation?"

"I'm day to day right now, don't know."

Later that night I have my phone in my hand. I should call, but I don't know what to say, so I text her like a coward:

I don't know what to say except that I'm sorry.

I don't get a reply.

* * *

DARCY

"Listen ladies, if you act all weird around me today because you think I'm in some kind of mental free fall, I'll kill you. I'm ok, I've made my peace with it. So I'm helping with hair and make-up, and then Rene, Cara and I are going to get drunk with a few other dateless wonders."

Jenna puts on a bright smile. "Don't you worry, Darcy, I'm going to make you my stylist, hairdresser, make-up artist and general all-around servant today. I'll be your wicked step-sister and bark orders at you."

"That's more like it."

I am managing to hold it together.

Word has gotten around pretty quickly that Tom and I are no longer together, but no one except my roommates and Tom's know about the baby. By three o'clock, I have two last-minute offers for a date to the dance. One of Tanner's roommates and a guy from my philosophy class ask me to go, but I decline. I know I'd be miserable company. I'm content to see everyone off and then head out with Rene, Chris, Cara and a few other friends. When six-thirty comes, though, I give Rene the pre-agreed upon sign, so she knows we're ducking out a little early. Suddenly the thought of seeing the boys all dressed up, here to pick up the girls they love—or lust after as in Caitlin's case—is too much.

As we're leaving I run into Dan, who probably came over early knowing my tendency to bolt. He hugs me tight. "I'm glad I caught you. I just want you to know that I hate this. He's making a huge mistake and I hope he gets his head out of his ass before it's too late."

"Thanks, Dan."

"I couldn't help myself. I told him that Brett and Jason asked you to the dance once they found out you were available."

I roll my eyes. "I'm sure he said something like, 'She should go, she should move on,' right?"

He shakes his head, laughing. "No, it wasn't like that at all. Let's just say I definitely touched a nerve, so mission accomplished."

I know Tom, know the thought of me at the dance with another guy would make him insanely jealous, but it doesn't bring me satisfaction. It's not even a hollow victory. It's nothing but a loss.

* * *

I'm glad I have at least a few people to commiserate with. In addition to us girls, Chris and his roommate Denny are along for the ride. Denny is pretty hilarious, so I actually wind up having a few laughs tonight even though a part of me feels like I'm dying inside.

I eventually confide in Chris because I know he won't blab the story elsewhere. He doesn't have a very high opinion of Tom these days, and for some reason I feel this ridiculous need to defend him. Despite everything, I know deep in my soul that Tom's intentions are good. That performance he put on last night was solely for the purpose of driving me away. It was an act, I'm sure of it, but it crushed me nonetheless.

At some point during the night, I see Tom's number flash on my phone. I hit ignore. I can't speak to him, can't bear to listen to another lame apology. I want to smash my phone against the nearest wall a few minutes later when I read his text:

I feel sick that you're missing the dance. I am so sorry about that.

Sorry about that. What does he mean? He's sorry about jilting me the day before the dance, but not about tossing me aside forever, like yesterday's newspaper?

My instinct is to forgive him, reassure him, tell him I understand. But I don't understand, and the pain he's inflicted sits heavy. I cannot reply to him. I won't.

I want *him* to know what it feels like to reach out and get nothing in return.

* * *

TOM

At six o'clock, I assume that Darcy is probably putting on a brave face and helping all the other girls get ready. At seven o'clock, I think of everyone getting on the buses and leaving her behind. At eight, nine, and ten, I imagine all of our friends dancing, laughing and having a great time. I want to be there with her.

After screwing with me, leading me to believe Darcy was going to the dance with some asshole lacrosse player, Dan let up and told me she was going out with a few other people who were skipping the event. I figure she's probably at a bar somewhere right now, unhappy.

I feel like shit. I deserve to feel like shit.

James is resting peacefully on my chest while I pretend to watch baseball. My mom sits next to me on the couch. "You want me to take him?"

"No, I like it when he sleeps on me like this. Anyway, he's my responsibility. I don't want this all falling on you." I force a smile. "Apparently, I'm a grown man now."

"Ok." She pauses and then asks, "Did Darcy wind up going to the dance?"

"No. I heard a few guys got wind of us breaking up and asked her today, but she said no."

"Would you have preferred she said yes?"

"I don't know. I want Darcy to be happy, but at the same time, the thought of anyone else with her..." hurts me so deep I can't form the words. "I feel terrible about what I've done to her, and not just about tonight. I mean, I do keep thinking about her looking at that new dress just hanging in the closet, but it's everything. I've failed her again."

"Thomas, why does it have to be all or nothing with you? Why can't you keep her in your life if that's what you want and it's where she wants to be? She doesn't have to be James's sole caretaker. You don't have to tie her down. Dad and I are here to help you."

"You don't understand."

"Then help me to see it your way."

"She never told me she got accepted into medical school." I turn to see my mother's surprised expression. "And not just got *into* med school, she got accepted into two extremely competitive programs."

"Why do you think she kept that to herself?"

"Because she didn't get into an east coast school."

"Wasn't she wavering on becoming a doctor anyway?"

"If Darcy got into NYU, where I'll be, then she'd still be entertaining the idea."

My mother looks lost in thought when she says, "She doesn't want to leave you."

"I'm giving her the opportunity to do it now." When my mother shakes her head, my frustration gets the best of me. "Why doesn't anyone see it my way? If she stays with me she'll be stuck, she'll miss out on everything."

"Oh Thomas, I know you think you're doing what's best for Darcy. I'm just saying that maybe you don't know what's best for her, only she does."

Chapter 22

DARCY

Graduation Day.

I know I sound like a drip, but I just can't wait for the day to be over.

Today is going to be all sorts of awkward. My parents are going to be thinking I'm on suicide watch, and Caleb and Luke, ugh, I don't know. I'm not even sure if my parents told them. If they did, then my brothers will either make a show of ignoring Tom or they'll confront him. All scenarios are negative.

Luke and Kate are bringing Rebecca. It suddenly dawns on me that Rebecca and James were born within one week of one another. How odd.

I'm in the shower, staring blankly at the tiles as hot water rains down on me. *If I make it through today without crying or puking, it will be a miracle.* Even though I feel like I have zero energy, I take my time getting ready because I am determined to look awesome today. My motives are pathetic. I laugh at my reflection in the mirror as I curl my hair with care and put extra time into my makeup. I want him to see what he's throwing away. I want him to see me and then decide he can't live without me. I want him to beg me to take him back.

Then I want to slap my own face. How can I let him ruin this day? Graduating from college is monumental, something to be proud of. The diploma I'm going to receive in a few short hours is the product of a lot of hard work.

Be proud of yourself, Darcy.

I repeat the mantra, try to shift my focus from Tom to the magnitude of this day.

By noon, everyone's parents have stopped by and are now making their way to the stadium for the ceremony. Rene puts on a brave face. I know her family isn't coming. She has a thick skin, but I know days like this have to be hard on her. I ask her to come to dinner with my family, but she's already going with Caitlin. I squeeze her hand and she squeezes mine back. I need the support to make it through today as much as she does.

Rene, Caitlin and I walk to the stadium together. Marcus came to get Beth already, and I know Jenna wants to go over with Dan. I'm just praying that I don't run into Tom. The girls purposely take a roundabout route to the stadium to make sure we don't pass his place on the way.

As we're making our way towards the entrance, my brother Caleb catches up to us. He's out of breath. "Hey, I'm glad I caught you. You all excited? It's a big day. And may I say, you all look *very* beautiful."

Caitlin winks at him. "Thanks, Caleb. You clean up nice yourself."

He laughs and then moves in a little closer to me. "Sis, how are you doing?"

"I guess you've heard?"

"Yeah, I heard. I mean, holy shit."

I can't help but laugh. "That was Tom's reaction."

"I feel awful for you, kiddo. I want to hate that fucker, but I feel bad for him too. I know he's a good guy."

"Caleb, if it was you, would you be so adamant about me moving on? Why can't he let me help him?"

He looks pained. "I don't know. I'm a bit of a screw-up in the love department myself, probably not the best person to be dishing out advice."

"Does Luke know?"

"Yeah, Dad told us yesterday."

"And?"

"Luke's taking a page from my book. He wants to shove Tom's head through a wall." When he sees my worried expression, he smiles and puts a reassuring hand on my shoulder. "Don't worry, he's mellowed with fatherhood. He won't do anything. He's just angry that you're hurt."

We've arrived. "All right, it's time. I better hear you hollering when they call my name."

He kisses my forehead. "Most definitely."

I'm D and he's F, so we're only separated by two rows. I don't turn around. The thought of him so close has me shaking at first. Thankfully, with Chris only two seats away, I have someone to calm my nerves and make me laugh.

It's hard to concentrate on the commencement speakers, but once they start calling the graduates' names, I'm focused on the finality of the day. When I cross the stage, I can hear my brothers above the crowd, and then Dan and the girls hollering my name. I think they all know I need the boost. I'm grateful in that moment that I have a lot of good people in my life. Even though I'm in the middle of a very rough patch, I am blessed.

When they call Tom's name, I feel a lump rise in my throat. Chris reaches over and squeezes my hand. Sad to admit, but I need the support to get through the rest of the ceremony.

I'm making my getaway, heading towards my family in the stands when he puts his hand on my shoulder. "Darcy, wait."

I take a deep breath to steady myself and then turn to face him. He looks like he hasn't been sleeping well, and I immediately feel bad for him, for us, for everything.

"Congratulations, Tom."

He takes my face in his hands. "Darcy, I…" He looks down and shakes his head.

"I know, Tom, you're sorry." Exasperated, I move his hands away. "If you change your mind about us, I'll be here. I know I sound pathetic, but I don't care. I love you."

He doesn't try to stop me, or come after me when I turn to leave. He's definitely cutting me loose, and it feels like a crushing blow.

I plaster on a smile when I meet up with my family. And then my smile is genuine when I see little Rebecca dressed in the most adorable outfit. I take her right into my arms and hold her close. I need to feel love, and she's it for me. After many hugs and congratulations from the rest, we make our way back to my place. Kate and Luke walk on either side of me, each holding one of my hands. They're treating me like I'm in full-on crisis mode.

"I saw him come over to you after the ceremony."

"Kate, it's such a mess. I know he's confused and miserable."

Luke asks, "Where do you two stand now?"

"He's pretty much indicated that we're done. He doesn't want me ruining my life, being tied down, blah, blah, blah. Whatever."

"Are you coming home with us tonight? I think you should, Darcy. Stay with us for a few days. Rebecca seems to take your mind off your troubles."

"Thanks, Luke. I'm actually heading to Rhode Island for a few days with Jenna, and then I'll be back down by the end of the week. She's going to give me a crash course in writing lesson plans so I can get to work on them. I'm meeting with the headmaster in a few weeks."

"You'll be fine. Bio is like your native language, nerd."

"I'm actually really excited about teaching in the fall."

Kate hugs me. "I think it's a great idea. And Prep is lucky to have you back."

"Thanks. Oh, and it's only part-time, so sign me up for babysitting. I'll have plenty of free time on my hands."

When we walk back into my place, it's packed with family. Caleb is talking with Rene, Caitlin and her mom are fussing over Rebecca, and Beth's parents are talking with mine.

Just as we're getting ready to leave for the restaurant, Mrs. Farrell walks in the door and wraps her arms around me. "I just wanted to say congratulations, honey."

I hug her back, tight. "Thank you, Mrs. Farrell. I'm so happy to see you."

"You looked beautiful today walking across that stage. And graduating summa cum laude...What an accomplishment."

"Thank you. Were the boys falling asleep during that hour-long commencement speech?"

"More like yawning and complaining."

"Oh, I just remembered. There's something I have to give you. Come upstairs with me for a second."

I pull the large box out of my closet. "I got some pictures from Mrs. McDaniel. There are a few great shots of James with his mother. I know these will be really special to him someday."

I just picked them up the day before, so I haven't had a chance to see them yet. I take one out of its protective wrapping to see what the framer has done with them. It's the candid close-up shot where Breanne is looking lovingly at James and he's gazing back at her. The framer used the larger black and white copy, matted in an off-white with a rustic wooden frame. I can't help but smile, so pleased with how it came out. I turn to see Mrs. Farrell's reaction. She's crying.

"It's beautiful, and you're so wonderful for doing this. Please, do me a favor and don't shut the door on you two."

Caleb knocks on the door and then peeks his head in. "You ready?"

Shaken up, I turn away from them both as I wrap the frame again and box it. "Caleb, would you walk this back to the Farrell's car? It's heavy."

I take a minute alone after they leave and come back downstairs to a nearly empty house. Everyone is gone except for my family and Rene. Apparently, she changed her mind and decided to take me up on my offer. And I'm so glad she's there. She keeps the lunch conversation from revolving around me and my mess of a life. That alone is a relief.

***

TOM

This day is turning out to be even crappier than I imagined, and I've run through some Armageddon-style worst case scenarios.

This is the first time I've been back on campus since my son's Jerry Springer-like arrival into my life. My head is all over the place, I just don't fit in here anymore, and running into Darcy means hurting her again. That's something I want to avoid at all costs.

She's only two rows in front of me, seven seats over. She knows I must be fairly close by, but she doesn't turn around. Not once. She looks gorgeous, just like she always does. I sit there staring at her the entire time. I don't hear the speeches, don't move when my row stands to receive our diplomas until the guy next to me practically shoves me. When I'm up on stage, I don't even shake the hand of the person handing me my diploma. No, I'm looking her way, and almost lose my shit when I see her lower her head. Better still, I have to watch as Chris reaches over to put a reassuring hand on her shoulder.

Screw avoiding her, I practically knock over a row of chairs to get to Darcy before she can run off after the ceremony. I'm a goddamn wreck, while she comes off as calm and clear-headed. And when she tells me she loves me, tells me she'll wait for me? What can I possibly say to that? I deserve the look of abject disgust she levels me with when I leave her hanging.

Everyone is partying together tonight and then going their separate ways tomorrow. I'm clearing out today, don't feel much like celebrating. I'm packing stuff into the car when I see my mother and Caleb walking towards me. I think Caleb chuckles a little when he takes in my reaction. Fucker probably thinks I'm afraid he's going to hit me. Truth is, I'm hoping he will. Instead, he puts a box into the trunk and then claps his hand on my shoulder.

"How are you doing?"

He's being nice to me? I can't take it.

Brendan runs over when he spots him. "Hi, Caleb."

"Jeez, Brendan, you look like you grew half a foot. You too, my man," he says as he tussles Terrence's hair. "What have you two monsters been eating?"

They're both looking up to him like he's their hero. Guess I've lost the right to be anyone's role model.

Caleb looks back to me. "Where's the little guy? I thought I'd get to meet him."

Terrence says, "He's at home with Aunt Mary."

"So you two are uncles, huh? Crazy, isn't it?"

Brendan nods, his smile forced. "You could say that."

"Gonna be great, though. Imagine in a few years when you're showing him how to pass a rugby ball."

Brendan smirks. "You mean, throw a football?"

"No, I mean, pass a rugby ball."

It's the first time I hear Brendan laugh this week.

My mom ushers the boys back inside to grab the last of my things.

"So what's your plan, Tom?"

"I don't know. I'm still trying to wrap my head around every-thing. But do you understand, Caleb? I mean, I don't want to hold her back, you know? Being with me...It's not fair to her."

"No, I hear you. You know she deferred her acceptances already though, right? She took a part-time teaching gig at Prep for next year while she figures things out. That was before everything with you went down. You knew that, though."

"I still don't think it changes anything. I want her to be like every other twenty-one-year-old. I don't want to burden her with some other," I pause, barely able to get the words out, "some other girl's baby. I want her to be happy."

Caleb looks away and nods. "Yep." He looks as if he's mulling something over before he says, "Listen, I wish I had some words of wisdom for you, but I don't. I just think sometimes when you think about things too much and try to plan it all out, you miss out on what's obvious and right in front of you. But hey, I gotta get back. If you feel like playing some rugby in the fall or if you need *anything*, I mean it, you've got my number, get in touch." With that he shakes my hand and leaves.

* * *

Back home in Connecticut, I stare at the ceiling from my childhood bed. My life has changed so drastically in just one week. One week ago, I had the world on a string. I was about to graduate, had found the love of my life, and was about to spend three amazing weeks with her traveling through Europe before starting a job I was excited about. Now I feel lost. I'm back to being dependent on my parents, and just in over my head in general.

I lie in bed staring at the ceiling long after James settles down for the night. I haven't slept soundly since I sent Darcy packing. I do nothing but think, my mind a jumbled mess of thoughts and memo-ries, both good and bad. I miss my brother Charlie, miss talking to him knowing he'd be able to give me some good advice. I think about Brendan and Terrence then, shake my head when I think about how many safe sex talks they're going to be subjected to thanks to their irresponsible older brother. Then my thoughts drift to that first time Darcy and I were together. How beautiful she was. How she trusted me. How good holding her and being with her felt. I finally drift off to sleep clutching a pillow, imagining my arms wrapped around her again, her body curled up against mine.

Chapter 23

DARCY

The idea of teaching? Wonderful. The reality of knowing I'll be tasked with guiding teenagers through an advanced biology curriculum in less than twelve weeks? Terrifying.

Sitting in Jenna's living room getting schooled in the arts of classroom management, learning theory, adolescent child development and lesson plan writing is humbling, but the girl is a godsend. She helps me corral a ton of information into a solid year's worth of lesson plans, and by the end of the week I'm back to feeling excited about this. I know the material like the back of my hand, and I'm glad I have something worthwhile to do with my time. I feel energized and excited, with zero regrets regarding my decision to put off med school.

Between banging out my course outline, Jenna and I spend a lot of time talking. I can tell she wants to reassure and console me, but I refuse to keep going over it again and again. Tom's one-eighty makes no sense to me, no matter what I angle I view the situation from. So whenever she starts in, I deftly shift the conversation back to her and her future. The plan is for Jenna to teach in Rhode Island for the year and then look for employment in whatever city Dan is transferred to after his year of training in Cincinnati. She's totally bummed about being separated, but they plan to see each other twice a month. Those two are solid. I have no doubt he'll be proposing sometime in the not so distant future.

I meet with the headmaster the week after I return to New York, and can tell he's beyond pleased with what I've prepared so far. He looks shocked that I have the full year laid out in lesson plans, complete with detailed labs. He tells me he's excited for me to join the faculty, as the last teacher covering this section was, according to him, a poor planner who was overwhelmed by the content and the precocity of the students. He expresses faith in me and believes the students are going to "benefit tremendously" now that I'm on staff. *On staff*—I like the sound of that.

And I dive right in because time on my hands equals time to stew, and I want none of that. I sign up for secondary education credits at Hunter College, and those summer classes are intense, as they're cramming a semester's worth of work into four weeks. Most days after class I head to Luke and Kate's. I scoop up my precious Rebecca and keep her until dinnertime. I know they're working on a new project so they're grateful for the help, but I'm not really babysitting as a favor to them. No, I need this. At night I settle in with my laptop and get to work, banging out my readings and assignments, and on the weekends I head out to the beach with my family, inviting Jenna, Rene or Kasia down to keep my mind off things. Don't stop moving, keep busy, avoid downtime at all costs—that's my plan and I'm sticking to it.

For the first two or three weeks of summer, I held out hope there was still a chance for me and Tom. With every day, week, and month that passed by with not so much as a phone call, though, my hopes diminished.

How could he do this to me? Not one phone call or text, no

communication whatsoever. Not even a reply to the text I sent him on his birthday. I spent the better part of that weekend crying. It's not that I wanted to be on that trip more than I wanted to be with Tom and James—I did not—but I couldn't help but think on that day that we should have been in Spain. I would have been surprising Tom with the concert tickets. We would have been so happy.

The silence is agonizing.

I put on a happy face for the benefit of my family, but the sadness is there, heavy and constant. Memories are the enemy. I see his beautiful face, and he's smiling as he stalks across the bed on his hands and knees towards me, the both of us laughing, tangled up in the sheets. It feels like being bathed in warm sunshine. But then the realization that he's gone hits like a freight train, the realization that he left me.

What is it that you don't understand?

Don't worry, Tom, now I understand. You've made it crystal clear that you don't want me.

The night before Tom is scheduled to leave for Chicago, my inner voice screams: *do not text him,* but I do it anyway. Nothing to lose. So what if he thinks I'm a hopeless loser pining away for him? I am.

Good luck in Chicago, you'll be great.

I thought there was nothing he could do to surprise me anymore, but I *am* surprised, after basically staring at my phone for four hours, when there's no reply. The next morning, so pathetic, I feel a spark of hope when I see Tom has answered me back.

Thx Darcy

That's all, folks.

If it wasn't official before, it is now. I need to come to terms with the fact that we're over. I was expecting, I don't know, something, anything.

How are you doing?

I miss you.

Let's get together when I get back.

He gives me nothing. Jerk couldn't even make the effort to spell out the word *thanks*. I vow to never write *thx* again in any form of correspondence.

I am empty.

I take his watch off my wrist and turn it over to look at the inscription before shoving it in the back of my desk drawer and closing it away. Yes, I have all the time in the world, but that no longer feels like a good thing. Now it just seems like a bland, interminable stretch ahead of me.

* * *

TOM

The month of June is spent taking James for walks, staying home, changing diapers, staying home, watching baseball with my brothers, staying home. You get the picture. History repeats itself. I'm in another self-imposed exile.

Turned down an invite to the Cape with Mac and backed out when Denny wanted to put a side in for a rugby tournament in Montauk. Dan invited me down to his family's shore house twice and I declined both times.

Talking to Dan, one of my closest friends in the world, is tough now. He's a harsh reminder of what a mess my life has become. When other people ask how you're doing, it's routine, perfunctory. When Dan asks, it's more like: What. Are. You. Doing. Asshole? One night I make the mistake of asking him how Darcy is doing. We're on the phone, but I can almost see his face twisting when he shoots back, "You *know* how she is, but if you really cared, you'd call her yourself. I'm not your fucking messenger boy."

His allegiance has entirely shifted to Darcy, and that's how it should be. I've lost the right to anyone's loyalty. During one conversation he adds, "Well, your loss is always going to be someone else's gain."

"What does that mean?"

"I saw Chris this weekend. He said Denny and his girlfriend had a great time in Europe. They especially enjoyed your birthday present." When I don't say anything, he adds, "Yeah, they said seeing Pearl Jam in Madrid was the highlight of the trip. Apparently, you had great seats. Denny said he was practically being pelted with Vedder's sweat."

I think back to the text she sent on my birthday. The text I didn't respond to. Does she know how much this is costing me? How much it hurts to cut myself off from her? Some days I literally feel like I'm dying.

When Dan interrupts my thoughts to ask if I'm still there, I say, "I didn't know. I hope she didn't have to eat anything more than the cost of those tickets. She probably hates me by now."

"Yeah, right. You know she still loves you, jerkoff. Jenna's been heading down to see her a lot. So have the other girls, for moral support. Like I said, Tom, your loss is going to be someone else's gain. Jenna said she's got no shortage of guys sniffing around. Her ex, Matt, has been dropping by all the time."

After that phone call I avoid contact with Dan.

My parents try to push me into going to Dylan's Fourth of July bash on Martha's Vineyard. I haven't missed one since junior year in high school. Dylan knows the state I'm in, but Dylan is Dylan. He doesn't wallow in heartbreak. He just doesn't get it.

"I understand why you cut her loose. I'd have done the exact same thing if I were in your shoes. And I'm not suggesting you go looking for a replacement. I'm just saying there will be some hot, willing women at the party who aren't looking to be your wife or James's mommy. Just come up here for a few days and get laid."

Yeah, I turn down that invite too.

* * *

I'm at the airport by six, alert but a little fuzzy. Ben dragged my sorry ass out last night for a few beers. One thing I love about Ben is that there's not too much depth there. The boy is loyal to a fault and will do anything for you, but he doesn't feel the need to dig into your psyche. Dan, on the other hand, would have spent all of last night belaboring the Darcy situation.

Two weeks. That's how long I'll be away. I'm surprised when a feeling of loss washes over me and I realize it's because I'll be missing James. It overwhelms me in a good way. He's the one thing that's made my life bearable.

James has started to smile a lot, and the look he gives me when I pick him up after a nap, well, it melts my heart. I've spent nearly every waking moment with him these past two months, so being away from him feels strange. I know he's in good hands with my parents and the boys, though. My mother and father fuss over him nonstop, and Brendan and Terrence will argue over who gets to feed James his bottle. Sometimes I walk in on one of the boys snuggling James or talking to him softly. It's pretty cool to watch.

I called Mrs. McDaniel yesterday, told her I'll be bringing James up for a visit as soon as I get home, and she sounded thrilled. "Will Darcy be coming along?" she asked, hopeful. Her tone changed when I repeated, yet again, that no, Darcy is back in New York now.

Waiting to board my flight, I look through my emails and see some texts from the night before. Ben sent me the name of a bar in Chicago that he couldn't remember last night. Dan reminding me, yet again, about the party at his shore house the weekend after I get back. He must think I'm planning to blow it off, and if so, he would be correct. The last one is a text from her, wishing me well. Fuck.

Thx Darcy

I go on to type a second message:

I miss you

I don't hit send on that one. I play this game almost every night. I write her an imaginary letter in my head telling her all the things I need to say. Tell her how much I miss her. How, every night, I hold onto that watch she gave me and rub my thumb over that word, *Siempre*, back and forth so many times that I'm surprised the engraving hasn't worn off yet. I beg her to come back to me in this imaginary letter, but in reality, I've pushed her away so hard and so abruptly that Darcy must believe at this point that I feel nothing for her. And absolutely nothing could be further from the truth.

* * *

Chicago is what I imagine a fraternity rush week would be like, with a lot of coursework mixed in. They're definitely looking to prepare you for the work hard, play hard atmosphere of Wall Street.

There are about thirty in our group, roughly ten females among us. The days are spent in class, learning formulas, strategic business practices and corporate ethics policy. Every night there's a dinner with plenty of booze flowing, and then more drinks after. You can read personalities right away. A few people are totally serious, but most seem like hard partiers who can still arrive at class at 8 a.m. looking sharp. One or two overdo it regularly, and catch the attention of the instructors when they can barely keep their eyes open in class. No impulse control.

I'm enjoying the nights, getting to know my new co-workers in this boot camp-style atmosphere, but I'm being smart. My father prepped me thoroughly before leaving. He told me they're watching us closely to see who can handle the atmosphere. Who can manage the after-hours, be socially engaging with clients, yet still maintain an air of self-control. I think his exact words were along the lines of: *Being the life of the party is one thing. Doing lines and hooking up with one of your new female co-workers is another. It's not 1985 anymore.* He's been known to lay it out straight like that when he believes it's warranted, and given what's gone down these past few months, he apparently thinks I need the not so subtle reminder.

You get to know a lot about everyone since you're practically together twenty-four-seven. I get to hear about where everyone grew up, some funny college stories, and the basic details of everyone's family life. I don't share my new parenthood status with anyone—don't want to deal with their reactions or to be questioned about it—but when someone asks if I have a girlfriend, I hear myself replying no. Besides feeling a deep sense of betrayal when I mutter that one syllable, telling the truth backfires on me.

She's pretty, but they all are. She's smart and has a sharp sense of humor too. We're grouped together with two others for a project, and I can sense it, she's giving off that vibe. I don't bite, but we're all up especially late the night before we're heading back to New York. I make my way back to my room at around three, and she's knocking on the door not five minutes later.

I shouldn't answer the door—I know this—but I do.

"Hi. I probably shouldn't be here."

"No, you shouldn't."

I guess my protest comes off as half-hearted because she just smiles at me, comes in and closes the door behind her. Samantha, or Sam as she prefers to be called, has her blouse and skirt in a pool on the floor within a minute. She stands before me in her heels and not much else. She's tall and curvy with long blond hair—totally fuckable. I don't make a move towards her, but my body is reacting to the sight of her. Nothing I can do to stop that.

"I know what you must be thinking, but we can do this. Just tonight, no strings attached. I want you."

She moves closer and presses herself against me, parting her lips and kissing me. My hands stay at my sides for a minute before they move to her waist and pull her in. I'm lonely, I'm sad, and I'm horny as hell. I run my hands over her ass, and she responds by rubbing me through my pants aggressively. I want this, I want the release, but in that moment something clicks.

Her ghost is in this room with us, and it's her taste I want in my mouth, not this girl's.

I won't be that guy anymore. Maybe I'll never be with Darcy again, but I'm not using someone as a substitute for her.

"I'm sorry, but I need you to leave." Sam looks ashamed. "Hey, it's on me. You're beautiful and..." I want to go on and reassure her, tell her everything that's great about her, but it's nearly three-thirty in the morning, I have to leave for the airport in a few hours, and I'm just too damn wrung out. "I can't do this, Sam. It's not a good idea for you, and I'm someone, co-worker or not, you should not be involved with."

She looks away as she slips back into her clothes. "I know guys, and you're a good guy."

"I come with a whole lot of baggage, believe me."

She sighs. "I don't believe that, but I guess you're right. This isn't a good idea for me." As she turns to go, she asks, "Is my momentary lapse in judgement safe with you?"

I motion to zip my lips. "Goodnight, Sam."

Good guy my ass. I have failed every barometer of *good guy* that's been thrown my way over the past few years.

Bunching the uncomfortable hotel pillow up under my head, I wonder, how *do* I see this playing out? Eventually my hormones are going to get the best of me. I'm no monk, that's for sure. And eventually, without Darcy, will I find myself drawn to someone else? Will she? Could another woman ever make me truly happy the way she does? Would some other man treat her right? The thought of Darcy being with anyone else, but especially someone who doesn't treat her like gold, someone like Nick Brunner—the thought of it kills me.

My thoughts flash back to Graduation Day. Every time Chris nudged her playfully or said something to make her laugh, I wanted to charge at him and beat him senseless. But I knew I had no right. I was treating her the way a cold-hearted bastard would, while he was showing her kindness when she needed it most.

There will never be a shortage of men who'd kill to be the center of her universe.

For the one thousandth time I ask myself, *What the hell are you doing?*

* * *

I'm tired, but I practically bounce out of the cab and trot up the driveway, eager to get back to James.

During my time in Chicago, I came to realize that all of this is for him. Now it's not just about my ambition, but my duty to provide a good life for him. And that's what I need to do. I need to focus on rising up through the ranks through hard work, and unfortunately, what I know will be some long hours. I don't care about the trips and the nights out I won't be joining in on. Every day off and every free moment I have is reserved for him, and I'm all right with that.

I spend my first hour back home hearing about all the funny and amazing things James did while I was away. Mom also fills me in on her visit with Mrs. McDaniel, noting that she seems weaker every time she sees her. Mom will continue to bring James up at least every other week, which is great, since I'll be swamped once I start work. My dad has taken the day off to hear all about my trip. We go for a slow, long run when James goes down for his nap, and I tell him about many—not all—of my experiences over the past two weeks. I also get to ask the seasoned pro a lot of questions.

I've got the weekend, but I'm due at my new office at 7 a.m. sharp on Monday. James is getting in some tummy time on my bedroom floor as I start to arrange my suits, shirts and ties for next week. I nearly trip over a large box in my walk-in closet, so I take it out to see what's inside. There are smaller boxes inside, and one looks as if it's already been opened.

When I peel the tissue paper back, I'm blown away. It's a picture of James looking up at his mother and Breanne looking down at him. It must have been taken when he was only a few weeks old. He looks so much bigger, so different now. It's a beautiful picture, but sadly, I feel no connection to the girl. I only feel sorry that a young life was cut so short, and that James will never know this person who obviously loved him so much. I unwrap the others, one by one. I have them laid out across my bed, and I'm just staring at the pictures when my mother walks in and picks James up off the floor.

"Isn't that a beautiful picture? Oh, you unwrapped them all. Let me see them, I haven't had a chance to look at the others yet."

"Where did you get them?" I ask, even though I already know the answer to my question.

She places her hand on my shoulder. "Darcy got the pictures from Mrs. McDaniel and had them professionally matted and framed. That was the box Caleb was carrying for me on Graduation Day."

I drop my head, rub my hands over my face. What am I doing? By pushing her away, I've made myself miserable and hurt Darcy in the cruelest way possible.

"Mom, you mind keeping James while I take care of something?"

"Sure."

I text Caleb to find out where Darcy is, hoping he's still somewhat in my corner. I could reach out to her, but I don't want to talk to her on the phone. I need to see her in person. I don't even know if what I'm about to do is right, but in the very least I owe her my honesty.

I'm already in the car heading south when Caleb writes back to let me know she's at the beach. I have no idea what I'm going to say, have no idea if she'll even see me, but I have to do this.

Sarah looks puzzled when she answers the door. "Tom?" Then she smiles and hugs me tight. "It's so good to see you. Does Darcy know you're here?"

"Uh, no, she doesn't. Is she around?"

"She just walked down to the shore with Rebecca. Go ahead, Tom. I know she'll be happy to see you."

Hope she's right. "Thanks, Sarah."

As soon as I hit the sand, I see her. Cute floppy straw hat, long golden wavy hair and a killer white bikini. She's holding Rebecca in her arms and pointing to the seagulls waddling along the shore. When I'm halfway down the beach, I slow my pace as two lifeguards jogging by in bright red board shorts stop to talk to her. I hang back and wait. One of them is falling all over her, and who could blame him? She's like a goddamn vision. I chuckle to myself as they start up again, and the one guy nearly trips looking back over his shoulder trying to get another look at her.

Darcy turns to face me when I'm still a few feet away. She doesn't look happy when she says, "I just had the weirdest feeling that you were here."

I study the sand, shove my hands into my pockets. "Yeah, I'm finally here." I look back up to her. She's wary, but her blue eyes also look trusting and expectant. "I'm so sorry for what I've put you through. You know I've loved you and missed you every day we were apart, but I just felt...No, I still feel guilty. Being with me has to be a burden, even if you'll never say it. But I've gone about this all wrong. I never wanted to hurt you." I'm trying to fight past the lump in my throat when I ask, "Did you mean what you said about waiting for me to stop being a dumbass?"

One corner of her mouth turns up in what I hope is a smile. "I'm still waiting."

Rebecca gets a death grip on Darcy's bikini top, trying to pull it down. I give Rebecca my keys to distract her, one of the many new tricks I've learned. I take a chance and move in closer to Darcy, putting one hand on her lower back. Being near her, touching her—it feels like electricity, like life is coursing through my body again.

"If you can ever find it in your heart to forgive me, I'll be here, and on your terms. I love you and I want you in my life, but I don't want you to take me on if I'm going to hold you back in any way."

She puts one hand on my chest to stop me from talking. "Just promise me you'll never say that again. I'll never see James as a burden. He's a part of you, and if I'm with you, then it's all of you. It's you, me *and* James. Do you understand?"

I nod and kiss her head, never more grateful for anything before in my life.

She pushes me away gently then, and looks up at me with steely, determined eyes. "And you can't pull this anymore. You can't pull the silent treatment and decide to push me away when things go wrong." Her eyes are watering when she adds, "You cannot do it to me again, Tom."

She's right. I've repeated the same shitty pattern, clamming up and closing myself off, time and time again. I make a silent vow to myself never to do it again before saying, "I promise."

She still has Rebecca in one arm when she buries her head into my chest and starts to cry. "I've missed you so much."

Her tears rip a hole in my heart. "I'm going to do everything I can to make it up to you. I love you, so much."

I have my foot in the door, and I'm beyond grateful for that, but I know I have a long road ahead of me. She might be hugging me back and saying she's missed me, but I know her, and she's mad as hell. I deserve whatever she plans to dish out, and I'll take it with a smile and a thank you.

Chapter 24

DARCY

Happy, relieved and angry, all rolled into one.

I'm not diving right back in. I'm not ready. And although it's killing me, I'm holding off on seeing James until I'm sure we're back on solid ground. I can't do that to him, and I can't put myself through the separation again if it doesn't work out between me and Tom.

It's not a done deal. What's happened has changed me. I think I've become a little more guarded, maybe a little meaner. He's going to have to listen to some harsh truths and then decide if I'm still the same girl he once wanted to spend his life with.

I cheated on Tom. Well, technically it wasn't cheating because we were broken up at the time, but yes, sweet Darcy Donovan made out like a porn star with some musician friend of Kasia's after watching him play a show in Williamsburg one night. It was a total rebound move. I spent a good portion of the night telling the guy my tale of woe, and I balked when he asked to take me out the next week. In truth, it wasn't the least bit fun, but Tom never needs to know that.

Childish, yes, but I get a teeny bit of satisfaction knowing that my confession will gut Tom on some level.

But nothing is a deal breaker for him. He wants me back, and says he'll do anything to prove it to me. In truth, he doesn't have to do much. I want him, and I want a life with him and James with all my heart.

It takes hours, days, the better part of the month of August, just talking. We meet up for dinner in the city after he finishes work some nights, and he comes to see me at the beach some weekends, driving back home each night. I don't invite him to stay over or to crash at the beach house with my family.

Still not ready, but I'm getting there.

When I go home to Connecticut with him one Friday night nearly two months later, I'm so happy to see his mother that I nearly bawl like a baby when she hugs me close. And James, I weep happy tears when I pick him up and he flashes me a toothy smile.

Tom creeps into his room wordless later that night, and slips underneath the covers with me. His hands burn a path across my skin. He kisses my mouth and my neck as his hands move across my breasts, smoothing over my hips and then back up to my face again. I can't help but cry, overcome with emotion because it feels so good to be with him again.

"I'm sorry, I'll stop. Are you all right?"

"Don't stop. I just...I've missed us."

He closes his eyes tight and rests his forehead against mine. "I love you so much. You deserve better than me."

"Just touch me, Tom, please."

He runs his hands over me gently and then kisses me hungrily as he guides himself into me. He feels so good, and I've never wanted anyone the way I want him.

"Darcy, it's you and me. I'll love you forever."

And then I dive back in. Can't help it, it's where I want to be.

* * *

Our routine is crazy, but it works for us. I work Tuesday through Thursday. I go home, pack a bag, and then meet Tom after he gets out of work. Occasionally we have dinner or meet for drinks with some of his colleagues, but more often than not, we jump on the Metro North and head back up to Connecticut. When Tom heads into work Friday morning, I give Mrs. Farrell a break and take over with James until I head back to the city on Mondays.

The Farrells converted the downstairs study into a bedroom for me. I'm fairly certain his parents turn a blind eye when Tom sneaks down to me in the middle of the night, and I admit, not sleeping together is so awful that I live for those nights when I hear him pad down the stairs to be with me. We're totally discreet, though. Mostly for the boys' sake, but I also don't want to piss off my future in-laws.

Those weekends with his family are everything I need to make me certain that this will be my forever. Autumn leaves color the landscape as we take James to watch Brendan's football games, take him for long walks, go to the park, shop—all the things young couples do with their baby. When winter settles in, we mostly just hang out at home with James. We're typically in Connecticut, but some Fridays I bring James back down to the city and we stay with my family for the weekend. Never for a minute do I feel like I'm missing out. Both the Farrells and my parents regularly push us out the door to meet up with friends whenever we make plans, but we're careful to make sure the weekends are about James. Tom always looks to make James a priority because his workdays start early and regularly stretch on past eight. James is usually sound asleep by the time Tom gets home on the train.

I'm grateful for the three weeks I have off at Christmas, grateful that I'm able to give Mrs. Farrell a real break. After Christmas Eve at my house, we spend Christmas Day with Tom's family, and James's first Christmas is insane. I mean, he's only ten months old, but we all believe he's getting into ripping the paper off the presents. We go a bit overboard for James and also for Rebecca. There's no way they'll play with half the toys they've been given, so Kate and I pack a suitcase full of toys up and take them along with us to donate to a children's charity in Puerto Rico.

My parents, Kate, Luke and Rebecca stay the entire two weeks at our regular rental house in Rincon with me and James. Tom can't come down for the trip. He's doing great at work, but he's new, so time off isn't an option. I torture him with pictures morning, noon and night. James sitting on a surfboard with Rebecca, James in the pool, James toddling after a gecko—he loves each and every shot. And I text Tom that I miss him, because whenever we're apart, I do.

He presses sometimes, asks me about medical school, asks if I can reapply to the east coast schools that were my first choice. He even hints that he's willing to relocate if I choose LA or Chicago. I always give a noncommittal answer or change the subject. First off, he'll uproot James and get a new job in another city while I'm in school full-time without family around for childcare? It's not feasible. Secondly, I'm almost one hundred percent certain that I've found my path, and while he may think that I'm settling, I don't feel that way at all.

I'm a good teacher. I know it when I see the look on one of my student's faces when they "get it" after struggling with a difficult concept. I know it when I get positive feedback from my more seasoned colleagues. And I truly believe that I'm good when the AP test results come back and my students have made impressive gains as a group over past years' classes. So when the administration offers me a full-time position for the upcoming school year, I feel validated.

But while I don't say it out loud, I also believe that I'm a good mother, and I see myself as James's mother in every way. So I ask to remain part-time for another year, knowing that our family works well with our current schedule, and I'm reluctant to rock the boat.

When Tom brings it up yet again late one night, I blurt out the idea that's been bouncing around in my head for months. "I'm applying for a master's in secondary education."

"I think that's a great idea, Darce."

"Yeah?"

"Oh, yeah." He grabs his phone off the table and moves in super close to me on the couch. "So is now a good time to tell you that I saw a listing for a great two-bedroom down in Battery Park?"

Life is as complicated or as simple as you make it sometimes.

Chapter 25

TOM

It's been one year. One year since we graduated, one year of getting my footing at the firm, and I believe that I'm doing better than just all right—I'm killing it.

So come July, it's vacation time. We spent a few days getting everything squared away at the apartment, and now we're at the beach, spending the remainder of the week with Darcy's family.

I'm pretty sure I have everything planned out perfectly. Jenna, Dan, Rene, Caitlin, Beth, Ben, Caleb, Luke, Kate, Chris, Cara and Kasia are all set to arrive for dinner. My parents are bringing Brendan, Terrence, Rob and Mary. It's going to be a casual engagement party, just our closest friends and family. I know that's what Darcy would want if she was planning it herself.

Taking a major risk? I guess I am making an assumption that she's going to say yes, but she's stuck by me through the past two crazy years, so yeah, I think she's in it for the long haul.

Darcy typically takes James for a walk along the beach after he wakes from his late afternoon nap. He started walking in February and has pretty much been running ever since, so it's a good way for him to burn off some energy. Darcy usually stays down there for at least an hour making sandcastles with him, chasing seagulls or collecting shells. She spent her childhood at the beach, so she's been teaching James about the ocean, marine life, and water safety from day one.

Darcy is always saying how smart James is. I'm sure she's prejudiced, but the kid does seem precocious. At seventeen months he's using a lot of short phrases, and he seems to have a good grasp on what we say to him. I credit Darcy with that, too. She's a great teacher and a great mother to him. That's what's going through my head as I make my way down the beach towards them.

"Hey, buddy."

"Da-dee!"

It's hard to describe the feeling. When he runs at me full speed, arms out so that I can lift him up, calling for me, Daddy, I get choked up every time.

I whisper in his ear, "I've got a surprise for Mommy."

Yeah, since James first started babbling I've been showing him Darcy's picture and teaching him to say *mommy*. The first time he called her mama, her eyes went wide and she cried so hard, but now it's second nature. And while I know in her heart she sees herself as his mother, she doesn't refer to herself as James's mom to other people. I guess it just isn't official to her. Doesn't matter to James, he calls her nothing but mommy and she happily answers to it.

I often catch her holding James in front of the photo gallery wall she made in his new bedroom. She points out each person, moving from one picture to the next. A large picture of Breanne and James hangs in the center, flanked by pictures of James with me and Darcy, with my parents, with Brendan and Terrence, with the Donovans, a really cute one of him and Rebecca laughing on the beach in Puerto Rico, and one of Mrs. McDaniel holding him on her lap just before she passed. That picture she always loved of me, Charlie, Brendan and Terrence on the beach is up there too, and Darcy always makes a point of singling out Uncle Charlie during her family tree sessions. I notice she always stops in front of Breanne's picture last, explaining to James that she's his mom too, and that she's in heaven watching over him. If Breanne is looking down on us, I'm pretty sure she's happy. James couldn't possibly be loved any more than he is.

"What are you two whispering about?"

With that, I get down on one knee. James follows, getting down on both his knees. He always imitates what I do, and it's pretty freaking adorable. I look up to Darcy and ask, "Will you marry us?"

She laughs and covers her mouth, nodding before tears prick at the corners of her eyes. I pull the ring box out of the pocket of my board shorts and slip the ring onto her finger. I was a little nervous about having Rene pick the style, but the girl done good. It looks beautiful on Darcy's delicate hand.

I'm sure James has no idea what's going on, but he's clapping his hands and jumping anyway, as excited as the two of us are.

I pick him up and then pull her in close to me, wrap my family up in my arms. I'll never take the goodness she brings to my life for granted. She has my heart and my soul, and I can't imagine living a single day without her.

* * *

DARCY

Walking into the backyard, Tom gives a thumbs-up and then we're greeted by hoots and hollers. I'm in shock for a minute as I take in the scene. Every person here has been witness to our highs and lows, and pulling for us through it all.

James runs straight to Rebecca when he sees her, just like peanut butter to jelly. Tom starts making the rounds, and I make my way to Terrence and Brendan, hugging them first.

Brendan, always the family spokesperson, says, "You're already a part of our family, Darcy, but I'm glad he's finally making it official." To which Terrence adds, "What he said."

It's a great night, just hanging out, beers and barbecue with the people who mean the most to us.

I grab Tom to the side and tease, "You think now I can spend some nights at your apartment?"

"Some nights? Oh no, woman, you're moving in ASAP. We're engaged now so we can do whatever we want. If it makes you feel better, I'll marry you at City Hall tomorrow. I just want you to be mine, legally, no turning back."

"I don't think my dad would be down with that, me being his only daughter and all, but Tom, I would like to get married soon. I don't want a long, drawn out engagement." I can't help but get emotional when I add, "I want to be James's mother."

He holds me close and kisses my head before whispering in my ear, "You know you already are his mother, but I understand. I'm with you. Name the date."

And by Monday morning, I'm seriously considering late September. I know it's the beginning of the school year and all, but taking an extended honeymoon vacation isn't in the cards anyway. I don't think either one of us wants to go away without James, and Tom still needs to plug along at work. It's only ten weeks away, but I'm low maintenance, not a bridezilla bone in my body.

Save the date cards are mailed out by the end of the week. A great winery loft space and the DJ are booked for the reception, and our parish Church has the opening. Nearly everyone at the engagement party is in my bridal party, and they're about as low maintenance as I am. I pick my wedding gown from small shop in Soho, and tell the girls to select any cocktail dress from the shop's bridal collection that they like. I pick the simple groomsmen's suits from there as well. James is going to look adorable in his custom-made little suit.

I guess you can make the process difficult and complicated, but there's really not much to stress about. As both of my brothers have advised me: the wedding is one day, marriage is for life.

And I'm not giving up my August at the shore to deal with drama. I taste one cake and it's delicious. Done. Surf and turf? Sounds good. Calla lilies or peonies? I go with the florist's opinion, with a reminder to keep it beach-themed.

After the invitations are mailed, we're done, and the rest of the summer is spent seaside. James and I pretty much move into my old bedroom at the beach house, and Tom comes out from the city most nights after work and on the weekends. Brendan and Terrence are here with us a lot, too. They love paddle boarding and playing football on the beach. They've made friends here, but Brendan and Terrence are also undoubtedly drawn to the beach by the adorable, bikini-clad teenage triplet girls who live on the block and play beach volleyball like they're bound for the Olympics.

Brendan will be a sophomore in high school this year and Terrence is finishing middle school. They're getting so much older, but they're great with James, so patient when he follows them around and imitates every single thing they do *all* day long.

Nights like this are my favorite. We're down on the beach just before sunset. I've made a tray of barbecued chicken and salads for an al fresco dinner. Eating dinner on the beach is the best because, hello, no clean-up. Tom and I sit there with full stomachs, passing a brownie back and forth between us while watching James chase Brendan and Terrence around. Tom is lost in thought.

"What's up?"

"I'm just thinking about how nice it is for James to have those two, but it's really great for Brendan and Terrence to have a brother so close in age. And I'm just missing Charlie. He would have loved you and loved James."

I rest my head on his shoulder. I'll never get tired of feeling his strong, powerful body next to mine.

"Darce, feel free to tell me no, or that I'm nuts, but do you think you might be ready to go off your birth control pills any time soon?"

"Wow, I haven't really given it any thought. You want this for James?"

He looks to me, hopeful and sincere. "Yeah, I really do."

After I think on it for a minute, I turn back to him. "Then I'm in."

He flips me onto my back in the sand and starts in on tickling my sides. "You mean it?" When I nod, he stops and leans down to whisper, "I promise I'm going to make this worth your while. I have moves I haven't broken out on you yet."

The next day I replace the pill with prenatal vitamins.

And he isn't joking. I mean, I love sex with Tom. He makes my body feel incredible and makes me feel like I'm the most desirable woman on the face of the earth, but now it's game-on. He's calling in favors with his parents and my parents, using wedding planning as our excuse for needing a babysitter. He makes sure that we have at least a few hours without James to be together. And I'm oh so down for this. I mean, we've spent the better part of this year holing up with our parents and sneaking in quickies whenever we could. They were good quickies, but in comparison, this feels like heaven.

We christen every room in the apartment. Sometimes he loves me slow and sweet, and sometimes it's a little rough and downright dirty. I love it all. One afternoon he even takes me the way I dreamed about before we first got together. Tom comes up behind me, kisses the base of my neck and presses his body into mine. He actually speaks the words I wrote for him in my fantasy. "Darcy, you know I love you, right?" He plants my hands on the wall above me and tells me to brace myself. He strips me slowly, like a sweet form of torture, and when I feel as if my legs might give out on me, he enters me, holding me up with both hands on my hips.

Reality is so much better than fantasy.

* * *

TOM

What a difference a year makes.

Last year I was struggling, felt like my life was spiraling out of control, and now I feel like I'm back on top. I'm on my game at work, my sweet girl is about to become my wife, and my son is thriving.

Just one more day. One more day until she walks down that aisle, one more day until it's official.

This afternoon the bridesmaids will be invading our apartment and I'll be exiled. Right now I'm here with her, though, so I'm getting my fill. Sitting on the edge of our bed, I fix my tie slowly as I watch Darcy get dressed. It's pretty hard to concentrate on anything else when she's smoothing a skirt over her hips or slipping into a sexy pair of heels. Today, as I watch her slide a lacy slip down over her body, I notice her breasts look extra full. Round and full, they're nearly spilling out of the cups. Besides being rock hard at the sight of her, I think maybe it's a good sign. I keep my mouth shut, though. I don't want her getting nervous about anything right before the wedding.

Chapter 26

DARCY

Mornings don't get better than this. James is half asleep, drinking from his sippy cup with his body nestled into mine. My little baby, in just a few more months he'll be two.

I haven't been to the doctor yet, but the drug store test was positive and my body feels different. I'm not nauseous and I don't actually feel anything happening inside of me, but I'm ravenous when I first wake up, and on both Saturday and Sunday last weekend, I went down for a power nap when James did.

I've been trolling pregnancy and baby sites, and the due date calculators agree that if all goes well, James will have a new little sister or brother around the end of June. James will be two years, four months. I'm so tempted to tell Tom, I know he's going to be thrilled, but I want to surprise him after the wedding.

By 10 a.m. all the girls have claimed a spot on the king-sized bed. After a late breakfast, the glam squad descends upon us to whip us into shape. I take a break after they set my hair to dress my little man. I thought he might fuss, being as he's usually in

269

sweats, shorts and tees, but he's smiling ear to ear standing in front of the mirror as I fix his tie and put on his belt. As I'm combing a little product into his hair, he looks back to me and says, "I like Daddy."

"Yes," I tell him, "you look just like Daddy."

"Poor kid," Caleb teases.

"It's time already?"

James runs into Caleb's outstretched arms and he lifts him up into the air over his head. "You look like a happening little hedge fund bro in this pint-sized suit."

"I handsome."

"You are handsome." Caleb nuzzles James's belly and he laughs. "A lady killer in the making."

"Ok, now one serious shot of you two together."

Tickling James, Caleb does his version of posing, which isn't the least bit helpful. When I scowl, he says, "We don't do serious." Gesturing to the clock, he adds, "And I think you should stop snapping pictures so you can get dressed. It's getting late."

"Oh!" I'm surprised when I see the time, and more surprised when I realize that I'm a little nervous.

"Jittery, sis?"

"No...I mean, a little?"

"I was just thinking this morning that we're lucky." He settles James in his arms and grabs the bag I've packed with his free hand. "You, me and Luke. We've all found that person, you know?" I nod, because I've thought the same exact thing on more than one occasion. He leans in to kiss my cheek. "He's a good person, and I'm happy for both of you."

"Thanks, Caleb."

He looks to James. "Say bye to Mommy. We'll see her in a few minutes at Church."

Caleb blows me a kiss and James imitates him, doing the same.

My apartment is like a revolving door today. The boys leave just as my father arrives to corral me and Sarah into the vintage car waiting downstairs.

Punctual to a fault, he sees that I'm still in my robe and looks down at his watch. "Hop to it. We're due at Church in fifteen minutes." But he's not too eager to get out of the car once we've pulled up outside. "You know this day will come, but you never imagine it will feel like this. It really is different with a daughter." I take his hand, surprised to see him so emotional. "That walk down the aisle means you're leaving us to start a new life."

"I'm never leaving you or leaving our family."

"No, it's a good thing. Change makes you wistful for the way things used to be, but I'm happy. You couldn't have found someone better suited for you than Tom. I feel blessed that you have someone who loves you the way he does." He smiles. "I'm not looking to make you cry, I swear, but I know your mother is looking down on you right now and she's so very happy."

I feel it too. Everyone in my life, my mother in heaven included, is around me, surrounding me with love. When I see Tom waiting for me at the end of the aisle with James in his arms, I'm overwhelmed with gratitude.

TOM

They say that if you find the right girl, that moment when she's walking down the aisle towards you is one of the best moments of your life. Well, I have the most spectacular woman on the planet making her way towards me in a dress that hugs her beautiful curves, and I can't help but smile, awestruck and amazed by it all. I'm a father, a soon-to-be husband, and I'm all but certain that my Darcy is nurturing a new life, a miracle inside of her body. I'm feeling content, blessed, and more at peace than I ever have at any point in my life.

It doesn't get any better than this.

When the priest pronounces us man and wife, we kiss and then turn to face the congregation. I think both of us are overwhelmed for a moment by the sight. So many people smiling back at us, family and good friends here to celebrate this day with us.

Walking into the loft space Darcy has basically transformed into a dreamscape, I'm amazed she was able to pull all of this together in such a short period of time.

Looking around, my gaze settles on my brothers. Terrence is goofing off with Caleb, while Brendan holds Rebecca with Luke looking on smiling. I'm so grateful for my family. And taking in the rest of the room, I laugh to myself, seeing as it's like a swanky college reunion—a far cry from freezer burnt dogs on the grill and beer pong.

It's bittersweet, the realization that we're all starting new chapters in our lives. I know Dan is planning to propose within the next few months, Chris and his girl Cara are moving to California for his new job at a tech start-up, and Ben is about to leave for an overseas assignment that will take him away for the next two years.

I am more than ready for our next chapter. We're now officially a family, we're making a home for James, and Darcy and I will spend the years to come raising our children together.

As we slow-dance together to the last song of the night, I remember that I still haven't given her my present. It's something simple, a locket with James's picture on one side and the other side empty, for now. We're spending the night at a hotel, so I tell her I'll give it to her tomorrow night when we get back home.

"You didn't have to get me a present. I feel bad now. I didn't get you anything."

"Yes, you did. You married me."

She laughs and then smiles like she's got a juicy secret. "Well, maybe I am giving you something."

I should let her have some fun with it, to tease me, but I can't help but blurt out, "I know."

She cocks her head to the side. "What do you know?"

I shake my head, try to stifle my laugh and school my expression. "Nothing. I know nothing, Darce. Now come on, what were you going to say?"

She holds out on me for a few seconds, but then gets up on her tiptoes to whisper in my ear, "We're having a baby."

I pick her up and spin her around. "I knew."

"You did not!"

"I did!"

"How? I just found out a few days ago."

I lean down to whisper in her ear, "Your breasts look phenomenal. They're huge, so I had my suspicions."

She hits my chest but she's laughing. "You're impossible, but I love you."

And swaying with her in my arms, I raise up a silent prayer that our hardest days are behind us. But I'm confident that together we can make it through anything. I have a woman by my side who is incredibly strong, and above all else, has the most loving, giving heart imaginable. I hold her close, never wanting to be apart from her ever again.

"You're the only one for me, Mrs. Darcy Farrell, forever."

The End, *for now...*

<h1 style="text-align:center">A Note From Lily</h1>

A heartfelt thank you for picking up *Let Me Be the One*, the first book I published in the Let Me series, which was also my debut. I sincerely hope you enjoyed reading Darcy and Tom's story.

Ready for more? Caleb and Rene's love story is heartbreaking, messy, sexy and uplifting—all rolled into one. The Let Me series continues with *Let Me Love You*.

**One chance meeting
One hot summer night...**

Caleb Donovan won't be seeing his sister's roommate again unless he makes it happen, and in his heart he knows that's not a good idea. She's too young, still figuring it out and trying to find her way in this world.

Infatuation, longing, guilt—he's nothing but a messed-up tangle of emotions he wants no part of. He tells himself the feelings will pass because they always do. Caleb doesn't do love, he doesn't believe in forever.

Rene has wanted Caleb since the day she first laid eyes on him, but it will never happen. He's got it all. What would someone like him see in her, a girl who's been struggling to keep her head above water since the day she was born?

**It's not always rainbows and sunshine...
No, some love stories are messy.**

Order your copy of *Let Me Love You* here:

Or visit my website to find out more:

LilyFoster.com